CW00859129

SANDMAN

Ian Kingsley

Iankingsley.com

'A gripping psychological read with characters that reach out and grab you. A real page-turner.'

'*Sandman* touches our primary emotions: jealousy, love, guilt, fear, hatred and grief. As a father, I related to Paul's unwavering commitment to keep his family safe. Kingsley has written an intriguing mystery/psychological thriller with interesting, believable and well-developed characters. There are twists, turns, red herrings, and a healthy dose of hair-raising fear and suspense to keep even the most fickle reader captivated. The dialogue is authentic, and, along with the scene-painting narrative, you'll feel like you're on the beach witnessing the unfolding action.

Just when you think you have it all sorted out, the author changes directions—successfully keeping you guessing until the final pages. When you begin *Sandman* make sure you set aside a good bit of time, for you won't stop reading until the last page is savoured. Highly recommended to readers who enjoy a great mystery!'

'With the yarn gathering force, readers can't help turn the pages compulsively, as we are seduced with small details and quick punchy dialogue... We are to discover, and a concept that underlies all good mysteries, nothing is as it seems...

What is intriguing about *Sandman* is that reading it made me think I was watching a movie focusing on several characters that all are subtly interwoven into the threads of each others' lives... Moreover, it is a novel that you may want to re-read, once for the sheer thrill of the story and again to fully absorb its implications.'

3

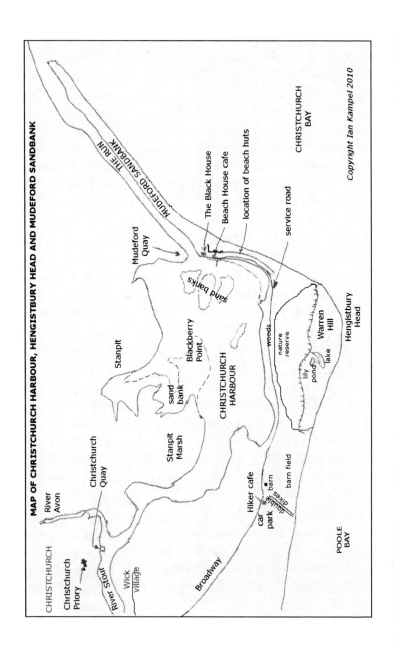

MAP OF CHRISTCHURCH HARBOUR, HENGISTBURY HEAD AND MUDEFORD SANDBANK

Copyright Ian Kampel 2010

CHRISTCHURCH BAY

The Black House
Beach House cafe
location of beach huts
service road

Mudeford Quay

sand banks

Warren Hill

Hengistbury Head

woods

nature reserve

lily pond

lake

CHRISTCHURCH HARBOUR

Blackberry Point

sand bank

Stanpit

River Avon

Christchurch Quay

Stanpit Marsh

CHRISTCHURCH

Christchurch Priory

River Stour

Wick village

Broadway

Hiker cafe
car park
barn
barn field
double dikes

POOLE BAY

MUDEFORD SANDBANK

THE RUN

4

Author's Note

This novel is set in the real and beautiful region shown in the facing map. This location is integral to the story. Settings used include Mudeford Sandbank, Christchurch town and Christchurch Harbour, Hengistbury Head and Wick village: all near Bournemouth, in England. This said, I must confess to using some poetic licence. Whilst the locations are real, buildings other than public buildings are fictional (as are all the characters). Consequently, you will not find specific houses or beach huts mentioned: although you can find the *Black House*, the *Hiker*, *Beach House* and *Soho* cafés, the ferry, the pond and the village. Even the beach hut on the cover is unreal. So if you visit this area just relax, enjoy the scenery, and remember psychological thrillers are meant to be scary; don't walk around in fear just because some of my characters do. So long as you are careful not to fall off a cliff, the worst that can happen is getting sand in your shoes; the best that can happen is to understand why I wanted the beauty of this location to shine through in the story.

Please visit my website at **iankingsley.com** to find out more. It includes pictures to get you in a suitable atmospheric mood, and suggested walks in case you visit the area. Better still, please tell your friends about the website and the book: for real and fictional entertainment.

Ian Kingsley, 2010

— — ∞ — —

Grief has limits, whereas apprehension has none.
For we grieve only for what we know has happened,
but we fear all that possibly may happen.

Pliny the Younger, Letters (c. 97-110)

About the author

Ian Kingsley was born in Peterborough, England, and has lived most of his life on the south coast of Dorset. He has written a number of non-fiction works on science and technology and has worked as an electronics design engineer, technical author, technical publications manager and webmaster. He is married with two children and four grandchildren. Details of his current writing are to be found on his website at **iankingsley.com**.

— — ∞ — —

To my wife, Hazel, for support and patience beyond understanding. To my daughter, Alison, my benchmark reader. To my son, Tim, my benchmark networker. To my friend and mentor, David, for support and understanding beyond patience.

Chapter 1

The crouching figure stared across the narrow strip of beach. Bright moonlight was forcing him to take cover in the shallow dunes. Although fierce flurries of sand occasionally stung his face, he considered conditions to be perfect, for the blustery wind would mask any inadvertent sound he might make. He was quite happy to wait for suitable cloud-cover. As always, the sea was his constant companion as it hissed and sighed in restless sleep.

Totally focused, he was ready to move. He knew his dark jacket and jeans made him practically invisible at night: ideal for a mission. Tonight, he needed to gather information and then get out by boat.

When a cloud finally obscured the moon, he slipped across the sand to the long line of beach huts. He knew he could now move down their entire length without being seen, just like the most highly trained member of the SAS. Time for an update on the hut-dwellers. At last, the mission was on.

— — ∞ — —

Paul Vincent was well aware his wife's tight little smile was the result of feasting her eyes on the sleek, wet-suited contours of Russell Gartland. Were it not for this, he could have relaxed and perhaps even been amused by the overpowering enthusiasm of the man with the spiky, gelled-up hair. Unfortunately, he knew Sasha's weakness only too well. Gartland was showing them his windsurfing training rig on the harbour shoreline. Paul felt almost under-dressed in his baggy red trunks.

'So remember the sport's called windsurfing, not sailboarding, and you're called sailors, not surfers,' said Gartland.

'Confusing,' muttered Leah, shaking her head. Paul watched

his daughter with some amusement. He knew she would want to get all the details like this correct. Dressed in a yellow bikini, she brushed long hair from her face. At only fourteen, she was not quite as tall as her mother and did not have the same toned body, but they were otherwise strikingly alike, except for her being a shade too skinny in his opinion.

Gartland grinned and shrugged. 'That's life, Leah. But windsurfing's a world away from board surfing, believe me. When you start out with displacement sailing, you're boarding through the water like a surfer, but when you're proficient and have learned to hydroplane in stronger winds, you'll be skimming across the surface of the water.' He winked at Leah. 'That's a whole new scene. It's fast.'

'Really?' Paul Vincent was impressed by this new piece of information; he also wanted to draw Gartland's lingering gaze away from his daughter. 'What speed can you get up to when you're hydroplaning, Russell?'

Gartland turned to face him. 'You can plane at around eight to ten knots, Paul, and you can even get to over fifteen knots with recreational equipment.'

'So can you do more with special equipment, Russell?' asked Sasha. Her black bikini revealed a figure almost as athletic as Gartland's, courtesy of her work as a physical education teacher. Paul noticed she moved a little closer to Gartland while enveloping him in one of her broadest smiles.

'Oh yes,' Gartland grinned. 'There's no holding back what you can achieve with special equipment, Sasha.' As they exchanged amused grins, Paul was sure of it. He reckoned he'd noticed their mutual admiration during the theory training Gartland had given them a week earlier, but now this seemed patently obvious as the man continued to hold his wife's gaze. 'It's possible to go right up to fifty knots, Sasha, but ideal conditions for recreational sailors are about fifteen to twenty-five knots.' He pulled up the sail of the training rig. 'So, we've done the theory. Now you need to develop balance and core stability. Stand up on the board, Sasha, and let's get some wind in your sails. You look up for it.'

Sasha stood on the training board but wobbled off when she

was distracted for a moment while smiling at Paul.

'Try again,' said Gartland. 'You can't walk on water, Sasha.'

Paul thought Gartland probably imagined that particular skill was restricted to him. As Sasha stepped back onto the board, a light gust of wind unexpectedly filled the sail, taking her by surprise. When she wobbled towards Gartland, he reached out to support her, one hand resting on her back and the other on her buttocks. Both were laughing uproariously as he pushed her upright again, with his left hand remaining far too long on his wife's bottom for Paul's liking.

'Steady on. Don't handle the goods.' Paul tried to make light of it, but annoyance was clear in his tone.

Still with one hand supporting the small of Sasha's back, Gartland grinned round at him. 'Why do you think I do this job, Paul? Wait till it's your turn, sailor.' He jokingly twitched one eyebrow, causing Sasha and Leah to dissolve into hysterics.

'Just don't push it, Russell, that's all,' said Paul. 'Especially with my daughter.'

Gartland's face now lost its humour and his tone became icy. 'I was only helping with Sasha's core stability, Paul.' He took his hand away from her.

'I'd just concentrate on your own core stability, Russell.' Paul held the other's gaze during an uncomfortable silence. No one was smiling now.

Sasha stepped back off the board, let the sail flop down onto the damp sand, and turned deliberately towards him, with hands on her hips and an exasperated expression on her face. 'Look. Cool it, Paul.' She glared at him. 'Russell only stopped me falling. That's all.'

'Okay, okay. I'm sorry.' Paul was annoyed with himself. He knew he'd over-reacted—and not for the first time—but it was tough being married to a woman who loved to flirt. It wasn't that he didn't trust her—he did—but he hated imagining what other men were thinking when she led them on.

Paul broke the impasse by stepping forward and pulling up the rig's sail himself. He turned to Russell. 'Try it with me, Russell. I'll not fall on you.'

9

Gartland managed to give Paul a weak smile. 'I think I could take it, even if you did. Anyway, start out by taking a firm grip, Paul.' He indicated the bar, but by their subsequent exchange of looks, both knew what he really meant.

Gartland then became more circumspect. He quickly regained his confidence and, by the time the family lesson had ended, they were all in good spirits again.

After they had said their farewells to Gartland, Leah peeled off to the café shop for an ice cream while Paul and Sasha wandered back along the harbourside towards their beach hut. As they walked, Sasha slipped an arm around Paul's waist. A few moments later she shook him playfully. 'You mustn't be so sensitive, Paul. You went way overboard with Russell.' She caught his eye. 'You've got to learn to cool it. He didn't mean anything. He wasn't exactly assaulting me, you know.' She grinned.

Paul put his arm around her, hugging her for a moment. 'Maybe not. But putting down a marker didn't do any harm, did it?' He smiled. 'I'm the only one licenced to correct your core stability, remember.'

Sasha laughed. 'Any time, sailor. I'll try anything once.'

— — ∞ — —

The little voice was barely audible. 'I *can't* believe I've killed him.' She creased her brow and then spoke out again, this time more confidently. 'I can't *believe* I've killed him.' Sighing, she searched her script for clues. Was the line better delivered without any emphasis? Pondering on this, she imagined herself in the scene and decided it perhaps required a rising intonation at the end. 'I can't believe I've *killed* him.' Satisfied at last, she dropped the script on the seat beside her and finally allowed herself to relax and enjoy the wonderful view. 'I can't believe I've *killed* him.' Her grin broadened into a happy smile.

The harbour glistened in the bright sunlight, a distant church tower gleamed white beyond the marshland, and red-sailed dinghies tacked to-and-fro across placid waters. Far to her right a colourful string of beach huts stretched out along a thin finger of sand. She promised herself to go there when she had more time. Below her, further down the hill, she saw a fenced wooded area she imagined must be a nature reserve; she thought she could make out a heron sitting at the top of a Scots pine. Taking it all in, she felt really pleased to have discovered Hengistbury Head; there could be no more inspiring place in which to relax while learning her lines.

Yet, despite the beauty surrounding her, her mind drifted back to the play: this time to the final curtain. Excitedly, she imagined herself bowing to an appreciative audience. Soon she would see 'Carol Davis' printed in a theatre programme. Her smile grew wider and, after a discrete look around to confirm she was alone, she punched the air. 'Yes!' At last she was a real actress and an exciting new career stretched before her.

A chilly wind began to ripple across the purple heather. Wearing a light cotton dress, it made her shiver. Picking up her script, she rose and decided to try to find the narrow path she'd spotted lower down the hill; it looked a pleasant way back to the car park. The track she was on led gently downhill to a hollow where she was surprised to discover an almost secret lake. On her left was the path she was looking for. She followed it around a discreet pond covered in delicate white water-lilies and then through an area where trees and shrubs provided dense cover on a steep slope that dropped away to her right. Although she was now sheltered from the breeze on the Head, she was still pleased to be heading back. Hunger pangs were making themselves known and she thought a hot snack in the nearby Hiker café would be a good way to celebrate her new job; after signing her contract that morning she'd been much too excited to think about anything so mundane as food.

Carol muttered more lines to herself while enjoying the pleasant wooded walk. She always sought solitude when rehearsing, and this was perfection. Areas of close shrubs and trees occasionally parted to frame delightful views across the lower fields to the harbour. It was all so beautiful.

Suddenly a loud rustle of leaves startled a blackbird that flew closely past her, chirping in panic. Carol halted uncertainly. Before she could assimilate what was happening, a

11

man sprang from the bushes and blocked the path. He planted his legs wide apart and outstretched his arms threateningly. To her horror she saw he was wearing a black balaclava. Frantically looking for some way to escape, and aware there was a sheer drop to her right, she veered to the left, but the ground immediately turned boggy. Small uncontrollable sounds of fear emanated from her throat, and her heart was pounding as she struggled back out of the mud. Only the path itself was passable.

The youth grinned and pointed to her feet. 'My, my! What a mess you're getting in. A shame for such a pretty little thing.' He paused to leer. 'Let's see your smile then.'

Carol ran back screaming along the path, but he was on her in a moment. One hand clasped tightly around her mouth, hurting her face, the other around her waist. The script flew from her hands as she tried to dig both elbows into him, but all her efforts were futile, he was far too strong.

'Stop struggling or I'll kill you,' he shouted angrily. She stopped, rigid with fear. 'Now just behave and I won't need to hurt you.' Still holding her tightly by the arm, the man moved around to face her.

Carol focused on the knife in his hand; it was pointing towards her, glinting menacingly. Looking up she saw dark eyes boring into hers through the jagged holes of the balaclava. Seeing her terror, the slit of his mouth twisted into a sardonic grin. 'Fancy walking here alone. Silly girl. Who knows what might happen?' He took his time to look her up and down. 'So what's your name, babe?'

'Michelle.' Almost subconsciously, she spat out the protective lie straight from her script.

'*Me*-shell.' As he drew the word out he seemed to savour the first syllable as if it were some fine delicacy. 'Nice name. Know what? You're almost *too* pretty to live, Michelle.'

— — ∞ — —

Paul never responded readily to the demands of his clock-radio, but, with the hazy, underlying realisation he was still on holiday, there was little chance of mere music having much effect. Groping the empty bed beside him, he confirmed Sasha was gone. She was probably already out running: limbs flying, heart pumping. He had time in hand. And yet... realisation dawned: there was no pushing this particular soundtrack into oblivion. Its significance snapped his mind into focus. It was their song: *I'll Say a Little Prayer*: a tune far too poignant to be ignored.

When he first heard Sasha sing it in karaoke, it had been her Irish lilt that drew his interest; closely followed by recognition of her exquisite beauty. But it was their meaningful exchange of glances during the subsequent applause that led to them both parting from friends, sharing solitary drinks in a dark corner, and later, each other, back at his Oxford digs. He had never been a pick-up artist, but things had been different that night. Sasha had been different, and marriage was the natural conclusion to a wonderful year of shared music and laughter. But this time the familiar tune was not casting its usual spell. Now each beat of the music seemed to modulate his conscience. He'd really made a fool of himself with Gartland the previous day: unfortunately in front of Leah. He must learn to count to ten. Okay, so Sasha flirted. So what? So did many people. It didn't mean a thing. Even *he* flirted, on occasion. Flirting was meant to be fun. On the other hand, Gartland *had* been 'handling the goods'.

The music finished and the DJ began droning on. Without music to mask it, Paul now heard the shower pounding in the bathroom. He guessed Sasha was back from her run. Surely it couldn't be Leah already? She was on teenager hours. Bleary-eyed, he squinted at his beside clock. It blinked onto 08:09 as he watched: late for a workday, but far too early for a holiday, albeit at home. This week was intended to be a complete break before the stresses of moving house. As a successful architect in a prospering partnership, it was not that he was unhappy at work, he loved it, but it was so different without his father at the helm.

Paul had been feeling very depressed lately. He put it down to the bitter-sweet sorrow of building the house he had designed for his family with his father only ever having seen the footings. It was such a tragedy. He could imagine how his dad would have delighted in it; how proud he would have been. Paul snuggled back under the quilt and only gradually permitted his mind to edge into thoughts of the new day, thankfully now to the accompaniment of a less provocative song.

It was Friday and, after making up with Sasha over his behaviour with Gartland—employing prone core stability— they'd decided to spend a long weekend at the beach hut. Paul wriggled happily while plumping up his pillow. Great. Two more easy days before Sunday's barbeque. Sighing lazily, he began transposing limbs into a posture that took full advantage of the king-sized bed, but his returning tranquility was rudely interrupted by strident music on Sasha's mobile phone: it infiltrated the bedroom with all the incessant energy of its owner.

Edging up onto one elbow, Paul listened carefully between the urgent musical bursts. The shower was still pounding, so calling her was pointless. Sighing, he levered himself across the bed and grabbed the mobile phone from her bedside table. A quick glance at the screen showed him it was someone called Glenn.

'Hi. This is Paul on Sasha's phone. She's not here at the moment. Can I take a message?'

The caller remained silent.

'Hello?' Paul could not prevent his impatience sounding. His peace was shattered, his space invaded, and now someone was playing silly games with him. It was way too early for hassle. 'So? Can I give Sasha a message?'

Still silence. After a shallow intake of breath, he heard a terminating click. It appeared Sasha had some very rude friends, although he'd never heard of this particular one. Frowning, Paul took an instant dislike to the man. He put the phone down and flopped back onto the bed. Glenn?

— — ∞ — —

It was over a week ago now, but Carol still found the whole ordeal constantly ran through her head, hijacking her thoughts. She knew she must stop it and find a way to blot the memory out—everything would be okay and he would be caught—but the horror was still too fresh.

By a great force of will, she managed to attend rehearsals, but she found she couldn't say her lines. She barely remembered them, and when she came to the murder scene she froze. The director said he understood but, as he put it, 'At the end of the day, I need a flawless performance, darling.' He was so sorry about her experience, of course. Why not contact him again when she'd got over it—and proven it—by playing in something else first? No, he hadn't exactly said 'proven it', but that was clearly inferred. She knew he needed to be convinced of her ability to deliver as an actress before he would risk her again. She was stuck in Bournemouth and fearful of going home to her parents in Canterbury, knowing full-well how that would lead to their nagging her to get a 'proper job'. She was determined to continue with acting, and going against her dad would prove so painful it would drive them apart in any case. Thank God they never heard anything about her attack in the news.

Meanwhile, she felt in limbo. She needed to get her head together and find another acting job, even if only a small bit-part: then, at least, she would be listed in the credits and have some evidence she was reliable again. But how could she regain her calm? The answer came in a flash of inspiration. *Act it*. Yes! It was the obvious way. She had all the necessary skills, so she simply needed to get into the right mindset. She would act it out. Act as if she were the person she used to be before the attack. Live the role of Carol Davis: the *previous* Carol Davis. After thinking about this for a while, she was sure she could do it. Heck, she'd had a lifetime of practice in the role.

Lying back on her narrow bed in the lonely B & B near Christchurch, she felt a tiny bit happier. All she needed to do was blot out the bad thoughts when they came. What if she imagined they were scenes from a film? Yes, perhaps she could get herself to think of it as a part she played in a film; the scenes that played through her head were very 'filmic', after all. Yes. She would play the part of former Carol Davis, and all that stuff that happened on Hengistbury Head was merely from a film: one in which she'd acted; quite brilliantly, of course. This allowed her to run it through her head once again; just once more, for it demanded to be played again. Just one last time, as an example of how good an actress she'd become. One more time before finally blotting it out. Why? Not because she enjoyed it, but because it was compulsive viewing: to see how she had portrayed that poor girl. Let's see, she was called Michelle.

This time the film played at crazy speed. The startled blackbird and its alarmed chirp; the man jumping out in front of Michelle as she walked the isolated path, his arms and legs forming a cross, a barrier; his creepy voice; the hand coming round her and almost suffocating her; the script, plopping into obscurity; the glinting knife; the way his hand tore and pulled beneath her vulnerably thin summer dress... she could still hear the ripping sound; the leering way he exposed himself with one hand while waving the knife in the other; the way he invaded and jerked her body; his scary, evil eyes—right in her face all the while—almost popping out of his head; the groan when he climaxed and she was, at last, able to push herself free from him, terrified, sobbing; the crashing sound as he vanished down a steep slope between trees and rhododendrons to the wooded area below; her run back past the lily pond, down the ravine-like slope to the road; the little green land train full of staring people that stopped when Michelle shrieked at it, waving her hands, calling 'help me' over and over; the ranger's Land Rover that pulled up right behind the train; at last, sympathy and understanding; the kind brown ranger driving her to his office in The Barn; the police arriving to take her away; the ride in the police car with embarrassed officers; the police rape suite with its all-too-clinical room; the horribly intimate questions; the examination: her skin, and worse, inside... hateful; the way they took her clothes away and loaned her a track-suit; the 'morning-after' pill they'd provided and the way Michelle couldn't even remember if she'd taken her contraceptive, or if she'd been taking it at all lately; the ride back to the B & B in the police car; the endless hot shower with its scouring jets and cleansing steam; the long night during which she just lay on the bed in a daze, with eyes that would not close in a room she couldn't bear to darken; the way she looked at every man on the street when she went out the following afternoon to walk and collect her car from the car park, looking for their eyes, the shape of their mouth...

It was all over now. She had played Michelle well, it had all been an act, and it had ended with a parking ticket: so beautifully mundane and ironic it actually made her laugh when she detached it from her windscreen wiper. She could handle that. She wondered if Sam, the nice police lady, could get her off that one, but it didn't really matter. It was only money, after all. True, she didn't have much of that, but she did have an accommodating credit card.

The part of Michelle was over. Now she was anxious for new roles. Firstly, she would play a much better part, a nicer part: that of Carol Davis, a confident, happy and bubbly girl: with a life so very far removed from Michelle's.

— — ∞ — —

Strangers could often prove more interesting than hut-dwellers; they were more unpredictable. Unpredictability excited him the most. Holiday-makers renting the beach huts never quite knew what was what; they blundered around uncertainly at night. Which was why he sometimes enjoyed being seen by them, so long as it was dark. When he reached one of the toilet blocks he saw a young girl approaching. It was a perfect opportunity. He hovered at the side of the building until he heard she was near and then strode around the corner, bumped into her and cursed in an Irish accent. Screaming with fright, the girl scuttled into the toilet. Grinning, he imagined her inside, alone, quivering with fear in case he followed. This move was always good for a laugh, especially with young girls. Sometimes it even made some of the lads gasp. Maybe he might follow a girl in one day. But then his face would be seen. No, he must never risk that.

Chapter 2

Sasha was in white: all white. She burst into the bedroom with a towel turbaned around her wet hair and wearing a robe: clearly nothing more. After going to the window and pulling back the curtains to flood the room with sunlight, she crossed to the bed, sat beside Paul and smilingly shook his elevated hip.

'Hi. So you're awake at last. Was this break a good idea, or what?' She smiled widely. 'Has it made you feel a bit brighter?'

Looking up at her, Paul put his hand over hers. He knew she was referring to his depression following his father's accident. 'Yes, it's helped a lot. Thanks for suggesting it.' She might be a flirt, but how could he not love her? As he expected, the unpleasantness of the previous day was now long forgotten. 'I've only just woken up, actually. Have you had your run?'

'I certainly have. It's such a beautiful sunny morning, Paul.' Her face sparkled with enthusiasm. 'And it's way time you were up. I've run to Boscombe Pier and back while you've been dozing.' She leaned down to plant a lingering kiss on his lips. Sasha was so brilliant at defusing tension.

Paul relished the kiss gratefully. 'Mmm! So much nicer than morning coffee.' Smiling, he slid his hand into the gaping fold of her robe. 'But what a waste of energy. Exercise could be far more pleasurable right here in bed.' Sitting up further, he kissed her again, this time long and lingering.

Giggling, Sasha gently pulled his hand away and smacked it playfully. 'Down, tiger. There's no time for that. I've hair to dry and calls to make. Let's go to the beach hut really early today. I don't want the holiday mood to end. I've arranged to get a lift with Lucy tomorrow to go to Sainsbury's from Mudeford Quay. Could you meet us when we get back on the ferry? I'll have a load up.'

Paul smiled. 'Of course. To be sure.' He loved kidding her about her Irish accent.

Grinning, she strode across the room while uncoiling the towel from her head. Sitting at her dressing table she toweled her blonde hair vigorously and then let it cascade around her shoulders. 'Unless you want to do the shopping today, of course?' She looked round at him, loosening her robe as she did so, shrugging it off to reveal seamlessly tanned skin. Picking up her hair dryer she waited for his answer.

Paul grimaced. 'I could. I will, if you want. But I really should call in at the build today to see how Charlie's progressing. I need to make some plans for next week. The move's getting near now.'

Sasha shrugged. 'Okay.' Looking back in the mirror, she switched on her dryer. Its roar filled the room as she teased-out her hair with its comb.

Paul allowed himself the luxury of admiring her exquisite body. It was no wonder she turned heads and provoked his green-eyed streak. He realised that was what the 'Glenn-thing' was all about, of course. She was a teacher, after all. She knew hundreds of people: colleagues, parents, pupils, university friends... other friends. The list was endless.

Sasha clicked off the dryer, pulled up her robe and looked round. 'Well, get a move on, Paul. You say you like to get into the bathroom before Leah. I heard her moving around when I came in. She won't be long.'

'By the way, you missed a call on your mobile while you were in the shower.'

'Oh?' Brushing her hair again, Sasha didn't seem particularly bothered.

'I answered it. Just deep breathing. No one spoke. Spooky. Do you often get deep-breathers calling you, Sasha?'

She laughed. 'I've no such admirers, I'm afraid. It must have been a wrong number.'

'Not many people get wrong mobile numbers.' Paul watched her expression intently in the mirror's reflection. There was no visible reaction.

'I don't see how you can say that. If a number's misdialed, it's just as likely to be to a mobile as a landline. I've had them before. Or perhaps someone I know accidentally selected the wrong person on their phone.'

'I don't get wrong mobile calls.' He paused. 'So hadn't you better check it out? See if it was important?'

Sasha lay down her dryer and brush and crossed to the bed. Picking up her phone she flipped it open and took it back to the dressing table. After flicking the calls button she shrugged and looked across at him. 'I don't recognize the number. It must be a wrong one.' She put the phone down and continued drying her hair.

Feeling his jaw tightening, Paul forced himself to relax. So casual. So smooth. Yet so naïve. A wrong number from someone already in her directory? She made it sound so insignificant. Why was she being devious?

His ponderings were cut short when the bedroom door was noisily pushed open by their dog, Shep, as he nosed his way into the room. He was closely followed by Leah. She was smiling widely. 'Hiya, crew,' she drawled, obviously still sleepy. 'Ready for the beach? Life's always a beach on the sandbank, isn't it?' She grinned. Her blonde hair straggled over her face and her lids were low. Shep came to the bed and Paul held out his hand to be snuffled and licked. After crossing to greet Sasha, Shep settled himself near the bedroom door, chin on the ground, his eyes raised to watch their movements.

Leah was wearing a white nightdress covered in coloured question and exclamation marks: more than hint of her love for books. Smiling at her, Paul yet again saw a teenage reflection of her mother's beauty and grace. She crossed to the bed and kissed him on the cheek. 'So, I'm first for the bathroom, okay?' She wagged her finger. 'It's only right, Dad. I'm out of bed first.' She headed across to her mother to exchange a kiss and a hug.

Sasha smiled at her. 'It'll be great when we move into the new house, Leah. When Dad and I have our en-suite, the main bathroom will be all yours.'

'Can't wait.' Leah grinned at Paul. 'So the sooner Dad gets his finger out the better.'

Paul held up a finger. 'Right. Finger out. And on the move.' He tossed back the quilt, leapt out of bed, and spurted for the door.

'Hey?' Big blue eyes followed him with indignation. 'Where do you think you're going?'

'I'll actually be the first one *in* the bathroom, Leah. And possession is nine tenths of the law. Bye-bye.' As he grinned back round the door at her indignant face, they exchanged well-practiced comic-glares.

— — ∞ — —

The lad with rolled-up jeans pushed his boat into the water from where it was beached near the end of his garden. Jumping in, he sat down and rowed with a slow, fluid motion. Golden reflections from the low morning sun danced on the calm waters, and the only noise he heard was the soft plop of his oars as they moved in and out of the water. A shallow mist hung low over marshland at the easterly tip of Blackberry Point; several horses dreamed by the water's edge as if floating on cloud. A light breeze caressed the boy's deeply tanned skin and he sensed the coming of a hot, sun-filled day. He savoured the freshness of the air greedily. It was good to be alive.

After a couple of minutes he stopped rowing, stowed the oars, and moved back to the stern where he sat by the outboard. In no hurry to start the motor, he was content to stare across glittering waters while the boat drifted gently. Squinting against the brightness of the sun, he looked towards the long sandbank that separated the harbour from the sea. Beyond, only faintly discernable through the morning haze, he could see the distant outline of the Isle-of-Wight. The beach huts along the golden line of sand reminded him of colourful beads on a necklace. Nature had painted a glorious picture here, but it was the touch of man that lightened the mood and confirmed it was a place of fun. Sand and sea; fresh air and the sound of breaking waves; it was a combination that created a special magic.

The sandbank seemed like an island to him because of the nature of its community: people who slept and lived out alternative life-styles: while paying handsomely for the privilege of their lazy days. This thought always made him grin; he practically lived his entire life there without cost.

Standing, he pulled the starter-cord and his outboard motor burst into a noisy life that startled some oyster-catchers into sudden flight from their feeding place off the point. In the distance, nearer to the nature reserve, and unfazed by the noise, he spotted a stationary heron standing majestically in the mist. Sitting back into the seat he headed down Hurn Channel. When he was quite near to The Run and the harbour-mouth, he turned around the immersed sandbank into Main Channel, observing the buoys. Finally he crossed the shallow waters of the open harbour towards the beach café and slowly approached his usual morning landfall.

His first visit was to the fisherman's hut near the Black House, but Tom Blake told him there were not enough net or lobster-pot repairs to warrant any work that morning. The fact there would be no money coming his way that day was of little concern. His financial needs were few, although he did have some serious long-term savings plans for when he could get a job with more pay. He was always asking at shops but they never had any job vacancies. Still, one day he might strike lucky.

Although the tide was wrong that morning, he happily spent a long while beach-combing and then stacking some smoothly-bleached logs into his boat; they would look great in his display. He imagined they were borne by the Gulf Stream across the Atlantic before drifting down the Channel; they might have originated from further up the coast, of course, maybe from Poole Harbour, or perhaps from France, but he liked the notion of America best. He was keen on America: 'land of the free... home of the brave'. He was brave, and he always wanted to be free. When he was older he thought he might live in America and be really free.

After buying a coffee at the shop alongside the Beach House café, and sitting at the strangely tall table there to drink it, he wandered down the sand-strewn service road to the foot of Hengistbury Head. On the way he had to step aside to let the little green land train pass by. He resented it. Why should it force him aside? He had as much right to be there as anyone;

more, really. Why couldn't the passengers walk like him?

He climbed the sandy steps onto the heather-clad headland and then lingered to gaze down along the coast to the east: his favourite view of Mudeford Sandbank. He always marvelled at the way it stood so strongly between the combined forces of two merged rivers on one side and the power of the sea's constant lashing on the other. How wonderful that tiny grains of sand, effortlessly moved around by wind and tide—even by people's toes—could jointly have the strength to form such a strong barrier. And what power the waters had. He knew it well. The fact people paid such enormous sums of money for their expensive beach huts also proved everyone else believed the sandbank would always be there. He reflected it was a good job there were never any tsunamis in Dorset. Or was it satsumas? He frowned uncertainly. He never mentioned the word for fear of embarrassment: he knew one or the other were oranges.

Gradually his eye was drawn along the colourful line of huts to the Black House, the last building on the sandbank. It stood next to the fast-flowing tidal waters between harbour and sea, the place where he loved to challenge its power in his little motor boat, especially when its engine could only just match the opposing current. Under these conditions it felt as if he personally overcame the power of Nature, thanks to his own strength and skill.

After a while he headed for his 'thinking seat'. He was a great thinker, or 'dreamer', according to his dad. That morning he dreamed of going to America and powering along Route 66 on the Harley Davidson he planned to buy; he always hankered for a more powerful motorbike. He imagined himself with an attractive blonde seated on the pillion, clutching excitedly to his waist, wholly dependent on his biking skills as he rode a ton to the accompaniment of that throaty roar. How he loved the sound of a Harley. He thought about the girls in his magazines: how attractive they were; how great they would be as girlfriends; what fun they would have with him crossing the States on his bike; what fun he would have with them at nights in motels. Yes, he would definitely do all that one day.

Then he visualised himself on nearby Poole Quay with his Harley and his long-haired girl, both in black leather, her wearing a short leather miniskirt, him the envy of the other bikers as they ogled her long, tanned legs. He also imagined what it might be like to own a *Sunseeker* boat, to moor in the South of France, to smile modestly at the admiring café people at the water's-edge. Which led to thoughts about the beach huts again, the happy families, the couples. Why did his life have to miss out on all that?

Hearing noises behind him, he glanced back to see who was coming. It was a family he vaguely recognised. They were happy and laughing. The man was tall, dark-haired and lucky: lucky because his woman was a real stunner with short blonde hair, now exposing a lot of sleek tanned stomach between her bright orange top and hipster jeans. The daughter was a fair eyeful too, although a bit young for him. She was also blonde, slim, shapely, similarly dressed to her mother, but her top was red. He knew they were hut dwellers. They had their boisterous dog with them, bouncing about all over the place, out of control, as usual. He didn't like dogs very much. They were too noisy and unpredictable. The girl was throwing a stick and the dog was fetching it and scampering around, barking excitedly, impatient for another throw: a dim, easily-amused creature. A family having fun: he couldn't abide it. Hunching over and looking studiously away from them, he gazed moodily across the sea towards the island. Mentally, he merged into the landscape so he would not be noticed.

Soon the family disappeared down the steps and he listened with relief to the fading sound of the girl's laughter and the dog's excited barking. Why had he never had a happy family life like that? Then it came to him. Rubbish parents, that's why.

— — ∞ — —

After lunch, Paul took time-out to cycle over to the new-build in Wick village. He felt guilty about leaving his builder-friend to fend for himself for a whole week, especially since he was only paying him 'mates-rates'.

Such concerns quickly evaporated when they were replaced by the warm feeling of pride that overcame him when he entered his new house. The tangy smell of plaster still hung in the air but the change in appearance was startling: at last it looked like a home. The new lightness hit him immediately for cold masonry had been replaced by beautiful plasterwork. While he had designed plenty of buildings far more ambitious than this, there was nothing as satisfying as designing your own house and watching its gradual realisation.

Paul climbed the polished wooden treads of the open staircase in the tall atrium area: the centre-piece of the house. As he did so, he once again admired the clean finish of the plasterwork; its perfect smoothness was a real achievement, given its unbroken height. Just as he had imagined it, the free-standing stairs seemed to float magically alongside walls that towered high above to the blue-tinted glass panels in the roof. This central light-shaft ensured the house would always be flooded with light by day; blue lighting down the walls would make it a completely different feature by night.

At the turn of the stairs, where a half-landing opened onto what he termed the 'day-level', Paul firstly glanced into the kitchen, pleased to see all the units were now fitted and gleaming. Then he went across the landing to the lounge, drawing nearer to scraping noises and the sound of a radio. Despite the white-clad figure busy working on the far wall, Paul's initial attention was drawn to the view through the fold-back doors. It was all as wonderful as he remembered it: fields, harbour, headland and, beautiful in the distance, the chalky whiteness of the cliffs on the Isle-of-Wight.

Paul gave a brief whistle, just loud enough to be heard above the radio, then approached his friend and cheerfully patted him on the shoulder. 'Hi there, Charlie. How's it going?'

As Charlie looked round, his deeply tanned face broke into a lopsided grin. 'Well, well. Look what the wind's blown in.'

It was good to hear that slow Hampshire drawl again. 'Can't keep away for too long,' said Paul, smiling. 'And I can see it's all going well. Very well, in fact.' They had known each other for years and were close friends and drinking buddies.

As Charlie continued with the plastering, he nodded towards the view. 'You've had a nice bit of sunshine, Paul. Pity us poor buggers left workin' though.'

Paul laughed. 'Enough of that. I feel guilty already.'

'And so you should,' drawled Charlie, grinning over his shoulder. 'Back-achin' stuff this.'

Paul turned his attention to the lounge, pleased to see Charlie had covered all the floor area alongside the walls with dustsheets: although dusty white footprints detracted from the natural beauty of the polished wood in the centre of the room. 'You've done a great job with the atrium plastering, Charlie. I didn't envy you that job.'

'But you didn't mind designing it.' Charlie winked at him. 'Anyway, I'm nearly finished in here. Then it's just decoratin'. It is going well, Paul. Be grateful I've been slavin' away here while you've been loungin' on the beach. All right for some.' Charlie smoothed off and turned to gather a further load. His forehead wrinkled into a myriad of creases as he bent to do this while looking up at Paul with his unfailing smile. 'Still, you'll be helpin' out next week, I've no doubt.' He rose with fresh plaster on his hawk. White plaster was speckled around the grey eyes that held Paul's gaze for a significant moment. 'We need a strong final push, Paul. You can't put the move off, remember.'

Paul nodded. 'I know. It's only ten days now before completion on the flat. So I'll be here every evening next week, and I'm hoping to take Thursday and Friday afternoons off as well, to help. You're still free all next week, aren't you, Charlie?'

The other nodded, then returned to his plastering, talking over his shoulder as he slid plaster effortlessly onto the wall with wide, graceful strokes. 'But not the week after that, remember. I've sealed all the remaining plasterwork ready for paintin'. There'll be plenty you can get on with, don't you worry.' He turned round and winked. 'Don't forget to let me paint the atrium. They don't call me Spiderman for nothin'.'

Grinning, Paul walked over to the partly open glass doors and stood in the gap, delighting in the view and the freshness of the breeze. The scent of cut grass mingled with the tang of the sea. It excited him to think he would soon be able to enjoy all this every day. 'I'm asking Sasha and Leah to help with the decorating next week. I'm even getting Leah to paint her own bedroom, although she doesn't know it yet.'

'You reckon she's up to that, Paul?' Charlie sounded doubtful. 'Has she painted a wall before? You've heard about a ha'peth of tar, I suppose?'

Paul laughed. 'Leah is a perfectionist, so it should work out. Especially if it's her room at stake.'

Charlie smiled at him. 'Perfectionist, eh? Now I wonder where she got that?'

— — ∞ — —

After Paul returned from the new-build, the family was quite content to relax for the rest of the afternoon at their beach hut. Many of their sandbank hours were passed like this, with their director's chairs planted on the hut's elevated wooden veranda. They just read, chatted, or simply gazed across at the bobbing boats in Christchurch Harbour. It was a great way to unwind before bed. Early nights were the norm; electricity was a precious commodity when you had to generate it yourself.

While all the beach huts were built for sleeping, they all had different arrangements. Theirs had two sections separated by a central work-surface and cupboards: to the front were double-doors and a comfortable seating area with a table that overlooked the harbour; to the rear was a small kitchen with a further door opening onto the narrow sandy strip that separated the parallel rows of back-to-back huts. Their seating and table converted into a double bed, and a wooden ladder in the kitchen led up to the roof-space which was Leah's private sleeping area and den.

Sasha was reading a magazine while Paul sketched the harbour on a pad. Sitting between them, Leah was engrossed in a paperback. As Paul drew with soft strokes of his graphite pencil, he periodically drifted into deep thought or momentarily smiled down at Shep who was watching them lovingly, his tongue lolling to one side of his mouth. A collie-cross, he was always alert, yet unknown genes did permit him to enjoy generous bouts of inactivity.

Paul focused on the distant tower of Christchurch Priory as he began sketching it, but after capturing it with a few strokes, he let his pencil rest. It reminded him of his father's recent funeral there; feeling himself welling-up, he fought to mask his emotions. It was so hard to believe such an experienced architect could have fallen from scaffolding. As he turned it over in his mind once again, he felt his eyes moistening. Alarmed, he surreptitiously wiped away a tear and tried to mask his emotions, but an indrawn breath softly pulsated into a sob that betrayed him. As a diversion he tried to look busy with his sketchpad. Yet Sasha had heard: or noticed.

'Are you okay, Paul?' She looked up from her magazine, concern etched on her face.

Paul smiled at her. 'I was drawing the priory tower and it reminded me of Dad's funeral.' He sighed. 'And the fact he won't ever see the house. He was so proud I was doing it. He was really looking forward to seeing the end result. Especially the atrium.'

Sasha leaned across Leah to rest her hand on his arm. 'It wasn't his fault, Paul. You know they said the scaffolding was loose.'

'But he should never have been leaning on it like that, Sasha.'

'Which is why you must learn to take very special care of yourself, for all our sakes,' she said. 'We love you too much. Hard-hat and take care. Always. Promise, Paul?'

Paul patted her hand, smiling his thanks at her concern. 'Promise.'

Sasha withdrew her own hand, but it was immediately replaced by Leah's. She had looked up to see what was going on. 'And Grandpa *will* see the new house.' She looked earnestly at him. 'You're not just dead when you die, Dad. Your soul lives on. He can come back and see it any time he likes.'

'True.' Paul smiled at his daughter and then grinned as he

thought of a way of changing the subject. 'And I was also thinking about how we must finish off the decorating next week.' He held Leah's gaze. 'Just think, sweetheart. We're moving-in the week after next. Excited?'

'Yes. I'm really looking forward to moving in, Dad. I love Wick. But it's such a pity my bedroom will be so much smaller than it is now.' She put on a dramatically forlorn air. 'I think you got that design detail very wrong, actually. Another metre would have been much better.' She smiled sweetly at him. 'And I'm worth it, after all.'

'Ah, but the plot's a bit narrow, so that's the price you have to pay for all the other advantages. Like the wonderful view you'll have from your bedroom window. You've only got a big bedroom at the moment because we're in an old house. So remember that view, Leah. Focus on the view. Location, location, location, remember. That's what Grandpa used to say, and he knew all about it, didn't he?'

Leah was now looking upset. 'Poor Grandpa.' Her bottom lip stiffened for a moment. 'Anyway, I do appreciate the view, Dad, so don't worry. It is a good location, and I guess the lack of space is the price I'll have to pay for going minimalist.' And with that she returned to her book.

'Minimalist?' Paul chuckled, exchanged an amused glance with Sasha and looked fondly back at his daughter. The prospect of Leah going minimalist was laughable: she was the greatest hoarder alive. That apart, she was his secret treasure, but this was not all down to her beauty. He loved her gentle, selfless nature. She had her mother's flashing smile, although hers opened more languidly, like a blossoming flower in the sun. She did most things in slow motion, but often with great precision and care. Her blue eyes also came from her mother; these usually only seemed half-open, hidden behind deep lids as if she were half asleep, often lending her a dreamy air. Because of this, and the fact she mostly came across as extremely laid-back, her appearance often lulled people into a false sense of security; but when riled, the lids opened wide, she pulled her hair right back and the monster from the deep lagoon arose, ready for anything until she eventually backed off to take stock.

Paul could see her mother's same sleek body in Leah. Sasha worked-out and ran most days; squash and surfing were her favourite pasttimes. Paul had even built a small gym into the ground floor of their new house, alongside the integral garage. Leah sometimes ran with her, but not with the same obsession. As for himself, apart from swimming and surfing, Paul preferred mental exercise.

Leah brought him out of his reverie by getting up and announcing she was going to fetch a coke. While she was inside the hut, a couple of teenage lads dressed in black wetsuits strolled past carrying surfboards. Paul couldn't miss how they muttered, laughed and grinned at each other as they openly eyed-up Sasha. Clearly Sasha noticed this too, for she looked up and smiled at them before going back to her magazine. Cool, as always, thought Paul. While Leah and he were dressed in jeans and T-shirts, Sasha still wore her black bikini bottom and a short, orange, T-shirt top that too plainly revealed there was nothing beneath it. Paul guessed the lads were laughing at the 'MAKE ME AN OFFER' message emblazoned in blue across it, and he felt sure they'd love to do just that. Why did she have to wear such a thing? Even worse, she encouraged Leah to do the same. He figured it was asking for trouble, but he never said anything. He was not ready to be branded an old-fogy at 36.

Leah returned with a can, but Paul continued to watch the retreating figures, squirming at the lustful comments he imagined the boys were probably now exchanging as ribald laughter drifted back to him. One of them stopped, turned back and made an obscene pelvic thrust that provoked roars of laughter from his companion. Even from the distance, Paul imagined he could distinguish their evil grins. When they turned to walk on he wanted to chase after them and give them a piece of his mind. Gritting his teeth, he forced himself to look at the harbour instead.

He never found that kind of thing easy. Like the mysterious 'Glenn' phone call. He imagined the worst and then beat himself up worrying about it. A few years earlier, while waiting in a hotel lobby, he overheard a smart businessman describing Sasha as 'stunning' to his colleague. Even now it was still true. He felt angry at the leering looks she sometimes provoked on the one hand, but proud she was his wife on the other. It was not so bad if people simply glanced and passed on by; he could handle that. What he hated most was when people stared and obviously talked about her. The two lads were an extreme example of this.

After tea, Sasha and Leah went for an evening swim while Paul read a book inside the hut. When Sasha's mobile phone rang he grabbed it quickly. His worst fears were fulfilled when the name 'Glenn' came up on the screen again. As before, the man hung up as soon as he spoke. He began to feel very unsettled. It was probably nothing, but it did seem strange Sasha would not admit the name was in her phonebook. If there was nothing to hide, why did this Glenn remain silent? And why did Sasha try to make out it had been a wrong number on the previous occasion?

When Sasha returned with Leah, Paul mentioned her phone had rung. She checked it and shrugged. 'Another wrong number, I guess.'

Without consulting her, Paul stood and silently began converting the seats and table into their night-time bed. He simmered quietly to himself. He was determined to think of a way of getting to the bottom of the Glenn mystery.

— — ∞ — —

He moved silently between the backs of the two rows of huts, peering into windows. The next one rewarded him with the sight of a girl: a teenager, a beautiful blonde with a shapely little waist and a bottom that wiggled as she descended some varnished steps from an upper level. He liked the way she moved. Tight blue jeans. Very nice.

Then he realised this was the hut of the family with the bouncy dog. The beautiful woman was doing something at the sink with her back to him, and the man was moving things around at the front of the hut.

31

It took him by surprise when the girl jumped down the last few steps and turned towards him. He saw her eyes widen as they engaged with his. He grinned back at her before ducking away from the window. Time to go.

— — ∞ — —

Leah's scream startled them all. 'Dad!'

Shep immediately started barking and shot towards the rear door, scratching at it wildly to get out.

'What's up?' Paul looked round to see Leah facing him, wide-eyed with shock, both hands over her cheeks. 'Someone was looking in at me, Dad. A man.'

'You sure?' Paul darted around her, nearly falling over Shep as he headed for the rear door. He practically wrenched it off its hinges as he flung it open. Still barking, Shep barged his way out, closely followed by Paul.

The retreating figure was barely discernable in the pale moonlight. He was running between the two lines of huts, something bulky clutched under one arm. Suddenly he disappeared between two huts. Shep was now almost upon him, still barking loudly. When Paul rounded the same corner he stumbled over Shep. The dog was snuffling and pawing at something on the ground. Ignoring him, Paul ran out onto the service road to look for the fleeing figure, but there was no sign of him. He had vanished into the darkness. Paul strained to listen for footsteps, but the noise of the wind, the zinging of wires on dingy masts and the crashing sea made it impossible to hear anything so subtle. A shower of sand stung his face. Now and then the wind whistled eerily through the blades of a wind turbine on a nearby hut. The beach road was deserted. The man could be hiding anywhere and could easily weave between the numerous huts or hide in the hollow space beneath one of them.

Shep went up to Paul, whining, bouncing to-and-fro, nuzzling his hand, constantly looking the way they had come, clearly urging Paul to follow him. He led him to the object that so intrigued him before. Paul watched with interest as Shep began scratching and biting at what appeared to be a bag.

Catching hold of it confirmed this. It had strange contents that rattled, so Paul took it back to the hut for a closer inspection. He guessed the fleeing man must have dropped it and that this was what had diverted Shep.

Entering the hut, Paul dumped the bag inside the door and went over to Leah, to whom he gave a comforting hug. 'No sign of him. He's well gone by now, sweetheart.'

'Chasing him like that might have been dangerous, Dad,' she scolded him.

'I'm a big boy now. Are you all right?'

Leah smiled gratefully up at him. 'Yes, I'm okay now, thanks. It gave me a shock to see him looking right in at me. We had eye-contact. He even smiled at me. Can you believe that?' She was incredulous.

Seeing her eyes were still wide and anxious, Paul gave her a kiss on the forehead and stepped back, holding both her hands at arm's length, a concerned look on his face. He shook his head, sighing. 'It's just some nutcase, Leah. And Shep gave him a real scare. He won't be back after that.'

Sasha came over and put an arm around them both. 'Leah's right, though, Paul. You should be more careful. Anything could happen in the dark.' She stood back and pointed at what Paul had brought in. Shep was snuffling at it, still intrigued. 'What's that?'

Paul picked up what they could all now see was an orange Sainsbury's shopping bag. He immediately found out what was interesting Shep so much: an opened packet of chocolate digestive biscuits. 'No, no, you're not allowed chocolate, Shep.' Paul put the packet onto a work surface and reached for a tub of dog treats on a shelf. He gave some to Shep as a consolation prize: twenty seconds of lip-smacking heaven.

Paul also discovered a red vacuum flask, a transparent bag of breadcrumbs and a collection of shells and beach pebbles inside the bag: an unlikely hoard. 'I think the peeper was carrying this. He must have dropped it when Shep chased after him. But it's a funny load of stuff for a man to be carrying around. I mean, just look at it. More of a kid's collection.'

'Actually he was more of a boy than a man, Dad,' explained

Leah. 'Anyway, well done Shep.' She knelt down to hug the dog around the neck. 'Good boy.' Shep licked her face and looked from one to another of them, wagging his tail wildly, clearly very pleased with his night's work.

'Eaaah!' After rubbing her cheek clean and grinning, Leah examined the shopping bag more closely. 'Looks as though Shep bit it,' she said, pointing to a stretched part of the bag that showed the imprint of teeth. 'Shep snatched it away from him. Clever Shep.' She ruffled the dog's fur and he licked her even more enthusiastically in response.

'Shep only did it for his supper,' Paul observed. 'He could smell chocolate. That's what I call self-interest, Leah.'

'Pity he didn't eat the man for supper instead,' said Sasha. 'Silly Shep.'

'No, no, don't be cross with Shep,' pleaded Leah, crouching down and hugging the dog all the more. 'He did his best. And that's all any of us can do, isn't it, Dad? That's what you say, isn't it?'

Paul nodded and gave her a weak smile. 'Too right.'

'And he still needs to go out, I suppose. Did he do anything?' asked Leah.

'Only catch his supper,' grinned Paul.

Leah made as if to go to the door. 'I'll take him out again, then.'

Paul caught her arm. 'No you don't, young lady. I'll take him out tonight.'

'And you be careful, too,' warned Sasha. 'Take your torch.'

'I'm always careful, darling. Always careful.'

'Like now? Chasing after some pervert in the dark? Yeah, right. You're always so careful, aren't you, Paul?'

Paul grinned and winked at her. 'So long as you know it, sweetheart.' He picked up his torch from a shelf and turned to Shep. 'Come on, boy. Time for a proper walkies.'

Chapter 3

Stevie Clarke's hut was known in the family by the rather grand name of 'the garden house'. Formerly a red-brick fisherman's workshop, the little ivy-clad building had been lovingly converted by his dad into a self-contained home: complete with a combined lounge and kitchenette and a separate tiny bedroom with an en-suite toilet and shower room. It was raised above a shallow enclosed base for flood protection. The base included double-doors giving access to space originally used for net storage. These were just high enough to allow him to get his motorbike inside for protection from the elements. The entrance door to his living accommodation was reached via four wooden steps. Thanks to his dad's inspiration, both Stevie and his parents had been much happier as a result of this conversion. Stevie had hated living in the house and much preferred his own company.

Situated right next to the narrow strip of shoreline where Stevie moored his boat, the garden house could not have been better located for him. He was really happy there. He could sit outside on an old wooden bench and gaze across the harbour to Hengistbury Head any time he wanted. He often ate sandwiches or fish-and-chips there. It was also his favourite place to while away the time looking at his magazines, or simply to think. It was also the place where he could most easily chat with his mum or dad: the place where they all seemed the most relaxed.

Breakfast was nearly always early in the Clarke household because Stevie's father usually took the early morning shift in his jointly-owned taxi. His mother had it ready for six o'clock sharp. Spot-on time, Stevie walked up the garden path towards the house with his usual air of anticipation: and a raised nose that soon detected the reassuring smell of fried bacon. Sometimes Mum would insist they just had toast and cereal—'for the sake of your dad's arteries', as she put it—but this morning he was confident it would be a full English breakfast.

The bacon would come with egg, sausage, beans, fried-bread—all the things he adored—plus piping hot tea and toast. Mum did it really well and it set him up nicely for the day. It was his favourite meal.

The garden consisted of a graveled area next to his garden house, a small kitchen garden behind this, then a narrow strip of grass on either side of the path that lead to the kitchen door. As he walked towards the house, his mother smiled at him through the window and waved. She was busy at the sink doing some washing up. He entered the warm room, brushed his feet vigorously on the mat and plucked his breakfast plate from the warming grid over the cooker. Taking it to the old pine table he sat opposite his father.

'Mornin' Dad. Mum.'

The delicious smell got his taste-buds going immediately. Dad was tucking into his own breakfast, his eyes constantly drifting to the kitchen clock. 'Mornin', Stevie. Just in time before it gets cold.' His wide mouth worked as slowly and remorselessly as a cement-mixer; egg-yolk began to dribble from it in a bright yellow trail that slowed across a bulbous chin until it was halted in its track by a stubby finger. Stevie noted with amusement that his father's glasses steamed up when he took a sip of tea from his enormous red mug. He chuckled.

'Something funny, lad?'

Stevie shook his head. 'Nope.'

Dad stared at him for a moment and replaced his cup on the table. 'I'm hopin' one of these mornings you'll oversleep an' I'll finish yours up as well,' he grinned, nodding at Stevie's plate.

'That you won't, Frank,' retorted Mum indignantly, turning from her washing-up. She waved a finger covered in suds at her husband. 'One of those breakfasts is bad enough for you, let alone two. You should have toast and cereal every morning like me. Look at your belly, man. Can't even get your belt round it no more.'

'Absolute rot, Mary. I'm wearin' it now. See!' Frank half stood, a thumb hooked into a belt slung low beneath his huge beer-belly. 'And I need me full-English.' With clear delight he chomped the end off a sausage held up on his fork and sat down again. 'With all that drivin' to do, all that manhandlin' stuff, a man needs a decent cooked breakfast. No taxi driver worth his salt could survive without one.'

'Nor without a mid-morning snack of bacon-baps as well, I'll warrant.' Mary placed the clean frying pan onto the drying rack and joined them at the table. She shook cereal into a bowl and poured milk over it. Spoon in hand, and contrary to her protestations, her little button eyes watched with obvious satisfaction as the two men tucked hungrily into their meals.

Having taken a few mouthfuls of her cereal, Mary concentrated on Stevie. 'I'm going shopping this afternoon, Stevie, so if there's anything you need then let me know soon.' She looked quizzically at him. 'Soap? Toilet rolls? Anything you can think of?'

Stevie paused for a moment, fried bread hovering over his runny egg. 'My magazine, Mum?' He sounded uncertain.

'Tuh!' His mother tossed her head indignantly. 'If you think I'm getting your mucky magazine for you you've got another think coming, Stevie Clarke. Not that Sainsbury's would have such a thing, anyway.'

'It's not mucky, Mum. It's got film reviews and all sorts of stuff for men in it.'

'I know very well what stuff for men is like. Lots of mucky pictures of girls, mostly without any clothes on.' Mary poured herself a cup of tea in a flurry, spilling a little onto the table as she did so. 'Time you grew up and read some decent magazines or books. Motor cycle maintenance or something.' Her voice had risen a clear octave, a sure sign of her agitation. Stevie hated it when she squeaked: it always meant trouble.

Frank, who had just finished his last mouthful and had cleared his plate aside ready for toast and marmalade, now found time to intervene. He winked at his wife. 'It's only top-shelf stuff, Mary. Best let the boy be. Not get him too excited, like. Better to goggle at that stuff than worse.'

'Worse?' Mary looked at him crossly. 'Worse magazines? Worse behaviour? What sort of worse, Frank?' Stevie's eyes drifted from one to the other of them during this exchange, but his eating continued unabated. They were always talking about him as if he were not there. So annoying.

Frank frowned at Mary, mouthing urgent words that Stevie easily interpreted as 'shut-up'. 'Better to dream, than act,' Dad hissed. 'Leave the lad be.'

'Cheers, Dad,' said Stevie. Why could Mum never let him be?

— — ∞ — —

While Sasha and Leah went off shopping with their friend Lucy Forbes, via the Mudeford ferry, Paul undertook a few chores. One was to re-mount a freshly painted name-plaque on their beach hut proclaiming 'Brief Respite'. Doing so brought Sasha's parents to mind. The hut was still theirs, but they had passed on usage to them when they went to live in Australia a couple of years earlier. Sasha's father had called the hut 'Brief Respite' in the traditional humorous tone: choosing the name because, as a lawyer, he relished lazy spells well away from legal matters. The exorbitant cost of these beach huts— probably the most expensive in the world—meant that, was it not for this piece of luck, it was highly unlikely they would ever have had the use of one. Paul's spending was far more prudent.

After doing a few more chores, he headed off with Shep for a relaxing coffee at the Beach House café. It was a pleasant vantage point from which to watch out for the return of Sasha and Leah on the ferry. Sitting with his coffee on the café veranda, he went over details of the forthcoming barbeque in his mind. Normally they only invited beach hut friends, but this time, at Sasha's insistence, they had also invited people from their 'real lives': including a few teaching friends from Sasha's school and Paul's recently widowed mother—not that widowhood, to his chagrin, prevented her from still enjoying life to the full.

The coffee was good, the view was interesting, and it was entertaining to vaguely listen to the loud chatter of two young girls on the adjacent table. He always felt disgruntled when he thought about how quickly his mother had continued her hedonistic lifestyle after his father's death. With some effort, he put her out of his mind and told himself to remember what Leah always kept saying: 'life's a beach'.

— — ∞ — —

The cool south-westerly breeze brought with it the salty tang of the sea. The sun shone brightly in a clear blue sky and it promised to be yet another delightful day. Stevie heaved a bleached log into the bow of his boat and turned again to look at the two girls seated on the veranda of the Beach House. It seemed they couldn't take their eyes off him. Both were stunningly attractive. It was clearly an opportunity not to be missed. Despite his best attempt to appear casual as he strolled across the sand towards them, he felt as awkward as a crab.

'Nice mornin',' he announced, stopping near to them, looking up to their elevated position, adjusting his lips into the best smile he had practiced in front of his bedroom mirror. His finger and thumb briefly stroked the designer-stubble on his chin. He'd seen Kevin Costner do that. By now the girls were feigning not having seen him, but he was used to that. 'Not seen you two here before. Come here often?' Stevie was not that easily put off.

'Hey, Julie,' said the girl with long blonde hair. Stevie thought he recognised an Australian twang to her accent. 'Did you hear something then? Do you reckon we'll come here often?' She grinned at her companion and winked.

'Well, hard to tell, Cass, since this is our first morning,' replied the dark-haired girl. She was definitely English. She smiled down at Stevie. 'Although, I expect a big strong boatman like you spends a lot of time here. And sooh brown,' she purred. Looking at her companion she caught her grin and they both began to giggle.

'And boy, sooh handsome,' winked the Australian girl. 'I bet you catch lots of big fish. I bet it makes your big muscles ripple a fair treat.' More sniggering from both of them.

Stevie shuffled uncomfortably in the sand. He had the

feeling they were teasing him: but perhaps not. Perhaps they were genuinely interested in his physique; he knew it was good. It was always hard for him to tell if people were teasing him. 'I'm not really a fisherman, see. But I can fish. No problem. That's my boat,' he said proudly, pointing to where his motorboat was beginning to bob in the deepening water. 'I go right out to sea in it. Honest. Man, it's a good boat. I go way out, even when the waves are really big.' He demonstrated their size with a sweeping gesture. 'I can catch fish if I want.' He stepped closer to the veranda and rested a hand on it. 'You on holiday here, girls?'

The blonde girl nodded. 'You got it. All the way from Sydney, that's me. A week on this desert island. If we don't get too bored. Trouble is, tell you the truth, I'm getting kinda bored already.' She made a dramatic yawning gesture and the dark girl giggled in response. 'There's a lot more beefcake on Bondi, that's for sure.'

Not understanding this remark, Stevie ignored it. Did she mean barbeques? 'If you're bored, you could come out in my boat,' he offered eagerly, looking shyly down at his boots. Colour rose to his cheeks. He straightened as a new idea struck him. 'Or on my motorbike. I'm a biker, see. We could go really fast on my motorbike.' He looked excitedly from one to the other of them. Surely this would appeal. 'Of course, one of you would have to stay,' he pointed out. He didn't mind which one came, they were both stunners.

The girls grinned at each other. 'We do have this terrible trouble choosing when it comes to hunks,' pouted the dark-haired girl. 'Especially bikers,' and the two of them broke into peals of laughter and table-slapping.

'Too right. We don't like making each other jealous,' said the Australian, provoking further hilarity.

Stevie felt uncomfortable again. He was not keen on people laughing. Generally he thought they were laughing at him, which must usually be the case since he never told any jokes. He could never remember jokes; he didn't even understand most of them. He looked from the girls to the boat, then back again. 'Tide's comin' in. I need to pull the boat up a bit further,' he muttered. He turned and went back to his boat while he thought it out. The girls' laughter rang in his ears as he walked across the sand. Were they interested in him or just poking fun? He thought they did seem interested in his bike. He wondered if he ought to tell them it was only an old Triumph in case they expected something new and shiny. Yet he didn't want to risk putting them off. He decided to keep quiet about that.

Stevie heaved his boat further up the beach, glancing back covertly to check the girls were still watching him as he did so. He was trying to look casual and experienced. He snatched the grapnel from the sand and casually tossed it further up the beach until the rope pulled taut and it snapped sharply back into the sand.

'Heeeey! Watch it, you idiot!' Looking round, Stevie realised the shout came from a man standing next to the two girls on the café veranda. 'That's my daughter.' The man was gesturing wildly, and this made Stevie turn to see a young girl had tossed herself backwards onto the sand nearby. She looked scared, and her foot was extremely near the embedded grapnel. A shopping-bag had spilled its contents onto the sand.

'Good grief, that nearly hit me,' said the girl, her eyes huge.

Meanwhile, the shouting man had let himself out of the gate on the café veranda and had run across to them. 'You damn idiot,' he shouted at Stevie. 'You nearly killed my daughter with that thing. You need to look what you're doing.'

Stevie recognised the family. With an embarrassed backward glance, he noticed the girls were now standing to see what was going on. Their laughter had ceased. He knew he'd been careless, but it was difficult to concentrate when people were watching: especially if they were pretty girls. Angrily, he felt the colour rising to his cheeks again, and he could see the man looked real mean. Out the corner of his eye he saw the girls were not missing a thing.

— — ∞ — —

Realising how close she had come to serious injury, Leah's

heart was pounding with shock. She suddenly felt so vulnerable, wearing flimsy shorts and flip-flops. The vicious spike had embedded itself into the sand no more than eighteen inches from her foot. Looking round she saw her mother was busy balancing her own shopping bags against each other on the sand, presumably so she could come to her aid. But the next thing she knew was that her father and Shep had appeared from nowhere. Shep was barking madly and Dad was shouting at the lad while he helped her up. She winced as a sharp pain shot through her ankle.

'Have you hurt yourself, sweetheart?' Her father turned his full attention onto her, really concerned. He bent to examine her foot, touching it softly, making quite sure she was not injured.

'I'm fine, Dad.' She managed to give him a reassuring smile, despite a sharp pain in her ankle. 'Really, it's okay.'

Her father snapped at the lad. 'You need to look what you're doing, you senseless idiot. Apologise to my daughter. You could have seriously injured her.'

Leah looked from her father's angry face to the lad's. His detached expression suggested he felt he was being unfairly criticised. Leah wondered if he was in another world or just plain careless. His eyes looked normal so he probably wasn't on drugs. In some ways he was not bad looking, although he had rather thick lips for her liking. His forehead and eyes were framed by two large quiffs of blond hair, one practically obscuring his left eye. Somehow, he looked familiar. His mouth hung open rather stupidly, exposing yellowing teeth amidst the shadow of several days' stubble, and he had the deeply tanned appearance of someone always outdoors. She guessed he was in his early twenties. Then she remembered where she'd seen him before, and she could not help staring to confirm it. When he took a brief glance at her and noticed her attention he quickly looked away.

Suddenly feeling strong, Leah spoke out to him. 'Actually, I agree with my dad,' she said firmly. 'The least you can do is to apologise for being careless.'

'But I didn't see you,' the lad snapped, glancing sullenly at her. 'Fuck me.' He scuffed the sand with his shoe.

'And that makes it better?' asked Leah.

'You heard her?' prompted Dad.

The lad tried to shrug the incident off as if he were not involved. He looked at her father with defiance. 'I didn't see her, right? Fuck me.'

'You must be stupid as well as blind,' said Paul. 'And watch your language in front of ladies. You need to look before you chuck a dangerous thing like that around. So be more careful in future and say you're sorry to her.' He gestured towards her. 'To the girl you almost maimed for life.'

Trust Dad to go overboard. The lad scowled, but quickly regained attitude. He pulled his head back, glared and thrust his arms out in a gesture reminiscent of an indignant Frenchman. 'Look, cool it, man,' he snapped, loudly. 'Or do you want to make somethin' of it?' He stared defiantly at her dad.

Leah hobbled over to tug at her father's arm. 'Dad, he didn't mean it. He is sorry. It was an accident. Just leave it now.'

Her father pulled away from her grasp, never taking his eyes off the youth. 'Well? An apology is not too much to ask, surely?'

Why did her dad have to be so confrontational? Then, to Leah's relief, her mother stepped forward to intervene. As a teacher, she was used to playing mediator. 'Look, my husband just thinks it would be nice of you to tell my daughter you're sorry. He's worried and upset about what might have happened if there'd been an accident. You could just say 'sorry' to Leah, couldn't you? Then everyone will know you didn't mean it to happen.' She said all this in soft but clipped tones, with special emphasis on the word 'nice'. Leah recognised this as her school warning voice, but she hoped her mother understood school playground rules did not apply here. Her tone, however, was quite calming. Leah desperately looked from her mum to the lad, hoping this more passive approach would work.

The youth turned his glare onto her mother for a few seconds. 'What would be nice is if you all pissed off right away from here, you silly cow. Don't you get involved as well. You're too pretty to get messed up.'

Leah gave an involuntary shiver at this response.

'Don't you dare talk to my wife like that.' Her father was looking really angry. 'Now we need two apologies.'

Leah's heart sank when she saw her father set his jaw and firm his stance. She knew he anticipated violence and was prepared for it. The previous year she had seen him in a short fight at a pub when a drunk shoved him out of the way. Dad had flared-up and punched out at the other. Thankfully friends had pulled the drunk away and calmed them both down on that occasion. There were no such calming influences around now.

'*Two* apologies?' The lad spat again, the large gob of sputum foaming on the sand. 'You'd be lucky to get *one*, you stupid tosser, never mind two. But I've got somethin' else for you. See here!'

Leah almost fainted when she saw the sudden glint of steel in his hand.

Chapter 4

Paul often regretted his stubborn streak. He reckoned it came from his father. Once committed, he always found it difficult to turn from a given course. Something deep within him now drove him on to make the insolent youth back down and apologise. The boy needed to realise how his carelessness might easily have lead to a far more serious outcome. The thought of one of the grapnel's spikes penetrating his daughter's flesh really angered him.

The sudden appearance of the knife surprised him. It seemed to come from nowhere. He had never figured this sort of thing could happen to him, but this ignored the fact that when pushed too far, he inevitably snapped. Having not faced this kind of threat before, Paul tried to ignore the shiver of fear that ran through his body. The knife glinted ominously in the sunlight as the youth tossed it from hand to hand; it was obviously a well practiced routine intended to be highly confrontational.

'You'll get it now, you bastard!' The lad hunched down like a wrestler. The knife, now firmly held in his right hand, was about six inches long: wide and lethal.

Paul realised he'd been foolish beyond measure. He tried to keep his voice calm and his tone measured. 'Put the knife away, lad. Calm down.'

'No one treats me like this, yeah? No one. No one tells me what to do, man.'

Paul was thankful when Sasha came to his side, and he felt some reassurance as she squeezed his arm, but he was unexpectedly fazed when she snapped at him. 'Leave it, Paul.' She looked at the lad and spoke to him in calm and deliberate tones. 'I'm asking you both to end this now, before it gets out of hand and someone gets hurt. This is stupid and unnecessary.'

Paul feared looking weak, so when he did step back it was only one step: yet it was a pace further away from the flashing blade. He jerked his head at the youth, signalling him to go. 'Go on then. Leave it at that, if you'd sooner flash a knife than apologise like a man. Cut anyone with that toy and you'll be banged-up for life. Look around. There are plenty of witnesses.' This was true. Quite a few people were now watching from a safe distance.

'He's right,' added Sasha, after a long pause.

The youth's anger finally broke. He lunged theatrically towards Paul with the knife, emitted a frustrated sob and quickly stepped back again. Paul sensed the other's attitude was far more blustering than offensive and he took great comfort in this. The two glared at each other in silence for a while. The youth waved the knife around as he shouted angrily at Paul. He sounded unbalanced and emotional. 'That's it! For the last time, don't mess with me. I'll cut your fuckin' head off next time.' The boy glanced towards Leah who was now standing awkwardly on her own, all her weight on one foot. 'You've got a stupid dad, right? I didn't mean it, yeah? It was an accident. I didn't see you, yeah?'

Paul watched his daughter nod; she even gave the lad a brief smile. 'Sure. I know. But be more careful with it, yeah?'

The lad nodded deliberately at her, as if giving this deep thought, and replaced the knife in some hidden sheath inside the band of his trousers. Without looking at Paul again he turned and headed across to the café.

Hardly believing it was over, Paul watched the youth closely. He stopped by the café veranda and looked up at the two girls who were standing by their table; they had obviously seen the entire encounter.

'Stupid shit,' the boy said, intentionally loud enough for Paul to hear, now jerking his thumb back towards them. He raised his voice even more, so everyone could hear. 'Some people don't keep their kids under control. Or dogs. It's dangerous around boats. You need to watch out.'

'You're the stupid shit,' shouted the blonde girl, angrily shaking her finger at him. 'Man, you're plain crazy.' She made a spiraling motion against her head. 'You've got a screw loose.'

'A big brave biker when you've got a knife, huh?' jeered

her dark-haired friend.

Even from where Paul was standing, he could see the youth turning the colour of a ripe plum. Why the girls were getting more deeply involved was a mystery. By now he realised how stupid he'd been to bait such a dangerous idiot, but their opposition was only going to make matters worse. Sure enough, the youth span on his heel and angrily headed back towards them.

'Oh, no,' gasped Sasha, tugging on his arm. 'Don't hang around for a second helping, Paul, or I'll be pulling that knife out your ribs. Let's get out of here. Just run. And I mean *now*!'

Paul resisted her and stood his ground.

Leah hobbled over and tugged his other arm. 'Yes, come away, Dad, or he will stab you this time.'

Thankfully, the youth walked right past them towards the grappling-iron. Pulling it out of the sand, he carried it to the boat, tossed it in and pushed the boat backward into deeper water. Once it was afloat he turned it around before staring back at Paul.

'Don't you ever annoy me again, mister, or I'll get you. When no one's around to see.' He wagged his forefinger aggressively. 'I'm warnin' you. I'll kill you next time you cross me.' He turned back to the boat and leapt in.

After pulling a cord, the outboard motor kicked into life and the boat powered away leaving a huge, foaming wake. Everyone watched its departure with relief, but then it swerved sharply back towards the shore and the youth briefly cut the throttle so the craft lay low in the water. Paul would never forget the hard, menacing glare the lad then aimed at him as he pointed aggressively with his knife. 'I'll get you!' drifted across the water, barely audible above the idling motor. Then the youth opened the throttle fully, the engine roared again, and the bows of the boat rose up as it swerved and headed away across the harbour in an angry, creamy wake.

After making sure he was gone, Paul turned his attention to Leah, trying to make light of matters. 'So how's the ankle, sweetheart?' He tried to sound bright but realised he just sounded stupid and brittle.

'It's absolutely fine, Dad. Really.' Leah managed a weak smile and demonstrated she could hobble on her foot. 'But boy, you were so silly. I couldn't believe it. You nearly got yourself carved up there. Didn't you realise that, Dad? You don't mess with that kind.'

'Well, listen to this, sunshine. No one messes with my little girl, either. No one. Especially someone like that.' He winked. 'Mark my words.'

Leah and Sasha exchanged exasperated glances, but these turned to smiles of relief as Paul grasped them both and hugged them together. He was buoyant in his relief. 'Now is the time for a great big lunch, girls. I don't know why, but I seem to have worked up quite an appetite.' Sasha gathered up her shopping bags from the sand, nodding to the spilled bag. Paul repacked Leah's bag and picked it up. 'Now, I need to replace a whole bunch of calories.' He turned to Sasha and stuck on a posh voice. 'I do insist, my dear. We shall dine at the Beach House. Where, incidentally, I fled without paying my bill.' He was well aware that everyone knew it was false bonhomie, but at least it helped him.

Sasha looked at him is disbelief. 'How can you possibly joke after that, Paul? I'm surprised you can even eat? Don't you realise your daughter might have saved your life today?'

Leah grinned at this. 'Oh well, I'm like that. Words are better than fists, you see, Dad. You should know that by now. Peace and love, yeah?'

'Come on, do us a favour. I was only asking for an apology because he nearly killed you.' Paul exchanged exasperated glances with them both, but his turned into a relieved grin. 'Come on, girls.' He put out an arm to support Leah. 'You lean on your old dad, who was only fighting your corner. We need caffeine now. Double shots.' He looked down at Shep. 'And come on, Shep. You were useless as usual.'

'Sensible, as usual,' said Leah.

They went directly to Paul's veranda table at the café, next to the two girls who were now seated again. Shep lapped some water from a nearby dog bowl.

'That got very nasty,' said the girl with an Australian

accent. 'That guy had a dangerous looking knife.'

'He's a danger to be let out on his own,' Paul answered, as they sat down. 'Do you know him?'

The girl's head shot back and she stared at them in horror. 'No way! He even tried to pick us up. But he's a no-hoper, for sure.'

'You took a big risk annoying him, then, girls. You should be more careful.'

Paul saw Sasha pull an 'eyes-up' expression at the girls who grinned and laughed back at her. Sasha nodded towards him. 'Get him. Pity he doesn't listen to his own advice. He was the one pushing things. He'd stay around to have an argument with a charging bull.'

'No, no, I'd just show a bull the red card,' grinned Paul. 'Well I would, be fair,' he said, joining in the general laughter. 'I never like to pre-judge.'

'I guessed that guy was a sandwich-short-of-a-picnic,' said the dark-haired girl. She blew out her cheeks and looked across at her companion. 'Dangerous place, Mudeford, or what?'

'Yeah,' grinned her friend. 'Much safer on Bondi Beach.'

'And much hunkier,' laughed Sasha.

The blonde girl caught her friend's arm and pointed to where two wet-suited surfers were strolling past with their boards. 'Oh, I don't know about that,' she said with a grin. 'They look quite hunky.' Paul looked across to see the two youths who had ogled Sasha at the hut the previous day. They were grinning and their waves were returned by both the girls and Sasha. In an instant, Paul's adrenalin-fuelled high was replaced by an immediate low as the green-eyed monster prodded him yet again.

— — ∞ — —

Leah invited her best-friend over on Sunday so they could enjoy a day at the beach before the barbeque. Marina was of Italian descent, a slim, pretty, dark-haired girl with a pony-tail and a striking tan. In the morning they had fun in the Vincent's little boat in the harbour, and in the afternoon they swam in the sea on the opposite side of the sandbank. Then, after drying themselves, they flopped down onto towels and lay back in their bikinis to enjoy the warming rays of the sun. As always, conscious of her complexion, Leah protected her face by pulling her T-shirt across it. They lazed to the calming sound of breaking waves modulated by the excited squeals of young children playing in the surf. Leah was enjoying the calm of normality after the previous day's crisis.

Marina's sudden tone of annoyance startled her. 'You're so quiet this afternoon, Leah. What's the matter? Did that boy worry you? The one who chucked the spiky-thing?'

Leah pulled the T-shirt away from her face, opened her eyes and turned her head towards her friend. 'No, not really.'

There was a pause while Marina thought about this. 'Was it the face at the window, then?' She sat upright, staring down at her. 'Look, I know something's bothering you, Leah. We always tell each other our problems, right? So what is it? Spill.'

Leah peered up at her friend through strands of blonde hair. She grimaced and sighed. 'I'm just a bit worried about something, Marina, that's all.'

'Worried about what?' Marina shook Leah's arm gently. 'Come on, let me help you, Leah. Tell me. Please.'

Leah sat up and hunched her arms around her legs. 'Okay, but this is an absolute secret, Marina. Absolute. Gold-plated.' She held her friend's concerned gaze. 'Agreed?'

'As always,' grinned Marina. 'So what's this about? It's about that boy Colin you fancy at school, isn't it?'

Leah was able to giggle cheerfully at this and her laugh carried the full harmonics of youth. 'No, you idiot. But it is to do with that lad who chucked that spiky-anchor thing near me. The thing is... I recognised him.'

Marina's eyes widened. 'Really? Who was it?'

Leah shrugged. 'I don't know his name, Marina. But I do know he's the same person I saw spying on me through the hut window that night.'

'Oh no.' Marina looked shocked. 'You mean you think the two things are connected? That he tried to get back at you with the spiky-thing for spotting him?'

'No, no, no.' Leah flapped her hand impatiently and shook her head dismissively. 'Nothing like that.' She brushed sand off her legs absently. 'He didn't even see me when he threw that thing, I'm sure of that. It was pure accident. He was looking the other way at the time. I think he had an eye for some girls at the café, actually. That's why it was so silly of Dad to go ballistic.'

Marina shrugged, palms upward. 'So what are you worried about, then, Leah? I don't get it. I really wouldn't read too much into the window thing. He's just a dirty old man—boy, rather—dirty little boy. He probably spies in lots of hut windows for kicks. It's probably a coincidence. Anyway, what does your dad think about it? Does he think they're connected?'

Leah slumped and heaved a dramatic sigh, laying her forehead onto her drawn-up knees. She straightened up again to look at her friend. 'The thing is, I haven't exactly told him. Or Mum. And nor must you.'

Marina rolled her eyes. 'Why?'

'I told you what Dad was like about the spike, and that was obviously an accident. I was going to tell Dad about it afterwards—I couldn't in front of that jerk—but imagine what Dad would be like now if he knew it was the same lad who looked in at the window. He'd go absolutely mental. He can be so protective, Marina. He's a dear, really, but a terribly silly one.'

'Der! And that's so bad? You wouldn't expect it? My dad would certainly be protective over something like that. He would be, like, raving mad, but I would just tell him to cool it.'

'That's exactly my point, Marina. My dad would not only be raving mad, he'd probably go after him. With a blunt instrument. He wouldn't listen to me. No way. And that lad's dangerous, I can tell that. I mean, really dangerous. He had this lethal knife, remember, and he looked like he knew how to handle it. He kept tossing it from hand to hand, like this.' She mimed the action for Marina. 'Dad could end up stabbed because of it. Like dead?' She shook her head. 'No, it's best to keep quiet.' She stared at Marina, reaching out to touch her arm. 'That's why you must promise not to tell anyone, Marina. Promise, right? Do you understand how important this is? On my dad's life?'

Marina nodded. 'I see.' She paused. 'So you don't intend to do anything about it? Even if he is dangerous?'

Leah shook her head, then flopped back down on her towel with a sigh. 'What can I do? Anyway, what would be the point? I'll keep a watch out. Mum was afraid Dad would get stabbed when he went on at the creep yesterday, but that's nothing against how he would be if he tied the two things together. He'd believe they were connected. He'd want to believe it. At worst, it would simply double his anger, and when he's angry he can go truly ballistic. We're bound to see that boy around the sandbank again. I've seen him several times before, now I come to think of it. He's often walking along the water's edge, beachcombing, or something.' Leah reached out and caught her friend's arm again. 'Marina, I love my dad. But I can't take the risk of him getting hurt. I have to keep quiet for everyone's safety. You must understand.'

— — ∞ — —

Paul and Sasha were meanwhile messing around in their boat on the harbour. Paul paused in his rowing and pointed towards the bluest of skies. 'Perfect weather for the barbeque tonight. Looking forward to it, Sasha?'

Sasha smiled at him. 'Of course. And thanks for inviting your mother. You can have some brownie points for that.'

'Plus some more, maybe. I saw Russell Gartland earlier on and I invited him, too. Does that even things up?'

Sasha's face brightened. 'Very big of you, Paul. Double brownie points for that.'

— — ∞ — —

Stevie sat on the wooden bench next to his hut and stared sullenly out across the harbour. A strong breeze was whipping the water into tight curls. Periodically, he glanced at the garden he'd constructed on the gentle slope leading down to the narrow public path along the shoreline. Admiring his handiwork brought him peace. There were sea-pinks and an ever-changing collection of shells and twisted, sun-bleached logs. He had arranged them on a bed of pebbles; through the middle ran a thick blue rope, curved like a wave. He was proud of that touch.

His boat was pulled up high on the shiny sand nearby. Beside him on the seat lay a large piece of driftwood. He periodically stabbed the point of his knife into it, driving it in hard, twisting, turning, gouging. He clenched his teeth tightly as he did so, all the while thinking about that terrible man and the humiliation he had suffered in front of those two gorgeous girls. It had ruined his chances with them, that was for sure; they were obviously interested in him before all that.

Stevie was so engrossed in his thoughts he didn't hear his mother approach from the rear. He jumped when she spoke.

'I do wish you didn't have that awful knife, Stevie,' she said, touching his shoulder. 'Do be careful with it, dear.'

'I'll only have an accident if you go creepin' up on me like that when I'm usin' it,' he grunted. 'Anyway, I need it for guttin' fish, Mum. And mendin' nets. It's my job.'

'I suppose,' she said, grudgingly. 'Now. This is your last chance. I'm off shopping, if that dreadful van of Dad's will start. Think of anything you need?'

'Yes.' Stevie looked up. 'I lost that Sainsbury's shopping bag overboard last night. I really liked it, Mum. I need a new one. And a new flask. And I need some more chocolate biscuits.'

'Need?' Mary's voice squeaked. She raised an enquiring eyebrow at him, waiting expectantly. 'And what's the magic word?'

'Please.'

'Good boy.' Mary smiled and patted her son on the shoulder.

'Yeah, yeah, whatever.' Her stupid word games bored him. An amusing thought popped into his head and it made him smile quietly to himself. Perhaps he should have his ear pierced and get an earring when he next went into town. He'd been thinking about it for some time. That would really annoy her.

Chapter 5

That Sunday evening brought a gentle breeze to sooth the hot skin of those who had spent most of their day in the sun: relaxed people who still exuded the sweet scent of coconut oil. Paul welcomed it, he was hot standing over the barbeque. Normally such a breeze just carried with it the salty aroma of the evening sea, but now it was masked by the pungent smell of fried onions and cooking meat. The previous day's drama by the café had been temporarily forgotten and all that bothered Paul right then was cooking the steaks to as near perfection as he could manage without simultaneously burning the sausages.

As usual, because of the close proximity of the service road to the Vincent's beach hut, they were holding their barbeque in front of the nearby Forbe's hut. This faced the sea and bordered a stretch of sand dunes that offered a much more relaxing venue. The arrangement worked well. Fred Forbes was ever-keen to enjoy the benefits of playing barman, while Paul supplied the booze and did the cooking. With a wide grin on his face, Fred kept repeating to guests it was a 'win-win situation' for him. This time the location had prompted Sasha to choose a Hawaiian theme.

'I can't wait to see how some of my colleagues and your mother cope,' Sasha had said when she suggested the idea, with a wicked expression on her face.

Paul had snickered at this. 'Don't you worry about her, Sasha. Surely you know she can rise to any occasion.'

Sasha and Leah wore grass skirts over their bikini bottoms. Leah mainly stuck with a few of her beach hut friends and Marina, but Sasha was sparklingly alive and mingling happily with all their guests, popular as ever. Even Paul sported a grass skirt over his trunks, although he began to doubt the wisdom of this given unpredictably spitting fat and the nearby flames. As he cooked, he watched Sasha unselfconsciously gyrating and swaying to the music, a dazzling smile on her face, obviously enjoying every minute of dancing and chatting with their friends. She had the easy confidence of someone totally relaxed in a body she knew others admired. Parties always brought her alive.

A little later, Sasha drifted across to him, en-route to collecting drinks. She took the opportunity to introduce someone he'd never met, a dark-haired young man called Roger Lines, whom she said was a teaching colleague. 'He's new to the area and starting at the school next term, so I thought it would be nice for him to come along to see the natives are friendly,' she grinned.

Paul shook his hand. 'Good to meet you, Roger. You knew Sasha before, I assume?'

'She was a colleague when I was teaching at Southampton a few years back. It's kind of you both to invite me.' His voice was surprisingly deep. 'Do you teach as well, Paul?'

'No. I'm an architect.'

'And building our new house, right now.' Paul noted pride in her tone. Sasha smiled at him and then took Lines' arm. 'Come on, Rog. Let me get you a drink and introduce you to a few of your future colleagues.'

Paul got back to his cooking. When he had time to scan the groups for Sasha again, he saw she was alone and in animated conversation with Lines. Apparently there was no haste to introduce anyone after all. She seemed to be hanging—and laughing—on his every word, occasionally touching his arm while she laughed. Not that this meant anything, of course, she was always 'touchy-feely'. Sasha was a party animal who somehow always managed to keep a half-full glass of white wine in her hand and the full attention of whoever she was addressing. She was also a person whose spirit grew in proportion to the alcohol she consumed. Sasha liked to have fun.

Paul's covert observance ended abruptly when Fred Forbes brought a can of lager over for him. Taking it, Paul clinked it against Fred's and cracked it open. 'Cheers, Fred. Thanks. Ever the attentive barman.'

'You know it's my favourite occupation when I'm not

paying.' Fred grinned and winked at him.

The two chatted until Paul's mother appeared from between the nearby beach huts.

'My, my, Paul. So you're wearing the skirt tonight,' said Connie, with a raised eyebrows and a mischievous grin. 'How very daring of you.'

Grinning back at her, Paul noticed her multi-coloured outfit, complete with bare midriff and slit-skirt. Why couldn't she act her age? 'Hardly as daring as you, though, Mum. I'm getting into the spirit of things. Sasha chose it for me.' He exchanged a kiss with her. 'Nice of you to come so dressed for the part.'

'I imagine Sasha would expect nothing less.' There was a sudden iciness to her tone.

Paul comforted himself with the thought his mother's costume might have been much worse in the ancient cleavage department. Gesturing towards Fred, he introduced him. 'Fred's a good friend and he's acting as barman. We always borrow his beach space because there's more room for parties.'

'Please to meet you, Fred.' Connie shook his hand.

'I'll fix you up with a drink in a sec, Connie,' said Fred. He pointed towards his hut. 'The bar's over there. We've some very nice punch I can strongly recommend.' He winked. 'Mainly because it's strong.'

'It's nice to come to one of Paul's beach parties at long last,' said Connie. Thin-faced, with a fringe of silvery hair lying across her brow, Connie was wearing her usual bright red lipstick on cupid lips: plus the wounded expression she had so perfected. 'We've never met before, have we, Fred? I don't get to come here very often, you see. But it's nice to see how you all manage without any proper facilities. I'm normally only invited to their garden parties, you know.'

'Mainly because we know you like your proper facilities,' said Paul, winking at Fred.

Connie glanced at him for a moment but disdained to respond to this remark. She continued her conversation with Fred. 'Of course, I don't know how you manage out here. It must be terribly difficult without proper facilities.' She gave Paul a pointed stare. 'Mind you, Paul is best at primitive cooking. People will always accept burnt offerings from a barbeque, won't they? I'm not too keen on them, myself. It's hard to decide which one prefers: undercooked or cremated. Although, I suppose, cremated is safer on the whole.'

'Actually, I think Paul does a splendid job of barbeque cooking. And we manage around here much the same as those in more civilised circles, you know, Connie.' Fred beamed ambiguously. 'We muddle along despite the lack of services. And we've lots of drinkies to choose from, and all Paul's, so you can drink as much as you like. I know I do.' He winked at her and raised his own can. 'Cheers, Connie, my dear. So very nice to meet you at last. I've heard so much about you.'

'Really?' Connie sounded suspicious.

'Oh yes. Chin-chin.' And with that, Fred tactfully departed to his makeshift bar.

'What a funny little man,' muttered Connie, once Fred was out of earshot. 'Who rattled his cage?'

'That might just have been you, Mum,' smiled Paul. 'I should warn you the beach hut owners around here are pretty sensitive about their investment. After all they've forked out for their huts, the last thing they want to hear is someone running them down. You buy a certain lifestyle here, even if there aren't full services in the huts.'

His mother blew out her cheeks. 'Lifestyle?' She raised her eyes to the heavens. 'I can tell you I prefer a bit of luxury in my lifestyle, Paul. All this is no better than a caravan site, despite the absurd prices. I can't abide sensitive people.'

'Good job you're not one, then, Mum.'

'Hi, Gran.' Opportunely, Leah suddenly appeared. She went across to link her arm through her grandmother's. Connie's eyes twinkled with delight as she patted Leah's hand. 'Sweet dear.' She looked down at Leah's costume. 'And so stunning, darling. Stunningly beautiful.'

'Thanks,' smiled Leah. 'Just like you, Gran.'

Paul turned to Leah. 'Will you take your grandma to Sasha so she can introduce her to a few people, sweetheart?'

'Or I could start by introducing you to some of my beach friends,' suggested Leah. 'You already know Marina, don't

57

you?'

'Of course. That would be lovely. I'm still very young at heart, you see, my darling.' Connie beamed at her granddaughter and glanced challengingly back at Paul.

'And I'm sure they'll all think that, Gran,' smiled Leah, with affected innocence.

Connie laughed at her uncertainly. 'Good. Good.'

As they departed, still arm-in-arm, Leah looked back over her shoulder at Paul with raised eyebrows and a conspiratorial grin.

Paul winked back at her and smiled. His darling daughter was growing up fast.

— — ∞ — —

It was dusk when a shadowy figure settled down snugly behind a dune overlooking the party. Stevie had binoculars with him that evening and he made good use of them as he lay on his stomach, peering between tall grasses. Appetising cooking smells drifted across to him, mingling tantalisingly with the ozone smell of the sea and the damp smell of the sand. It conjured up an aroma that titillated his senses and made him feel really hungry. He reached in his pocket for chewing gum, by way of consolation. While chewing it lazily, he panned around the different people at the party, stopping for a while to look at individuals, changing the focus until something caught his eye and his binoculars locked on the man doing the cooking. Stevie felt his anger rising. It was the tosser who'd embarrassed him over the grapnel incident and blown his chances with the two girls. He even looked as if he might be in charge of things, yet this was nowhere near his hut. Very strange. He'd watch a while longer. He liked watching parties anyway; there was nearly always some good talent to be found somewhere.

Knowing his number-one enemy was there, Stevie scanned around looking for the man's wife; worthwhile because he remembered she was a good looker. The light was poor, but there were several lanterns set up on poles stuck into the sand,

and at last he found the face he was searching for. Thankfully, she was standing near a lantern. It made him sick. That pig-head didn't deserve such a beautiful wife. Such a tosser married to such a stunner. Life was so unfair.

He liked the wife. She had been quite polite to him, really. And she had tried to calm the bugger down. Stevie had noticed her several times before, of course, sometimes on the beach and often at their hut. He'd once seen her changing in the hut, topless: beautiful, and he dwelled on the memory of that for a few moments. Yes, he would add her to the women he sometimes thought about at night. She was so beautiful: her face as well as her body. And that fabulous long blonde hair. Wow. A bit old for him, maybe, but still stunning, and she certainly had a body he'd like to get his hands on. The kind of person he liked to watch best of all, in fact. He liked to watch women move. She was such a desirable woman. A sexually experienced woman. A woman who knew she was attractive and wallowed in it. And why not? She was like those girls in his magazines. They wallowed in it too. It was right, what they said. If you had it, flaunt it.

Zooming out a little, he saw she was laughing and talking to a man with dark hair. Her hand moved to momentarily rest on his arm. Wow, she looked so fabulous in that bikini top and grass skirt. What would it be like walking along the beach with her, his arm around her waist? Maybe pulling aside the strands of that grass skirt. He felt himself begin to tremble with excitement at the thought of this and his breathing became deeper, slower, more urgent. His eyes remained glued to the scene. All alone, he felt inferior, pressed secretly to the sand, and he wanted to jump up and join them and talk confidently to her. He wanted to make her want him. To hell with that loser. If he could get closer, maybe he could even hear her talking. But how?

Suddenly an idea occurred to him. He knew it was cheeky, but the idea really appealed. Standing, he threaded his way through the party-goers and headed straight for the drinks table, careful not to look directly towards his enemy.

'Beer.'

The old man with boozy eyes looked at him suspiciously. 'You one of Leah's friends? You old enough for beer, sonny?'

'You kiddin'? Give me a beer, man.' Then, to forestall an incident, Stevie added, more politely: 'Please.' It felt like he was performing for his mother, damn-it.

The old man unhappily handed him a can.

'Cheers.' Stevie grinned and headed back through the merriment to the dunes – right past *her*. She was now talking to a muscle-bound guy he'd seen around. Tart. But in such a fantastic bikini!

Cracking open the can he sat with his back to a dune. He watched the shimmering moonlight on the sea and listened to the surf breaking to the undulating background music. He was really pleased with himself. Beer from right under the tosser's nose. How cool was that?

Chapter 6

Paul was finally able to extinguish the gas barbeque and relax. He looked for Sasha but she was nowhere to be found. Finding Leah alone with Marina, he asked her where her mother was, but Leah had no idea. He guessed Sasha had gone to the loo or back to their hut for something. His hands were still sticky from the cooking so he decided to go to the hut to wash them. Perhaps he would find her there. It would be nice to have a modicum of attention from her that evening. Happily inebriated, one of her lingering kisses would go down very well right then.

Passing between the Forbes' hut and its neighbour, he walked along the narrow space between the backs of the beach huts, heading towards their own. Because the sand was thick and soft, walking was slow-going. Moonlight made it possible to see vague outlines. Well before he got near their own hut he heard faint voices, female giggling, and then, as he drew closer, instinctively walking as quietly as he could, the giggles transmuted into soft, regular and satisfied tones he recognised only too well. He felt himself stiffen with apprehension when this was followed by a low male voice and joint laughter. With a sick feeling in his stomach, Paul threaded silently around a hut in the row next to the sea in order to look what was going on from a safer distance. It had fallen suspiciously quiet again.

There was just enough moonlight for him to recognise the outline of his wife as he peeped around the corner of the hut. He had no doubt it was her. She was kissing a man and, as her partner spoke again, now more loudly, Paul recognised the deep tones of Roger Lines. Some little cries followed from Sasha. Lines was holding one of her legs high. Shocked, Paul shot back, inadvertently making a noise as he stumbled over a kayak that projected from beneath a hut veranda. Aware this would alert them, and hardly knowing what he was doing, Paul hurried away in the direction of a nearby toilet block, half-running, half-striding, his heart pounding, his mind in turmoil.

For once he must not act hastily. Sasha sometimes called him 'Mr. Impulse'. Acting in haste now could mean the end of married life as he knew it.

Leaning back against the door in one of the toilet cubicles, Paul held his head in his hands and listened to a pounding within his own skull. Although Sasha's possible unfaithfulness had always been a lurking fear for him, he could hardly believe he'd now witnessed it with his own eyes. How long had this sort of thing been going on? Had it happened before? Or with anyone else? And what about that Glenn person? If she could do it once...

Had he totally misjudged her all these years?

—— ∞ ——

Paul walked briskly to the Black House in a vain attempt to clear his head. He sat on a bench there for at least an hour, staring across the narrow channel to Mudeford Quay. There was bitterness in his heart that people drinking and laughing outside the pub could be so happy. His emotions were sapped and he felt dead inside. Time seemed meaningless.

When he finally got back to the party, Paul heard Fred shouting a general warning the special ferry they had arranged would be leaving in fifteen minutes: at ten-thirty. It was early, but it was as late as they could conveniently arrange a chartered boat large enough for their guests. From the occasional bursts of laughter it seemed clear the evening had been a great success for everyone except him. This last ferry meant an enforced ending for the guests because it was their only means of returning to their cars parked across the harbour on Mudeford Quay. Sasha appeared at his side, all smiles, and they jointly bade farewell to their guests as if nothing had happened.

'Where have you been?' she hissed as they waited for the next couple to approach. She dug an elbow into him. 'You've been totally useless tonight, Paul. You've not circulated at all.'

'I did cook for everybody,' he snapped back. 'Anyway, you've kept them all very happy, single-handed, from what I could see. I was hardly required.'

Although Sasha gave him a strange look, he still judged she didn't suspect he'd seen her with Lines. He doubted she would dare be so crotchety with him if that had been the case. Paul noticed Roger Lines seemed to be hanging back.

Even Paul's mother had enjoyed herself that evening and she, on a high, gave Sasha and himself surprisingly warm hugs and kisses. She was tagging along with one of Sasha's older female school colleagues who had come with her husband. 'Lovely party, darlings. We've all had such fun, haven't we?' she said, looking round at her new friends. 'Although gin and tonic helps a lot, doesn't it?' The couple laughingly agreed with her as they shook hands with Paul and Sasha, then departing as a group.

Paul pointed to Roger Lines. 'You'd better tell your dear friend he needs to hurry as well or he'll miss the boat. He seems too dozy to realise.'

'You mean Roger? No problem for him,' Sasha drawled. 'He came by bike, apparently.'

Paul was surprised Lines had taken such an energetic means of getting there along the road at the foot of Hengistbury Head. 'I'm amazed he's got any energy left for that. Know what I mean?'

Sasha gave him a puzzled look and called across to Lines. 'Hey, Rog, come over here. Want another beer before you head off?' She looked back at Paul as Lines ambled over to them wearing a wide, rather bleary smile. He held a can of beer in his hand. 'I think he should have some more for... fortication, before he pedals off into the sunset.' Sasha was speaking unusually slowly, clearly having to concentrate hard in order to formulate her words.

'The sun set long ago, Sasha, but I guess you've been too busy to notice that,' snapped Paul. 'Anyway, Roger seems to be pretty well fortified already, if you ask me.'

'I suppose. We don't want him falling off his bycle, do we?' continued Sasha, oblivious of Paul's undertone.

'Bycle?' grinned Roger, drawing near. 'What's a bycle, Sasha?'

They both giggled.

'I mean... bi-cycle.' With some concentration she managed the word. 'Bike, Roger? That right, Roger Lines? So you can bike in straight lines.' Paul felt his anger growing as she giggled at her own pathetic joke; she grinned at Roger, placing a hand on his drinking arm. 'It's a bike, isn't it, not a bycle?' she laughed. 'They don't call them bycles any more, do they?' She looked round at Paul. 'Do they, Paul? Or push bycles?'

'The party's over, so you'd better push-off on your *bycle*, Rog, old chap.' Paul stared Lines in the eye. 'I should be very careful to steer in the right direction on that dark little lane or a tree might jump out and hit you. Do you live far away?'

Lines looked at him with a sudden wariness. 'Iford, actually.' He downed the remains of his can and handed it for Paul to dispose of as if he were a waiter, all the time holding his eye. 'Nice one, Paul. Yes, everyone needs to be careful these days.' He winked familiarly. 'Thanks for the invite. Everything went with a real swing, for me.'

'Or sway,' giggled Sasha, wiggling her hips.

'Or gyration,' laughed Lines, staggering slightly as some uneven sand took him by surprise while he was momentarily diverted by Sasha's cleavage.

'And you're certainly swaying,' observed Paul. 'But no grass skirt for you, eh?'

'Roger's too much of a man for skirts,' slurred Sasha, exchanging what Paul took to be knowing glance with Lines.

'Glad you think so, Sasha,' grinned Lines.

'Why not have a mineral water, Sasha?' suggested Paul. 'I think you've had a few over the odds. Clearly lost your judgement.' He called across to Lucy Forbes who was standing nearby. 'Have you got a mineral water left for Sasha, Lucy?'

'Boring,' Sasha pouted. 'Anyway, Connie really seemed to enjoy the party, Paul, so I'm glad she came. I sent Leah off to bed a while ago, by the way. She said she wouldn't sleep till we got back, but I bet she will. I let her have a couple of Bacardi and cokes. That should've helped.' Sasha took the bottle of mineral water Lucy brought over and pulled a face after dutifully sipping it. 'Disgusting stuff, but suppose I need to sober up a bit if I'm going to run. I feel sort of… rubbery.' She shook her head. 'Need to clear my head. A run will be good.'

'Run? Tonight?' Lines looked amazed and laughed. 'Surely a stagger back to bed would be more sensible?'

'Sasha will run to any lengths,' Lucy told him with a laugh. 'She even does marathons. She makes me tired just watching.' She looked at Sasha and gave her a disbelieving headshake. 'But you can't be serious, Sasha. Surely you're not running on your own in the dark?'

'But I am, Lucy. I often run in the dark. There's a moon and its never really dark here. Don't worry. I can take care of myself.' Sasha sipped her drink, looking slightly unsteady, and pressed the glass back into Lucy's grip. 'Need to do it now, though. Clear my head. Running does that… marvess-ly.'

'And I need to get pedalling along that dark road through the trees before the ghoulies and ghosties come out to get me,' grinned Lines. 'So I'd better be off. Unless you'd like me to escort you on the bike, Sasha?'

Paul waited with bated breath for his wife's response to this, watching her face closely.

'No, no, it's all right, thank you, Roger. I need to change first. You get off. See you when school starts.'

Paul responded gruffly to Lines' farewells and turned to Sasha after he'd disappeared between the huts. 'Come straight back to the hut and go to bed, Sasha. Please.' He made sure his voice only revealed concern.

Sasha put a hand on his arm and smiled into his eyes. 'I need to do this, Paul. I'm going to change and then run for fifteen minutes max.' She blew out a long breath. 'I'll never sleep otherwise. All fuzzy in head. So I'll see you soon. I'll tell Leah where I'm going if she's awake. See you later.' She jerked her head towards the nearby dunes. You'd better give Fred a hand clearing up. It's his sand, but our mess.' She sounded a bit more sober now. She kissed him on the lips, a long lingering kiss, and he felt himself returning the pressure despite everything. It made him realise what he could so easily lose. Then she was gone with a wave and a friendly smile to him and the Forbes.

Paul was not in the mood for small talk. He produced a torch from his pocket and flashed it around. 'I'll get on with a bit of tidying up.' Grabbing an empty bin bag he began searching for discarded cans and paper plates in the nearby dunes. The sad thought crossed his mind that he could, at least, still cope with the little practical things of life.

— — ∞ — —

Sasha had never needed a run more. She padded softly along the sand-strewn service road away from the huts, Shep scampering happily at her heels. A refreshing breeze carried the sharp tang of the sea. It was getting chillier and she felt pleased to be on the move. The blood pumped through her veins and helped to clear the fug inside her head but, in truth, the run was more about giving her time to think.

Who had seen her with Roger? Could it possibly have been Paul? He certainly seemed inexplicably sarcastic and snappy, but he often was after she had a good time with friends. The possibility he'd seen her with Lines sobered her up fast, though. She dreaded going back to the hut for she could think of no better explanation for his tetchiness or the fact he'd been missing for so long. Unless he just thought she'd spent too much time with Roger, or maybe someone else. Yet it was not like Paul to hold back from saying what he thought. So perhaps it had been someone else who'd seen them between the huts: someone who didn't matter. Probably no one could have recognised her in the dark, but she was cross with herself for having endangered a happy marriage for a few moments of fun. Why didn't she take more care about how much she drank?

It was a lovely night and the near-full moon laid a silver sheen across open stretches of the road. Gradually Sasha became more relaxed and fell into the familiar rhythm of running. Soon she entered a twisting part of the route where it threaded through a wood; here the moonlight could barely penetrate. Although very dark, she decided to carry on, for at least it was a far better surface to run on now it was absent of the blown sand that covered large stretches of the road by the huts. Thankfully, running was bringing back her senses. She needed to be particularly alert by the time she got back to Paul.

She had a sinking feeling Paul might ask some very awkward questions when she got back to the hut. It was good Leah would be there to prevent a full-scale interrogation. All around it seemed the trees were conversing in soft, animated whispers: probably about her.

The sound of footfalls behind her came as a shock. Sasha stopped running for a moment and, after hissing at Shep to be quiet, she held her breath to listen. They were getting closer, and fast, but a bend in the road, and the general darkness, prevented her from seeing anyone. She had never run there in the dark before and now she realised it was not exactly wise. It hardly compared with the illuminated streets of Bournemouth, her usual night-running scene.

A figure came into view around the bend, highlighted for a moment in a patch of moonlight. From initially running hard, the person suddenly faltered. Obviously she had been seen and, disturbingly, this person was reacting suspiciously. The person then began to run towards her again, now faster and more purposeful. Feeling very afraid, Sasha turned and began to put distance between them as fast as she could, but the other person was steadily gaining on her. She sensed it was a man: a very fit one.

Though her heart pumped and her lungs strained to bursting, the slap of shoes grew closer and closer. A hand grabbed her jogging top from the rear, dragging her to a halt. The man span her around and pulled her close to him. She could smell beer on his breath. Shep began barking loudly, but that was as far as his commitment went.

'Don't shout.' The man spoke in a loud hiss, obviously to disguise his voice. 'Come over here.' Sasha battled with him as she was dragged to the side of the road. After a short struggle she ducked and pulled him neatly across her hip, using her knowledge of self-defence and putting his weight against him. Cursing loudly, he lost balance, yet he still managed to retain a firm grip of her as he fell, pulling her down on top of him. Almost in the same motion, he rolled her over onto her back and scrabbled to sit on her hips, pinning her arms down with great force.

'Don't fight me or I'll kill you,' he hissed. 'I've got a knife. Best enjoy it, then you won't get hurt.' She felt him fumbling at her clothes. 'You're a lively one, aren't you? Anyway, you want it really, don't you?' He laughed and then viciously dragged her jogging bottoms down. 'Can't get enough of it, can you?'

Sasha heard a low rustling noise nearby—a moment of hope in her desperation—and she called out in case there was someone to help. Her heart sinking, she realised it was only Shep, who was now pounding around them, but doing little more than barking loudly.

'Shep. Attack! Attack!'

A hand smothered her mouth.

'Be quiet. Lay still or I'll kill you.' Now he sounded almost bored.

Sasha continued to struggle, but the other's weight was overpowering. She heard Shep bark and snarl. The man cursed and kicked. Shep whimpered in pain and scamper off, his periodic barking growing ever fainter. Her attacker was moving again, changing his position. Was it best to give in or to try to get him where it hurt and run? Sasha stopped struggling. She would use surprise tactics.

'That's better. Enjoy it.'

It might even work. He thought she was co-operating. She would regain some of her strength and catch him unawares with a sudden viscous retaliation when he least expected it. Meanwhile, she reckoned she must accept the inevitable if she wanted to live.

— — ∞ — —

When Paul let himself into their beach hut he found the light on and Leah standing by the kitchen sink in her pyjamas. She was drinking a glass of water.

'Good. You can always trust water.' Paul forced a smile.

Leah greeted him excitedly. 'That was a great party, wasn't

it? I think Gran really enjoyed it, too.'

'Yes,' said Paul absently. 'Did you see Mum before she went out?'

Leah nodded. 'She changed quickly and went off for a run. She woke me up, actually.'

Paul crossed to a cupboard for a glass and poured himself some water from a bottle. 'Did you enjoy your Bacardi and cokes?'

Leah smiled. 'They were great. So now you and Mum have set a precedent, Dad.'

'Precedents can be broken,' he said, putting an arm around her waist and smiling at her while sipping his water.

'Maybe,' she said, spinning round to look at him properly, returning a knowing smile. 'But I can't be broken.'

They both laughed.

Paul glanced at his watch. 'Now, up that ladder and back to bed, young lady. And make it snappy, before Mum gets in, or she'll say I'm keeping you up.'

Paul had kissed her goodnight and was returning her hug when Shep arrived at the back door, barking frantically. They both looked round in concern. Opening the door in surprise, Paul tried to quieten the dog down, but Shep wouldn't have it.

'Shep was with Mum,' said Leah in alarm. 'Something's wrong or he wouldn't have left her.'

Shep kept bouncing back-and-forth to tell Paul to follow. Like Leah, Paul's gut instinct was to imagine something was wrong. Shep was a fairly docile animal and such desperate agitation—especially so late at night—was completely out of character. Clearly the dog had been severely spooked.

'Dad, we must find Mum. Let's follow Shep.'

'Did she say *where* she was running?'

'Up towards the Head. That was... at least ten minutes or so ago.' Leah's eyes widened with fear and she flapped her hands in panic. 'Come on, Dad. Let's move.'

Paul took charge. 'No. I'll go and check alone. Listen, sweetheart. Stay here, whatever you do. It's probably nothing to worry about. And don't panic.' Inwardly that was exactly what he was doing, but he tried to maintain a calm exterior for her sake. 'Maybe Mum's sprained an ankle or something.' What he imagined was that she might have keeled over and hurt herself after all the drink, but he was aware it could be something much more serious in such a lonely spot. 'Stay here till we get back, Leah. Whatever you do, don't go outside. Have you got that? I don't want two of you to look for. And lock the door after me.' Thoughts of the face at the window still haunted him. As he departed, Paul looked back at Leah's worried countenance. 'Don't worry. We'll soon be back. Okay?'

'Okay... I suppose.'

Shep was way ahead of Paul, barking all the while. He kept running ahead, pausing, looking around, and scampering back to bark and hasten Paul on. All kinds of terrible thoughts ran through Paul's mind as he chased after the dog, but as he did so, he realised his growing fear and desperation for Sasha's welfare confirmed his deep love for her, despite anything he'd seen that night.

'Please God, may she be all right.' He had never been particularly religious, but he found himself praying this over and over as he ran: a desperate mantra. Shep was crazy by now so Paul felt certain it was something serious: but nothing could have prepared him for the reality. As the struggling couple came into sight it became clear how much trouble Sasha was in. Her screams for help sent fear shivering through his body.

'Sasha! I'm coming.'

'Paul! Please help me!' Her voice was filled with terror. There was just sufficient moonlight to outline a violently waving object clearly being used by one or the other of them as a weapon. He guessed it was a branch.

'Let her go!' As Paul approached, Sasha fell backward; her screaming ended abruptly and there was no further motion or sound from her. The dark figure turned to face him, waiting, poised, the long object held high above his head. Without thought of the consequences, Paul dived straight at him, his head to the other's stomach, a rugby tackle that made the other stagger backward, but then he felt a painful blow to his shoulder and, as he ducked to get out of the way, another blow struck his head...

Chapter 7

Paul's head was throbbing and his limbs felt a dead weight as he forced his eyes open. Fearful, he vaguely heard someone moving close by. As slowly and soundlessly as possible, he took the torch from his pocket. It was reassuring to have it in his hand, but he didn't switch it on. He painfully levered himself up onto one elbow. A beam of light was already directed on a body lying in the road. The blonde hair and the dark jogging top told him immediately it was Sasha. But she seemed far too still: desperately still.

Trying to sit up further, he groaned involuntarily when a sharp pain shot through his shoulder and head. The figure standing over Sasha turned in alarm and the powerful beam swept in his direction. As Paul switched on his own torch in response it spotlighted the other's face. Blinking hard, he knew it looked familiar. But who was he? Everything seemed fuzzy, his thought processes somehow frozen.

His energy depleted, Paul sank back onto the road. He was vaguely aware the light was coming closer. While he realised this heralded danger, he had lost all ability to move, and, strangely, even the capacity to care.

A new pain began when something struck the side of his head with a soft thud. The blackness of night descended once again.

— — ∞ — —

Two bodies lay at his feet. Unbelievable. Dangerous. He looked down at the man. He deserved a good kick in the head. But now he must get away, quickly and silently. It annoyed him he was trembling. This was no way to behave. He clenched his fists and gritted his teeth. He needed to stay hard, even though this was the most dangerous situation of his life. He'd never been involved in murder before. He listened intently for the sound of anyone approaching but there was no chance of hearing anything above the wretched dog's barking.

'Shut up, dog!'

The dog took no notice but continued to bark and dance around him, its teeth snapping. It scared him a little, but obviously the dog would have bitten him by now if that was going to happen.

Fortunately it had all happened well away from the beach huts so no one would hear or see anything. The bodies would be found in the morning, by which time he would be long gone. There would be nothing to connect him to it. With this knowledge he didn't fear running down the road towards the huts. Any other route would take too long in the dark and he needed to get away from the scene quickly and back to his boat. Worryingly, he heard the dog pounding behind him, still barking incessantly, so it was a great relief when he turned off the road and his torchlight picked out the path across the little footbridge and the mud flats; the dog didn't follow him any more but ran towards the huts. Gradually its barking grew fainter and he began to relax. The danger was over.

Soon he was in his boat, tugging the cord that brought its faithful engine back to life. His nostrils breathed in the comfortingly familiar smell of petrol as he sped away. Now the water was streaked with moonlight, trembling in its ripples. He felt safe again.

What a night. Sitting, he looked back in the general direction of Lob's Hole and the place beyond, where it all happened. Somehow he knew he could have done better. Had he done the right things? Would anyone know he'd been there? He definitely needed to think hard about it all. And to analyse. Yes, he needed to analyse everything. He would undertake a full debriefing.

— — ∞ — —

Leah felt almost numb with fear when she heard Shep barking and pawing at the back door of their beach hut. Wild thoughts ran through her mind. Where was Dad? Why was Shep alone again? Where was Mum? She let the dog in and tried to calm him down, but he was totally uncontrollable and hyped-up like never before. Despite feelings of absolute panic, Leah told herself to keep calm. She quickly tossed off her pyjamas and pulled on a T-shirt and jeans. Stuffing her mobile phone into her pocket and grabbing a large flashlight they kept for emergencies, she followed Shep through the door. 'Find Dad, Shep. Find Mum.'

Leah had to run quite fast to keep up with the panicking dog, first along by the huts and then around the bend at the foot of Hengistbury Head. Her weak ankle made this painful but she put this out of her mind. There was an unexpectedly cold wind and she wished she'd put on a jacket. It seemed like she was following Shep for miles, but she knew this was not so. She began to wonder if she was doing the right thing after Dad's firm instructions, but as Shep's continual barking became almost maniacal, she felt certain she was right. She had no choice. Something was very wrong.

The scene that faced her made her freeze in her tracks. Her lamp picked out two bodies lying on the road. Both were very still. She stopped hesitantly. After swinging the light around to make sure no one else was present, she cautiously approached the first dark form, trembling with fear. As soon as she drew close she knew it was her dad. His head was covered in blood and he was frighteningly still.

'No!' Flashing the beam onto his face she saw his eyes were closed. She swung the light across to the other figure and immediately recognised her mother's jogging top. She was naked below the waist and her jogging bottoms lay nearby. 'No, no!' Leah ran to her mother's side, crashed to her knees on the road, flashed the beam into her mother's face, saw the blood on her head, shook her body, screamed, then, checking herself in fear, staring at the half-open eyes. She knew this was a terrible sign. She listened for a breath, put her cheek to her mother's mouth to see if she could feel anything and desperately felt for a pulse: with little confidence in her own ability to do so. Yet it was obvious there would be no pulse. Leah had little doubt her mother was dead.

Dead. Her mother was dead. Deep inside, Leah also felt dead. Already the skin on her mother's face felt somehow strange. Why had Mum been crazy enough to run in the dark? Then a terrible thought struck her. Why hadn't she stopped her from going instead of meekly saying 'goodnight' when all along, in her heart, she knew it might be dangerous? Good grief, she was responsible for her own mother's death. Her world was ending now. With a sudden start, she looked behind her. 'Oh, God. Please, no.' Was her father dead as well?

Chapter 8

Stevie often cut Auntie Hilda's grass. She wasn't his real auntie, of course, but he'd always called her that since he was little. He liked her. She chatted to him and laughed *with* him instead of *at* him. She even made him tea and cakes. Better still, she treated him like an adult, which was only right now he was twenty-one. Auntie Hilda was lovely. In fact, thought Stevie, as he finished off, she was probably the loveliest person in the world. He got far more thanks for cutting her grass than he did from Mum or Dad for cutting their own. And it was good to cut her grass that morning. He needed to do something normal until the local paper came out. It almost seemed like an ordinary Monday.

As usual, Auntie Hilda timed it perfectly as he mowed the final strip. There she was, with her beaming smile, carrying her blue Isle-of-Wight tray with the blue mugs of tea and his favourite fairy cakes on a matching blue plate. Such a lovely blue: like the sky on a summer's day. And the cakes were always scrumptious. It was so reassuringly normal.

'I've brought you your tea and cakes, Stevie.' Despite the fact she had to shout above the noise of the mower, Hilda's smile was virtually continuous, a white crescent in a brown and time-wrinkled face.

'Thank you, Auntie Hilda,' called out Stevie. He hurriedly mowed the final strip of grass and released the switch to cut off the noisy electric motor. Silence descended on the narrow little garden apart from the enthusiastic chirping of a blackbird that had been competing with the noise of the mower. It now flew down onto the grass to hop and look for worms.

Laughing, Hilda pointed to the blackbird. 'It takes more than your din to frighten Blackie off when he wants a worm.'

Stevie nodded. 'It knows what it likes. Like me with cakes.'

Hilda chuckled. Her head had a continuous wobble about it and the tight little curls of her thinning grey hair reminded

Stevie of a scouring pad. He thought her wobble was a bit like an engine left running, all part and parcel of Hilda. Because her hands were also a bit wobbly, he helped her by taking the tray in case she spilled the tea. He set it down on the table and held her arm while she heaved each leg over the seat. She always had a job doing that.

'I need to get one of those new tables with seats you don't have to climb over,' she laughed in her quavery way. 'I'm getting far too old for this one.'

Stevie reckoned she might be right. Eighty-seven she was, that's what she'd told him on her last birthday. It was hard to imagine anyone being that old. Anyway, age wasn't important. It was how people were inside. Hilda was the best neighbour anyone could have. She always gave him a pound for cutting her grass. Always had, except when it had been less because he was little. She had always been kind to him. Better than his real aunties, for sure.

Stevie joined her at the table, facing Hilda and the harbour. The sun was hot that morning and he'd been sweating. The view down the lawn and over the water was beautifully clear. Now his work was done he felt like going out in the boat before dinner. A good way to bide some time.

Hilda handed him a mug of tea and, after he'd taken it, she offered the plate of cakes. Stevie chose one and took a grateful bite. There was a pound coin on the tray and Hilda picked it up after some difficulty chasing it across the slippery surface. She held it out for him. 'Here's the usual, if that'll pay you, Stevie. I don't know what I'd do without you.'

Stevie transferred the coin to the pocket of his jeans with a grateful smile and finished his mouthful of cake. The cream in them was beautiful: nectar to his tongue. 'Your cakes are so nice, Auntie. And thanks for the money.'

'You're very welcome,' smiled Hilda. She selected one herself and took a bite. Sometimes her teeth would slip when she did this and Stevie always had to stop himself from laughing, which would be rude, but he could never avoid looking out for it... there, it happened. 'I heard your boat coming back last night, Stevie. You were a bit late, weren't

76

you? Don't know how you find your way in the dark. But I suppose you're clever at that sort of thing.'

'It's never really dark. And I wasn't very late.' What was it to her? Although nice, she was also far too nosy. He knew she really wanted to know where he'd been, but that was his business; very much so. He changed the subject. 'Lovely day, Auntie Hilda.'

Hilda Redland looked at him closely. 'You seem a bit quiet, today, Stevie. Is everything all right?'

Stevie was cross he'd obviously given something away. Hilda knew him too well. 'Everything's fine.' Unintentionally, the last word almost came out as a shout, so he gritted his teeth and remained silent. He mustn't give anything else away.

'As long as it is, Stevie. You know you can always talk to your Auntie Hilda if anything is wrong, don't you?'

'Yes.'

Hilda sipped her tea and smiled at him. 'Yes, it is a lovely day, Stevie. And it's nice to see a young man who appreciates such things. And Nature.' They were both watching the blackbird as it pulled a long worm from the grass. 'You're a good lad, Stevie. It's lovely having you living next door.'

— — ∞ — —

Leah was tired and drawn. She had spent half the night at her father's bedside with her grandmother. The bandages around his head, and the various tubes connected to him, were so frightening. Eventually a nurse had persuaded them to go home until morning: which meant to Gran's home, not more than ten minutes walk from the Royal Bournemouth Hospital. They were warned there was no telling how long her father might remain in a coma: hours, days, even weeks. Leah refused to believe it would be long. Dad was a fighter. The good news was the brain scans had not shown any internal abnormalities.

Leah managed about two hour's sleep before both of them returned to the hospital at 10 o'clock in the morning. As she walked along the corridor she felt a curious sense of disbelief and detachment. Passing by an open door to a cupboard, the smell of disinfectant rolled over her like a wave, almost triggering nausea. Was this really her walking in the hospital? Did she really only have one parent? Would she ever lead a normal life again? Would her dad become a vegetable?

Sitting quietly by the bed in the separate intensive care sideward, Leah was either replaying the horrible experience in her head or sitting in a mindless daze. During the morning a very understanding lady police officer, called Sam Gold, had asked her more questions, but there was nothing new she could tell them. Once again, she repeated what she told a uniformed policeman the night before. She'd known something was badly wrong when Shep came back to the beach hut without her father. Shep had led her to the scene. She'd realised Mum was dead straight away. Concentrating on Dad and holding her ear against his mouth, she had heard his faint breathing; it had been then she'd called emergency services from her mobile phone.

Alone with Dad again, after her grandmother had left to do some shopping, and with time pressing heavily, Leah forced herself to analyse the events of the previous evening in case there was anything further she could remember that might help the police. The long wait in the dark until the police cars and two ambulances arrived had been the scariest time of her life. All the while she'd wondered if the murderer might be watching her. Sometimes she thought she'd heard things, but between the wind and her imagination, she realised there was no evidence anyone had been around. She'd been thankful for Shep's company. A policeman told her that if she'd not seen anyone, the killer would have been long gone by the time she got there.

It had been frightening in the ambulance with her father looking so terrible. After injecting something, the paramedics confirmed he was breathing well and would be all right when they got him to hospital, but she had her doubts right then. There was so much blood on his head and she had seen a branch lying near him, also covered in blood. It was obvious Dad had tackled Mum's killer and had been knocked unconscious during the struggle. Her mother's death was disastrous enough, but she feared her dad might never come out of his coma, or that he might end up permanently disabled. True, she knew Gran would look after her, but she was old enough by now to understand Gran was really only interested in her own life and pleasures and would not welcome her as a burden.

Leah's despairing thoughts were immediately forgotten when her father's eyelids fluttered open and his eyes momentarily looked around and then locked onto hers in a joyful and much prayed-for miracle. She could hardly contain her joy, firstly clutching his hand and kissing him time and again as he spoke to her with slurred speech. Her tears of joy spilled over his cheek and she wiped them with her hand, half laughing, half crying.

'Leah?' He gave a loud sigh and his eyes closed again. 'Where am I?' He sounded so tired.

'In hospital, Dad.' Leah pressed the emergency button on the bedside cord. 'Dad. Can you see me?'

Her father opened his eyes for a moment but closed them again with a sigh, as if the effort was too much. 'Oh, Leah.' After a pause, he moaned, 'I've got such a headache.'

'Can you move your hands and legs, Dad?'

Her father moved an arm and then a leg. He made to nod, but this movement provoked a cry of pain. He opened his eyes wider for a moment. Memory kicked in. 'Sasha! Mum? Is she all right?'

Leah burst into tears, gently clutching her father's head, her cheek pressed closely to his. 'No! Dad, it's terrible. She's dead.'

— — ∞ — —

DS Samantha Gold got into the police car alongside her gaffer.

Detective Inspector Jimmy Hughes looked at her with weary eyes. 'Well? Any joy, Sam?'

'He's coming round, but the doctor says we can't go near him.'

'Why?'

Gold shrugged. 'He's not up to it yet. Says we might be able to talk to him tomorrow. Can't expect much sense from him yet. Still heavily drugged. But it's looking good and he might even be discharged in a couple of days. No physical problems, apparently.'

Hughes reached for the door handle. 'Then there's no reason why he can't talk to me now. This is a murder enquiry.'

Grinning, Gold caught Hughes's arm as he began to open the driver's door. 'Not worth wearing out the shoe-leather, guv.' As Hughes looked round at her, she gave him a knowing nod. 'Really. Believe me. The doctor is even a tougher-cookie than you. You won't get past him, honestly.'

'I might get past a nurse.'

'No, really. Wait until tomorrow, guv. We'll phone the hospital then.'

'And you're sure the daughter can't tell you anything more?'

Gold winked. 'Sure as sure. She's a bright little cookie, though. A sassy one under normal circumstances, I'd reckon. If anyone can cope with this at fourteen, she will. You let me keep her sweet, guv.' She winked. 'She trusts me.'

'Whereas you don't trust me, eh, Sam?'

Gold laughed. 'You said it, not me.'

— — ∞ — —

Dad was obviously surprised to see him in the lounge when he came in from his taxi shift. He was carrying his usual copy of Bournemouth's Daily Echo. 'Why, Stevie, lad. Not out on the water, today?

Stevie tried to look relaxed. 'I have been,' he said. He nodded at the newspaper. 'Can I take a look at the paper, Dad?' He tried to sound casual.

'At the paper?' Frank looked at him in amazement as he flopped down into an ancient leather armchair in their little front lounge. 'What's brought on this sudden interest in the news, Stevie?'

'There's been some excitement on the sandbank, Dad. Police swarmin' all over the place. Loads of police cars. I want

80

to see if there's anythin' in the paper. Loads of blue tape blockin' the road off. Lots of rumours.'

'Were there now? Well, maybe this is it.' Frank held the newspaper towards him and tapped the headline. 'Teacher murdered while jogging. It's the headline.'

Stevie was transfixed as he stared at the newspaper. 'I did hear tell,' he said, distantly. Then, more loudly, 'Let's see what it says, Dad.'

Frank jerked the paper away from his son's grasping hands to see for himself. 'Hang about. I want to read it properly, too. I'll read it out, Stevie.' On hearing his wife in the hall, he raised his voice. 'Mary! Come in here a minute to hear the latest news. There's been a murder on Hengistbury Head.'

'Never!' Mary appeared at the door wearing an apron. She had a duster in her hand and the smell of furniture polish wafted into the room with her. 'Murder? When was that then, Frank?'

'Last night.' He showed her the headline. 'Stevie saw the police investigatin' today. Didn't you, Stevie, lad?'

Stevie nodded. 'Lots of police cars, Mum. Even two police motorbikes,' he said, his eyes gleaming at this. 'Big powerful bikes.'

'Well, read it out then, Frank.' Mary perched on the arm of the other armchair, and Stevie stood by his father so he could look down at the paper. There was a small picture of the woman. He recognised her at once. It showed her with some schoolchildren in tracksuits. She even looked gorgeous in this poor picture.

Frank began to read aloud. 'Local schoolteacher, Sasha Vincent, was brutally murdered late last night while out jogging with her dog. The killing took place on the service road linking Mudeford Sandbank to the main road at Broadway. Her husband, local architect Paul Vincent, was found unconscious alongside the body by their daughter, fourteen year-old Leah Vincent, who discovered the incident after being alerted by their dog. Mr. Vincent was taken to hospital unconscious and is said to be in a stable condition. A hospital spokesman said he was presently in a coma, with his daughter and mother at his bedside. The crime scene is currently cordoned off and public road access from Broadway to the sandbank is temporarily suspended. This is the second tragedy for the family in four months. Mr. Vincent's father, a well-known local property developer, fell to his death from faulty scaffolding in April.'

'Well, well, well. Fancy that.' Mary looked from one to the other of them. 'Stupid woman joggin' in the dark on a road like that. Just askin' for trouble, I'd say.'

Stevie tugged gently at the paper. 'Can I see it now, Dad?'

'If you like.' Frank released it reluctantly.

Stevie stared at the picture again. She looked so happy with her schoolchildren. A pity it had to come to this. She was much too young to die. And way too pretty. If she hadn't fought so hard she might still be alive.

— — ∞ — —

While staying at her grandmother's flat, Connie showed Leah a copy of an old Daily Echo containing a news item about an incident that had taken place a couple of weeks earlier on Hengistbury Head. Apparently an actress had been attacked and raped by a man wearing a black balaclava.

'It's got to be the same man,' Connie said firmly. 'It must be. So don't you go anywhere near Hengistbury Head alone, Leah. Or the beach huts. Stay well away.'

Leah shook her head at her Gran's lack of understanding. 'I won't be going anywhere while Dad's the way he is,' she replied. 'I'll be visiting the hospital while he's there, and at home looking after him when he comes out.' She waved at the newspaper. 'Can I keep that, Gran?'

'I suppose so. But don't dwell.'

It was a great relief for Leah to return home a couple of days later with her dad. Already the huge bandage on his head had been replaced by a large sticking plaster. She helped him fight off her grandmother, who wanted to stay over, but once this battle was won and Gran had left, Dad became frighteningly quiet and inactive. Apart from his dramatic plaster, he seemed reasonably fit and was fully coherent: but only when he wanted to be, which was not very often. He spent most of the time sitting in an armchair in the lounge, staring into space. The most active thing he did was to listen to classical music, something he had not done for a very long time. Once, when she looked at him enquiringly during a particularly loud passage, he grinned and explained, 'Music is food for the soul, Leah. It calms me. It diverts my thoughts.' She finally understood. It did the same for her—although her taste in music was very different.

Eventually Leah decided to show her dad the newspaper article about the earlier rape on the Head. When she told him Gran thought it must be the same man, he merely shrugged and said, 'Maybe.'

'But they got DNA from her attacker. It says so in the paper. So that should help find him, Dad.'

'Maybe.'

Leah agreed with her grandmother's suggestion not to mention the local TV news item they'd seen about the incident on Monday evening. It didn't amount to much other than an appeal for witnesses by a police inspector called James Hughes, but since there were no further developments, it no longer made the news.

Her father had been prescribed antidepressants by their doctor. Leah made sure he took them every day. The fact that all thoughts of a funeral for her mother were postponed on police orders hardly helped; apparently everything had to wait for an autopsy. How terrible they would poke over the remains of her poor mother. And how could anyone come to terms with her death with everything that hung over them? The police had briefly questioned her father the day before he came out of hospital. They said that because of the remote location and time, it was unlikely there would be any witnesses coming forward; apparently it would prove a difficult case.

Now her dad merely sat gazing out at the garden. He hardly ate anything of the simple meals she prepared, although he was touchingly grateful for her efforts. The fact the completion date on their flat was due in a few days, and there were still countless jobs to be done, didn't seem to bother him even when she tried to persuade him they needed to do more packing. Nor had he contemplated going back to work. So Leah spent a lot of time packing things into cases on her own and feeling wretched. Her father hardly noticed.

Each day Leah grew more desperate. She wanted her dad back. When he was not around, she sometimes allowed herself the luxury of lonely tears. She missed her mum more than she could ever have imagined. Yet she tried not to show it and knew she had to remain strong to pull her dad through. Hardly speaking now, he seemed a broken man. They had shared tears and hugs a couple of times, but all he could manage were words to the effect he would always be there for *her*: despite the fact it was presently the other way round.

'And I'll always look after you, too, Dad,' was all she could reply to this. And she meant it. Thank goodness Marina was always to hand via email or phone. Marina helped her to keep sane.

In final desperation, given their imminent move to the new house, Leah phoned her dad's friend Charlie to ask him to call round. He came the following Friday evening. When she answered the door to him and he asked her in a low voice how her father was, she whispered back, 'Pretty low, actually, Charlie. Perhaps you can stir him out of it. I've told him we need to do the final packing this weekend, and I've already packed what I can myself, but he's not interested.'

Charlie put his arm around her shoulders comfortingly. 'He couldn't wish for a finer daughter, Leah.' He winked at her. 'I'll see what I can do, but I can't promise anything, like.'

Leah smiled back gratefully. Feeling very guilty, she hung around in the hall after showing Charlie through to where her dad was sitting in the lounge. She listened intently to Charlie's commiserations and the way he gently steered him into thinking about the coming move and the urgent need for packing.

'It's not as if you've any option, Paul,' Charlie said. 'The van will come, and if you're not already packed, they'll bung stuff into boxes any-old-how and move you across anyway. Then you'll be in a terrible muddle and never find anything you want. Loads of hassle.' He paused. 'I've done what paintin' I

can, like, but there's not time for me to do it all. I was hopin'
you could still do the two main bedrooms before the furniture
arrived.'

'Yes. At the weekend, Charlie.' Leah was surprised by the
long pause that followed. Finally her father continued. 'Sit
down, Charlie. I'm really grateful for all you're doing, you
know that. But I can't seem to face anything at the moment.
But I'm definitely going back to work next week. I know I've
got to get on with things.' Leah heaved a sigh of relief at
hearing this.

After another uncomfortable pause, Charlie spoke again.
'Such a terrible thing, Paul. I can imagine how devastated you
must feel.'

'Even if you can imagine how devastated I might feel at my
wife being murdered, Charlie, I doubt you could imagine how
devastated I might feel if you knew I'd seen her having sex
with someone behind the beach huts a bit earlier the same
evening. Just an hour or so before she was murdered.'

Leah practically stopped breathing. She felt her knees going
weak during the following silence and she held onto the wall
for support; her mouth was open in shock, her eyes wide.

'No, Paul. You can't be right.' Charlie sounded shocked.
'Maybe that bang on the head has confused your thoughts, like.
Sasha would never have done that.'

'But I saw her, Charlie. I even heard her. It happened.'
There was another long pause. 'And I know who with.
Someone called Roger Lines. One of her old colleagues who
came to the party.' His voice became stronger and more bitter.
'Now can you understand why I'm in this state? But you've got
to keep quiet about it. I don't want Sasha's memory sullied or
Leah finding out about this. It would be far too distressing for
her.'

Leah heard a sob from her father. She wanted to go to him,
to comfort him, but it was as much as she could do to remain
quiet. Hurrying silently up to her bedroom she went in, closed
the door and flung herself onto the bed in floods of tears.

— — ∞ — —

There was a small and carefully engineered gap in the hedge, half-way down the garden. Mary Clarke thought this was the perfect compromise between privacy and access to their neighbour, Hilda Redland. Frank regularly cut the hedge to maintain this gap, so she could chat with Hilda: but only when she wanted to; Hilda would talk all day if access became too easy. Stevie was not allowed to use the shears; they feared he would become over zealous and widen the gap.

When Hilda cleared her throat in her noisy 'here I am' tone that signalled she wanted to talk, Mary stood up from her weeding, glad of a rest. She walked over and popped her head through the gap in the hedge. 'That you, Hilda?'

Hilda was pretending to adjust the pegs on her rotary clothes line when she heard the call, and she turned, beamed and walked over to the hedge. 'Hello, Mary. How are you? And how's Frank?'

'I'm all right, but Frank's moanin', as ever. Says business was down last week. More people walking 'cos the weather was nice.' She tut-tutted. 'I don't know. If it was bad weather he would be complainin' about that. Anyway, how are you Hilda? I see Stevie cut your grass yesterday.'

'He's a good boy,' said Hilda smiling, her hand pulling down a wisp of hebe that was partially blocking her view. 'He does a good job.'

'He would do anything for you,' grinned Mary. 'You have a way with him like nobody else.'

Hilda laughed. 'I only listen to him. And he knows the garden's a bit too much for me now. Is he all right today, Mary? I thought he wasn't quite himself yesterday.'

Mary grimaced. 'Won't ever admit when anything upsets him, of course. I reckon that murder on the Head did, last weekend. He saw the police cars and everythin' on Monday mornin'. All cordoned off with blue tape, it was. Even saw blood on the road, he said. Hit home, I think. He's a sensitive lad, is our Stevie. And there was that rape of some actress on the Head the other week. They'd be connected, I reckon.'

Hilda shook her head and closed her eyes for a moment in

distress. 'Such a terrible thing.'

'No woman's safe on their own, these days, I reckon. Stevie couldn't wait to read the Echo about it yesterday. Headlines, it was.'

'Still, Mary, it is his life, that sandbank, isn't it?' Hilda chuckled. 'How he loves that beach and the stuff he finds there. Getting quite full, that sea-garden of his.'

'I wish he could do somethin' worthwhile with his life, though, Hilda. I know he comes across as a bit simple, poor lad. And he's out all hours. I'm worried about him, sometimes. He's not really sensible enough to look after himself.'

'The murder was on the television news,' said Hilda. 'Poor girl. Local teacher. But such a silly young thing to go out jogging in the dark like that.'

'I know,' said Mary. 'And on that lonely bit of road through the trees, as well. I sometimes worry Stevie's out too late at night for his own good, but he likes the water at night and watching the moon and stars, he says. He even uses the boat to go to the pub on the quay, the lazy thing. It's only ten minutes walk. Yet he'll run miles when he's doing his training.' She shook her head. 'Funny lad, really. Glad you understand him, Hilda. There's not many as do.'

'But he's got a kindly heart,' said Hilda. 'I sometimes think he's got things more to rights than most folk. He doesn't want much more than his boat and his bike. And he always looks after me.'

Mary raised an eyebrow. 'Count yourself lucky, Hilda. He doesn't cut our grass, lest we tell him. And we're not going to pay him. He needs to do something for his keep, I say. What's your secret with him?'

Hilda winked. 'Fairy cakes. Keeps him coming back every time.' She laughed. 'So don't you go making them or I won't have anything left to tempt him with.'

'Temptin's not generally a good idea though,' said Mary. 'Only understands instant gratification, our Stevie. He's got no self-control, see.'

Chapter 9

That Saturday Paul decided to get a grip. 'Four days to go, Leah. And I need your help with some jobs, sweetheart,' he announced over breakfast. 'Are you up for painting your bedroom walls? Have you got other plans?'

Leah looked up from her cereal and beamed. 'I was going shopping with Marina, but that can wait. We do need to crack on.' Paul was aware that normally she would have made some ironic remark about him asking her to decorate, but clearly she was still being extra kind and considerate. He appreciated it. 'Would Marina like to give you a hand?'

Leah grimaced. 'Yeah, right. You think I'd trust Marina to paint *my* walls?'

'What? So you're an expert decorator now?'

Leah grinned. 'Believe me, Dad. I will be after that job.' She gestured towards Shep, who was lying on the kitchen floor looking very forlorn. 'Poor Shep. He's been so miserable lately. He's really missing Mum, too.'

Paul sighed. 'Life doesn't seem real any more, does it?'

The ringing of the doorbell cut-off any reply from Leah. She got up from the table. 'I'll get it. Maybe Marina's come early.'

Paul smiled his thanks and went across to the toaster to collect his toast.

Paul could hear the exchange at the front door well enough to know it was the police, not Marina. It sounded like the inspector who had visited him in the hospital. Shortly afterward, Leah brought a man and a woman through to the kitchen. Although they seemed familiar, Paul realised he'd not taken much notice of them before, probably because of his condition. Yet he did vaguely recall how pallid the female detective looked and how penetrating the eyes of the inspector seemed.

'DI Hughes and DS Gold, to see you, Dad,' said Leah, in a very adult manner.

Paul exchanged handshakes and invited them to sit at the table. Hughes had thick dark hair, bushy black eyebrows and a determined slit of a mouth. Paul imagined he was quite unemotional. The female sergeant had short blonde hair, a ready smile and seemed much more approachable. Leah had already told him how nice she'd been to her on the night of Sasha's death and he exchanged a pleasant smile with her, thankful on Leah's behalf. 'Can I offer you tea? Coffee?'

Hughes shook his head: for both of them. He slid onto a pine chair at the table. The sergeant sat alongside him and produced a notebook and pencil. 'No thank you, sir. I'm sorry to trouble you again. Just a few more questions, if you don't mind.'

'Can I ask one first?' said Paul. Leah had remained standing by the hall door.

Hughes' piercing eyes focused on him. 'Of course, sir.'

'It's about my wife's funeral. Can I go ahead soon and make the arrangements?'

'I'm afraid that won't be possible, sir,' said Hughes. 'In cases like this there has to be an inquest, and I would expect the coroner to open it shortly and to formally adjourn it pending criminal proceedings. The Coroner sends a form to the Registrar of Deaths to allow the death to be registered within five days of the Inquest being adjourned. The prosecution and defence will need to gather evidence. There'll be an autopsy. So the funeral will be on-hold for quite a while, I'm afraid.' He shrugged. 'I'm sorry, sir, but in cases like this you have to be patient and wait.'

Paul sighed. 'I see. Can you guess how long all that might take?'

'I'm afraid not, sir. I understand how painful it will be for you, so I'll let you know immediately circumstances change. Meanwhile, you must try to get on with your lives.' He looked from Paul to Leah sympathetically.

'Are there any developments, yet? Did anyone see the man who killed my wife?'

'It's very early days, sir, and it's a very isolated spot. There wasn't likely to be anyone around at that time.'

'But people from the huts come and go to the toilet blocks all the time. Someone may have seen something.'

Hughes nodded. 'We will be questioning hut owners. But what about you, sir? You didn't hear a car or any other form of transport after your attack, I suppose?' He looked from Paul to Leah, who shook her head.

Paul didn't like the inspector's stare. 'Ordinary cars can't get past the barrier to the Head without a key. And I was unconscious from when he hit me until I woke up, a day or so later in the hospital,' he said, frowning. 'But then you must know all that.'

'Ah, yes, of course.' Hughes exchanged a glance with his colleague, who was scribbling in her notebook. 'But you did have at least one convenient lucid moment after he hit you, sir. Right?'

Convenient? What was he getting at? 'Only the brief one I told you about. I saw this light in my face and so I flashed my torch up at him. I briefly saw his face.' Paul massaged his forehead with his fingertips, trying to recollect the face. 'But I can't remember what he looked like. I've been trying really hard to remember, but I can't. I only remember falling back onto the road. That was when he hit me again, or maybe kicked me, I think. I don't remember anything else.'

Hughes paused. 'The party you had earlier that night, sir. Would you be kind enough to write down a list of everyone who went to it and either drop it into the station, at Gloucester Road, or call us so my sergeant can collect it?'

Paul looked round at Leah. 'Was there a list, Leah?'

Leah nodded. 'Yes, I know Mum made one. I think it was loose in her diary. I can look for it.'

'If you could add addresses and phone numbers that would be very useful,' said Hughes, looking from Leah to Paul. 'We need to interview everyone who was there in case someone saw something suspicious that night.'

'But they would all have gone back to Mudeford Quay on the special ferry by the time Sasha was attacked,' said Paul.

Hughes held up a finger. 'Ah, but did they? We need to establish that.'

After a pause, Leah piped up. 'Excuse me. Can I ask something?'

'Of course you can, Leah.' This time it was the sergeant speaking. She sounded kindly. 'What is it?'

'My grandmother showed me a newspaper cutting about an actress who was attacked on Hengistbury Head recently. Do you think there's any connection?'

Gold and Hughes exchanged glances. It was the inspector who answered. 'There might be, Leah, but it's too early to tell. That's one line of enquiry, though.'

'So are there any developments on finding her attacker?' asked Paul.

'Not yet,' admitted Hughes. He pushed his chair back. 'But we'll keep you informed. Meanwhile, we'd appreciate that contact list as soon as possible.'

Sam Gold also stood and, as she passed Leah, she paused to rest a reassuring hand on her arm. 'How are you coping, Leah?'

Leah managed to return a small smile. 'I'm keeping busy. We're moving house next week, you see. There's lots of packing still to be done.'

On hearing this, Hughes turned to look at Paul. 'Then we need to have your new address now, sir. Is it local?'

'I'll write it down for you.' Paul went across to a pad they used for shopping lists. He had to choke back a sob when he found one of Sasha's half-completed lists on the top sheet. Tearing off a blank sheet beneath it, he scribbled their new address and handed it to Hughes. 'It's in Wick village.'

'Mum was really looking forward to moving house,' said Leah. A single tear trickled down her cheek. 'It's so nice.'

'Oh, you poor thing.' Gold shook her head in sympathy and rubbed Leah's arm. 'How dreadful for you.'

Leah sniffed, wiped the moisture from her cheek and managed a weak smile. 'Never mind.' She waved vaguely at the cooker. 'It's better than thinking it was normally Mum cooking in here. I seem to be the cook now.'

Gold smiled at her. 'And are you good at that?'

'Better than Dad,' she grinned. 'Boiling an egg is his limit. And that's pushing it.' She exchanged an amused smile with

Paul.

Paul saw the police out on his own. Stepping outside the front door as they left, he spoke to Hughes. 'Can you tell me? Was Sasha raped in the attack?'

Hughes looked him in the eye. 'I'm afraid the evidence suggests she was, sir.'

— — ∞ — —

Working at the new house was good for both Paul and Leah. It gave them little time to dwell on their sadness. Neither of them wanted the inconvenience of painting after the furniture was in. Charlie helped out all over the weekend because he had other work booked the following week. By 11 pm on the Sunday night they had finished. Paul was thankful this gave him a chance to get back to the office the next day. He needed to pull his weight before his partner became too disgruntled.

They moved into the new house on the following Wednesday. When Paul's mobile phone rang at lunchtime he almost didn't bother to answer the unfamiliar number but, given he was already resting on the balcony with a cup of tea, he hit the green button. 'Hello.'

'Hello. Is that Paul?'

The voice sounded vaguely familiar, although Paul couldn't quite place it. 'Yes. Who is this?'

'Russell Gartland. I'm sorry to trouble you, Paul, but I can't seem to raise Sasha on her mobile. She gave me your number as well, so I thought I'd contact you. It's just a reminder. She said she'd call me about arranging the next windsurfing lesson for you all. She hasn't done, I'm afraid.' He paused. 'The thing is, I get pretty booked up.'

Waves of emotion flooded over Paul. How often would this kind of situation arise? Finally he managed to form some words. 'You're not very well up with the news, Russell.'

'I'm sorry?'

'Sasha's dead.'

'*Dead*?' Gartland sounded shocked. 'Really? I'm so sorry, Paul. I didn't know.'

92

'So you'd better cancel all our lessons, Russell. I'm sorry.'

'No, no. I'm sorry, Paul. I quite understand. Please accept my sincere condolences.' He paused for a tactful moment. 'I assume it was an accident?'

Paul swallowed. 'Yes. Thanks for calling, Russell. I've got to go now. Goodbye.' He ended the call abruptly and slid the phone back into his pocket. Sighing deeply, he stared at the view across the harbour. With binoculars he would probably be able to pinpoint the very spot they had begun their windsurfing lessons. They had all advanced pretty well by the end of the previous session and had been really looking forward to getting out on the water in their next lesson. Such reminders were painful evidence of just how much life had changed in a week.

It rained for the last half-hour of unloading the removal van; rain that began lightly had gradually gathered in force. Paul and Leah had to dry the furniture with towels. Once the removal men had departed and all the drying was done, they were both exhausted. It seemed quite surreal when they boiled a new kettle in a new kitchen and sat on familiar furniture holding familiar mugs in an unfamiliar room. They looked out through angled rain across wildly billowing trees: not the view they might have hoped for on their first day. It was not even possible to see Mudeford Sandbank, and the Isle-of-Wight was totally hidden by a grey murk. Clearly their view for all seasons would change dramatically with the weather.

Grinning, Paul pointed out of the window. 'What did I tell you, Leah? I told you we'd love the view.'

Leah smiled back and got up from her armchair to join him on the sofa. After sipping her tea, she leaned across to place her mug on the nearby coffee table and cuddled up against him, putting her head on his shoulder. 'We never figured moving in would be quite like this, did we, Dad?'

'No way, sweetheart.' As Paul thought how much Sasha had been looking forward to this day, he felt himself welling up. He put a comforting arm around his daughter.

Leah looked up at him, her face hauntingly sad. 'So soon after Grandad, as well.'

'At least Grandad's death was an accident.' Paul's voice

cracked a little. He squeezed her gently. 'Thank God I've still got you, Leah.'

'And me you, Dad. We've got to be strong and look after each other.'

They exchanged fragile smiles. Wiping moisture from his eye, Paul kissed Leah on the forehead. 'Yes. We do have to do that and be strong, sweetheart.' Afterwards, she settled back against his shoulder again while he sipped his tea.

It was quite some time before Leah spoke. 'I know how tough this is for you, Dad. And you know you'll always have me, don't you?'

He looked down at her earnest little face. 'How come you're fourteen, going-on twenty-five, all of a sudden? I should be saying this stuff to you, young lady. It's just as tough for you.'

'Stuff like this makes you grow up fast, Dad.' Leah paused. 'You see… I know about Mum.'

Paul looked down at her with a puzzled expression and leaned across to put his own mug down. 'You know about Mum? What do you mean, Leah?'

'I'm sorry, but I overheard what you told Charlie the other day.' Leah's tone gradually increased in pitch. 'About Roger Lines?'

Paul stared at her. 'You heard what?'

Leah looked down. 'Don't make me say it, Dad. I heard you tell him what you saw her doing with him.' She bit her lip and began to gabble. 'I'm so sorry, Dad, I didn't mean to spy on you or anything, I was worried about how you were. I wanted to know if you were going to help Charlie again…' Her voice faded away. She looked up briefly but could only meet his eye for a moment.

The shock of what Leah knew tore Paul apart. The thought of how long she had kept this knowledge to herself pressed him further over his emotional cliff. And as tears began to roll down his cheeks, so they did hers, and then they were both holding each other tightly, sobbing. Heavy rain began a fierce rattling on the windows as if the heavens were crying with them.

'I wondered where you were that night,' managed Leah, eventually.

'I went to sit by the Black House to think things out,' said Paul, trying to pull himself together for her sake. 'I was thinking I loved Mum too much to let her know I'd seen it. I didn't want to risk us breaking up, Leah. I didn't know how to handle it. I wanted it to stop.' Another wave of emotion broke over them both as they clung to each other.

'Mum was a bit of a flirt,' said Leah. They exchanged understanding looks. 'But I don't think she could help it, Dad. Most of the time it didn't mean anything, you know. She only really loved you.' Then, as a shy afterthought, she added, 'Proper love, that is.'

Paul could not think of anything to say. All he could do was squeeze her again.

Leah continued in a soft voice. 'But I have been wondering if Roger Lines had anything to do with Mum's death.'

Paul pulled back from her. He took a handkerchief from his pocket and wiped his eyes. Leah had found a tissue to wipe her own. 'Why do you say that?'

'Maybe he tried to force himself on her again, afterwards. We don't know. Mum must have been tiddly when she was with him before. But I think the police ought to know. Just in case. Do we know if Roger went back on the ferry?'

'No. Apparently he had a bike.' This idea had not occurred to Paul. To him, Lines' involvement was merely another thorn to pierce him. But perhaps Leah had a point. Lines would have taken the road through the woods to get home.

'Really?' she looked up at him. 'So when did he leave?'

Paul sighed. 'A bit before Mum went back to the hut to change.'

'You see?' Leah looked at him pleadingly. 'I think the police need to know this, Dad. He's a definite suspect.' She paused. 'And I thought he seemed a slimy individual.'

'But I don't want anyone knowing what Mum did,' said Paul. 'I don't want to sully her memory. It would be too horrible if that came out.'

'Not if Roger killed her, it wouldn't. It would be imperative for the police to know. We have to help them find the killer.' Leah pulled the hair back from her eyes to gain better eye-contact with him. 'Honestly, Dad, they need to know this.'

Paul shook his head. 'No. I can't admit I saw them together like that, Leah.'

'Then there's only one answer. Tell them anonymously. Phone Crime Stoppers, or something. Tell them how Roger Lines was involved with Mum that evening. As if you're some anonymous person who saw them. Disguise your voice, Dad. Then they'd have to investigate him.'

Paul was still uneasy. 'I'm not so sure that's a good idea, sweetheart.'

Leah shrugged. 'I suppose you keeping quiet can be explained. Like you said: so you don't sully Mum's memory.' She looked at him sternly. 'You are one-hundred percent sure it was Mum with Roger Lines, aren't you?'

'Oh, yes. And now you can see why I was so knocked sideways by this, can't you, Leah? I don't even know what to think about Mum any more. And I feel guilty about having the wrong emotions, sometimes. Then there are periods when I'm completely dead inside: kind of hollow. My head's all over the place.'

Leah reached out to squeeze his hand. 'Tell me about it, Dad.'

— — ∞ — —

Three times a week, Stevie ran early in the morning as part of his self-imposed training regime. Usually it was on mornings he knew he would be getting a proper cooked breakfast. It worked up a nice appetite. He felt really sporty in his black tracksuit and would run from his house to Mudeford Quay, along to Friar's Cliff, up the slope at Steamer Point and through the woods to Highcliffe Castle, then retracing his route back home. He liked to be able to run without getting puffed, although he always increased his pace on the last stretch home from the Quay. It was necessary to always keep fit for his missions; maybe not quite as fit as the SAS, but fit enough. And tough. He must always stay tough.

Chapter 10

Leah and Marina were sitting in front of the computer in Marina's bedroom. At Leah's insistence, they were both wearing plastic gloves she had grabbed from a filling station while her dad had been paying for petrol. Leah was not allowing any chance of them leaving fingerprints on the paper or the envelope.

Marina reached across to her printer and extracted the sheet it had printed. She was wide-eyed as she read it. 'Are you quite sure about this, Leah? It's pretty dramatic stuff. There's no going back once it's posted.'

Leah nodded. 'Dad won't do anything himself, and it might well be Roger Lines.' She turned to her friend and put a hand on her arm. 'Look, Marina, Roger was pretty tipsy when he left the party, and so was Mum. And he did cycle back along the road, and he did know Mum was going for a run shortly afterwards. What if he waited to see her and things went wrong if he got too pushy? It seems the most likely thing to me. The time and place fit. That's why the police must be told he was there. I think he killed my mum.'

Marina shrugged uneasily. 'But doing this behind you dad's back? It's like... betrayal.'

It was now Leah's turn to look wide-eyed. 'Betrayal? You've seen how the police always look to the husband as the prime suspect in cases like this. You know, when husbands go on television in tears, pleading for witnesses, and it turns out they did it all along. I'm going to tell Dad not to do that, by the way. The thing is, if there is any chance it might be Roger—and the time and place do fit—we need the police looking into it. I'm sure DNA evidence can rule Roger out if he's innocent.'

Marina shook her head. 'Hardly. If he had sex with your mum just before, it's more likely to incriminate him.'

Leah had her mind made up. 'If they don't know about this they'll be concentrating on my dad. He doesn't seem to realise that. There's only my evidence he was unconscious when I found him. They might think I'm lying and give me a rough time, too. No. It's best if they know all the facts.'

Marina shrugged. 'Be it on your own head, Leah. But I'm not happy with this.' She waved the paper. 'But I guess they'll think it could come from anyone.'

Leah smiled in relief that her friend was at least going along with her. She grabbed the paper, folded it and slid it into an envelope on which they had already printed an address. 'I'll take the spare paper and envelopes when I go and get rid of them. There won't be any evidence they can use to trace it back to us.'

'You're so devious, Leah. And that's why you're using my printer, I presume. To incriminate me.' Marina put on a mock angry face.

Leah laughed. 'There's no way they'll check your printer out, and if they do, I'll confess, I promise. But they might check out our printer at home. Now. Next thing. Delete the letter from your computer. We must remove all the evidence. I'm not even admitting this to my dad, so you know you're dead if you mention it to anyone, don't you?'

Marina grimaced and deleted the letter. 'What if the police question me?'

'Why would they?'

'Der. I was at the party.'

'Then tell them what you saw. Which is *nothing*. Right?'

Marina nodded. 'I guess so.' She shrugged. 'I saw nothing.'

'Except that Roger was a bit tiddly, maybe? But only if it comes up.'

'Maybe.'

— — ∞ — —

When Paul's phone buzzed and the receptionist told him there was a Miss Carol Davis to see him, he thought the name sounded vaguely familiar. 'Could you ask her what it's about, please, Jackie?' He was really too busy to see people without appointments.

There was a brief pause before Jackie's hesitant reply. 'She says it's in connection with your wife, but that it's private.'

Paul was immediately on his guard. 'Do you think she's a reporter, Jackie?'

'No, no. I'm pretty sure not.'

Sighing, Paul asked Jackie to show her in. He was still suspicious that reporters might infiltrate although Jackie had fended them off very well so far.

Carol Davis looked to be in her late twenties and was a short, fresh-faced girl with neatly-trimmed dark hair, high cheek-bones and brown, almond-eyes that hinted of an inner anxiety as they flitted around his office; when they finally came to rest on him they appeared to be assessing him in some way. She wore pale pink lipstick with a hint of pink eye-shadow. She was slim and smartly dressed in a long black skirt and white blouse. She greeted him with a pleasant smile but a timid manner as they shook hands, her grip soft and yielding; Paul felt it would be all too easy to crush the pale hand that lay within his own. After inviting her to take a seat in front of his desk, he sat down in his own deeply-padded chair.

'How can I help you, Miss Davis?'

'I'm so sorry to trouble you, Mr. Vincent, but I had this strong feeling I should contact you. I'm guessing my name doesn't ring a bell for you?' The rising intonation of her statement made it come over as a question. Her voice was soft but seemed edged with an underlying tension. She spoke rapidly.

Paul raised an eyebrow for a moment. 'To be honest, your name does sound familiar, but I can't think why.'

Carol nodded, as if expecting this. She seemed to steel herself before going on. 'I was the person who was raped on Hengistbury Head three weeks ago.' Their eyes met again as remembrance of the newspaper article came to Paul; then hers sank in obvious embarrassment.

'Oh dear, I'm sorry. Yes, I did read about it.' Paul paused uncomfortably until the girl looked up at him again. 'It must have been a terrible ordeal for you. I believe I read you're an actress, right?'

Carol nodded. 'Sort of. I was meant to be playing at the Lighthouse theatre in Poole last week. It was my first proper acting job in rep and I totally blew it.' The girl's shuddering intake of breath warned Paul how fragile she was. 'I wasn't confident enough and I had trouble remembering my lines during rehearsals, so they revoked my contract. It was my big chance and that man ruined it.' She paused and wriggled in the chair, dabbing at her eyes with a tissue. Paul felt uncomfortable but, thankfully, she soon pulled herself together. 'There was an attack and murder in the play, you see. I couldn't hack it so soon afterwards.'

'How awful for you.' Paul felt agitated and wondered why she had come to see him. 'Can I get you anything to drink? A glass of water, perhaps? Or tea?'

Carol managed a smile. 'No, no, I'm sorry, Mr. Vincent. I've got to pull myself together. But it was a frightening experience. And I'm so sorry for you. I can barely imagine how terrible you must feel at the loss of your wife.' She paused. 'I can't help thinking that might have been my fate if I hadn't got away.'

Paul raised a sympathetic eyebrow. 'Please call me Paul, by the way.' He tried to be as gentle as he could. 'How do you think I might be able to help you?'

The girl now found the confidence to hold his gaze. 'I thought we might help bring this man to justice by combining our efforts. I imagine you'd agree it's almost certainly the same man involved here.'

Paul could now see there were others just as deeply affected by the killer as himself and Leah. 'I hadn't thought, but yes. It's far too much of a coincidence, otherwise.'

'I heard you were an architect, so I made a few enquiries to find you. And since I gather you're a beach hut owner on Mudeford Sandbank, you must be quite knowledgeable about what goes on there. If there are any rumours about who might be involved, you would get to hear them, right? I'm a stranger here, you see. I come from Canterbury. I'm staying in digs for another week in the hope the police might get somewhere, but they don't give me a lot of confidence, to be honest.' She paused. 'Have you heard of any developments with respect to your wife?'

'The police are going to interview everyone who went to the party we held the night Sasha was killed. When they see fit to get around to it. I take it you haven't heard anything that helps?'

Carol shook her head. 'Nothing at all. The fact is, I was all shot to pieces by this. I'm now terrified of men in general, to be honest.' She looked up at him with a timid smile. 'Sorry. Nothing personal.'

Paul smiled back. 'I can well understand. Maybe it would be best if you went back to Canterbury and tried to put this behind you.'

'Put it behind me?' Her voice cracked. 'Can you? Can you put your wife's murder behind you?'

Paul became flustered. 'No, no, of course not. I'm sorry.'

Carol waved her arm. 'No. I should be sorry. I was rude. It's just that I would like us to stay in contact so we can tell one another about anything we hear that might help. He's got to be caught, you see.' She fumbled in a black leather handbag and pulled out a folded piece of paper which she pushed across the desk. 'My mobile number. Could I have yours, please... Paul?'

'Of course.' Paul picked a visiting card from a holder on his desk and handed it across the desk to her. 'Use the mobile number. I'll certainly let you know of anything useful and whether I think the police believe it's the same person. Did you get the impression they do?'

'The inspector did say it was one line of enquiry.'

'Typically non-committal. Was that Detective Inspector Hughes, by any chance?'

Carol nodded. 'That's right.' She rose from her seat. 'Anyway, I'm sorry to have taken your time.'

'Not at all. I'm pleased you contacted me. I'll certainly be in touch.'

Carol shook Paul's hand limply, gave him the flicker of a smile and allowed him to show her out of the office.

Paul found it really difficult to get back to work after her visit. Realising what this man had done to her made the thought of what he probably did to Sasha seem all the more terrible.

—— ∞ ——

Paul stopped for lunch early that day. Carol Davis' visit had been unsettling. It got him thinking about the sandbank, wondering if a visit would lead him to any rumours. Taking a sandwich box from his drawer he began eating, although he quite forgot about tasting. His thoughts drifted back to the murder scene and his mind seemed to be flickering around the experiences of that night, all the while getting tantalisingly closer to remembering what was somehow cloaked by the protection of his subconscious. He was just getting up from his desk, to make a cup of coffee, when a brief image came to him like seeing a face momentarily caught in flashlight photography. It was the face he'd seen when he temporarily regained consciousness and shone his torch onto the attacker.

The image flickered once again in his subconscious and he sat bolt upright in his chair. Now he remembered. He was about to reach for the phone when he faltered. No. Too soon for the police. He needed more facts first. He must visit the sandbank.

Chapter 11

Paul was finding it hard to concentrate on work. He kept thinking about how dreadful it was that Carol's experience had shattered her promising new career. He was also struck by how fragile she seemed as a result, and the fact resolution of these crimes was as important to her as it was to him. Which was why he called her at three o'clock that afternoon and suggested she accompany him to the sandbank to make some enquiries.

Paul anticipated her reluctance at the idea of going anywhere with a strange man, especially near the place she'd been raped, but he explained he might have a lead—although there was insufficient information for him to tell the police yet. Hesitant at first, Carol finally agreed to meet him outside the Hiker café at the end of Broadway, the road leading out towards Hengistbury Head.

After they met and he had discreetly found out where she'd been attacked, he suggested they take the little land train to the sandbank. He explained it would not only save twenty minutes walking, it would also get them quickly past the area near where she'd been attacked: and the place where Sasha had been killed. It would be an emotional journey for them both.

While they sat on a seat by the café to wait for the train, Paul told Carol about the incident with Leah and the grapnel, and how the face he now recalled from the murder scene was that of the same youth. 'He threatened me with a knife on the first occasion and he said he'd kill me the next time I annoyed him.' He exchanged a meaningful glance with Carol at this point. 'He's obviously unbalanced. Afterwards, we talked to some girls at the café near where it happened, and apparently he'd been trying to chat them up earlier. They said he was a real weirdo. It all seems to add up, Carol. It must have been him. He's a mean one, that's for sure. And he has a knife, just like your attacker. What can you tell me about him?'

Carol grimaced. 'Nothing very much. He was medium

height, wore blue jeans, a blue T-shirt and a black balaclava.' She shivered. 'He looked really scary. The police asked about his shoes, but I didn't notice those.'

Paul nodded. 'Medium height would fit.' He couldn't help noticing the strain on the poor girl's face. What an ordeal she'd had.

'If you say he's often around on the sandbank, I'm a bit worried about the fact we might see him,' she murmured nervously.

Paul gave her a reassuring smile. 'It's unlikely we'll actually see him. But if we did, and if he saw you, his reaction might give him away, which would be a useful confirmation. Don't worry, I'll look after you.'

Carol smiled uncertainly at him. 'You'd better.'

The little green train arrived five minutes later and, because it was hot, they chose an open carriage. Paul was quiet during the trip, well aware they would both be suffering their own painful memories. He avoided drawing attention to the spot where Carol said she came across the train after she was attacked, and he felt a cold shiver run down his spine when they passed the place where Sasha had been murdered. He noticed it was marked by a huge patch of sand. 'To cover the blood, to cover the blood,' kept going through his mind. He was relieved when they finally reached the stopping point. After leaving the train they walked along the last part of the sand-strewn service road by the huts that faced the harbour.

'So why have we come here, Paul?' asked Carol, stepping out to keep up with Paul's fast pace. 'Why don't you tell the police about your suspicions?'

'I want to find out who this youth is first, and I've a friend who might know. Fred Forbes. He owns the beach hut where we had our barbeque that night and he practically lives on the sandbank. His hut is in the row facing the sea. It almost backs onto ours. We can drop in at our hut for a cup of tea afterwards.'

Thankfully, Fred and Lucy Forbes were sitting in front of their hut when they arrived. Because the whole point of them being there was to enjoy the isolation of the sandbank, Paul knew they didn't have mobile phones, hence the need to go in person. Paul introduced Carol and, after appropriate commiserations and sympathy from the Forbes to her, he explained their joint quest was to gather information that might help the police. He told them about the confrontation he'd had with the youth after the grapnel incident and explained why they thought there might be a link between the two crimes. 'He's a rough lad with blond hair; very tanned. Thinking about it since, I realise I've seen him around the sandbank from time to time, usually walking along the beach right next to the sea. He often has driftwood under his arm. Do you know who I mean, Fred?'

Fred nodded and wagged a finger at him. 'I do. "The Sandman". Well, that's what some folk around here call him, apparently. A beachcomber, really. An odd lad. Always hanging around and staring. That'd be him, for sure.'

'Yes, yes, that's right,' confirmed Lucy Forbes. 'He does odd jobs for Tom Blake. I've seen him mending lobster pots at Tom's hut.'

'Which hut is that?' asked Paul, pleased to be making some progress.

'You know, the old fisherman's hut near the Black House,' said Lucy. She jabbed her finger towards the end of the sandbank. 'Tom might even be there now. It's worth a try.'

'Do you know the name of the lad?' Paul looked from Fred to Lucy but they both shook their heads.

'Tom will be able to tell you,' said Fred. 'There's nothing Tom doesn't know about the sandbank.'

— — ∞ — —

Ten minutes later, Paul and Carol were thankful to find a well-rounded character wearing a blue peaked cap sitting on a weather-worn, red plastic chair in the open doorway to his hut; he was smoking a briar pipe that emitted an almost tangy fragrance. When Paul enquired, he cheerfully confirmed he was Tom Blake.

'What can I do yer for?' he asked with a grin. He had

bulbous red cheeks and skin like leather. Thick greasy grey hair protruded from his denim cap.

'I gather there's a lad who helps you out here,' said Paul. 'Blond tufty hair. Got a motorboat. I'm trying to locate him.'

'Are you now?' The fisherman looked at him curiously. 'An' why would that be, squire?'

'About something that might interest him,' said Carol.

'And what might that be, then, lady?' Blake turned his attention to Carol. It was difficult to tell whether he was suspicious, protective or merely curious.

'I gather he collects a lot of driftwood,' said Carol. 'I'm a landscape gardener, you see. Always on the look-out for interesting pieces I can use in people's gardens.'

Paul exchanged a grateful smile with her, impressed by her inventiveness. He was beginning to regret not having prepared a story for this exchange himself.

'Aaah. Right.' Blake took out his pipe and now seemed more relaxed. 'His name's Stevie Clarke. Lives across Stanpit, next to the harbour. Moors his boat right at the bottom of his garden, lucky sod. I'll write down his address for yer. He might be right pleased if there's money in it.' He got up and went inside his hut. They saw him scribbling with a pencil and he shortly returned with a scrap of paper he held out to Carol. 'Real keen on his old bits o' wood, is Stevie. Mind you, he might not want to let any of 'em go, he loves 'em so much.' He laughed. 'Funny lad.'

'Is this the only work he does?' asked Paul, in a conversational tone.

Blake nodded. 'Reckon so. Big ambitions, but a bit short of the wherewithal, if you know what I mean.' He tapped the side of his head and grinned. 'Simple needs and a simple mind, has Stevie. But he's not so bad if yer treat him right.' He winked at Carol. 'What would yer name be, then? So I can tell him.'

'Anne. Just say Anne.'

'I'll tell him tomorrow morning. He'll look forward to hearing from you. Or you could catch him here, middle of most mornings.'

Carol smiled. 'Thanks a lot, Mr. Blake.'

'Someone told us he's called "The Sandman", said Paul. 'Is that right?'

Blake laughed as he sat on his chair again. 'I was first to call him that. I called out "Mister Sandman" to catch his attention when I wanted to sound him out for work. He's always combing the sand, that's why. It kinda caught on. I'd bet he's got a real store of wood by now.' He winked at Carol. 'You should be all right there, love. Give him a good deal, though, lady. It's only fair to him.'

— — ∞ — —

Paul handed Carol a steaming mug of tea and sat on the seat opposite her inside his beach hut.

Carol looked appreciatively out through the open doors to the view across Christchurch Harbour. 'What a wonderful place you have here, Paul. Almost idyllic.' She looked at him with a shocked expression. 'Oh dear. I'm so sorry. I didn't mean to sound insensitive. My being here must be so traumatic for you, after Sasha.'

Paul smiled wearily at her. 'Lots of things are traumatic right now, if we let them be, Carol. Look, if we're in this together, there's no point in us both carrying on as if we're walking on eggshells. We're both bruised, but we've got to feel free to say anything, within reason. We've both got to learn to talk about what's happened. We might be able to help each other to move on. Agreed?'

'I know what you mean. Yes, that's fine by me. Actually, it's a great relief to have someone to talk to about this. I'm alone here, you see. I don't know anyone in this area. But you'll have to forgive me if I have the occasional wobbly.' She smiled nervously.

'Ditto.' Paul returned her smile. 'And it seems to me you'll make a great actress. You'll even cope with forgotten lines, judging by the way you can ad-lib. That stuff about being a landscape gardener. Where did that come from?'

Carol laughed. 'I really don't know. The only thing I could think of was that he was a beachcomber. It was down to word-association: beachcomber, driftwood, landscape gardening. It all seemed to fit.'

'And you fitted your part perfectly. I'm sure there'll be many starring roles to come for you.'

'I hope so. If I haven't blown it too badly. But I am out of work now. I quit my other job when I was offered an acting contract and I know they won't have me back because sales are slack.'

'What was your previous job?'

She grinned. 'If I tell you, you'll understand why I quit. I was just a sales assistant in a shoe shop. Spent all my time fetching the other shoe. And wore my own shoe-leather out doing it.' They both laughed. 'Plus, I did some amateur dramatics work, of course, which is how I got a taste for the smell of greasepaint. And I like pretending I'm someone else,' she added, wistfully. She caught his eye. 'Never very happy at home, you see. Had an elder sister who was Mum's favourite, and a younger brother who was Dad's. I don't think they really needed me. I didn't feel I amounted to much. I was a spare part.'

'Poor you. So will you go home, now? To Canterbury, wasn't it?'

She nodded. 'Yes, I've been living there with my parents. It's cheaper,' she grinned. 'I didn't earn much. I was the only fledgling still in the nest, but restless about it. This was meant to be my great escape. Such a shame I messed-up.'

'You didn't mess up. You were messed-up.'

'A pro would have been able to carry on by wearing their acting head. The show must go on, et-cetera.' She sipped her tea. 'The thing is, I can't face going home now. Fortunately it was only on local news and that seems to have bypassed Canterbury. I can't contemplate the fuss they'll make if they discover I was raped. I'm thinking of getting a temporary job in Bournemouth until some other acting job comes along. I'll be able to tackle it next time. I've put out some feelers at the theatre and the people with the digs I'm in are ex-theatricals, with contacts. But I'll need to look for somewhere cheap to rent as soon as I get a job. I can't afford to stay at the B & B for too long.'

Paul smiled at her. 'I'm glad you're sticking around. This has also knocked me off course, at work.'

They drank their tea in silence for a while.

'So tell me a bit about yourself, Paul. Obviously you're a successful architect. That must be very rewarding. What kind of buildings do you design?'

'All sorts, but mainly houses. Often luxury pads. That was my dad's speciality, you see. We worked together. I joined his partnership to add architectural design to property development. It was a strong team.'

Carol looked at him hesitantly. 'Why the past tense, Paul? Is he no longer in the business?'

Paul stared glumly at the view. 'He died recently.' He sighed and looked round at her. 'An accident. Leant on some dodgy scaffolding and it gave way. Fell to his death.'

'Oh, Paul, how terrible.' Carol put down her mug and joined him on the opposite seat, resting a comforting hand on his arm. 'What a terrible time you're having.'

'We've recently moved into the house I designed for us. Just my daughter and me, now, of course. Everyone was so looking forward to it. Leah's only fourteen. She seems very strong on the surface but I know how cut-up she is inside. Dad was longing to see the house completed. He only saw the footings.'

'Your dad's death must have been such a shock for you. And for your mother, too, of course. How is she handling it?' Carol let go of his arm rather self-consciously and moved slightly farther away.

Paul went quiet, concentrating on the view. In the centre of his vision was Christchurch Priory: a reminder, once again, of his father's funeral. He turned to her. 'I sometimes think my mother was partly the cause, Carol.'

'What? Why?'

'All my mother has ever been interested in is socialising. Dancing. Having a good time. The problem was that Dad was usually far too busy for all that, but it didn't stop Mum. There was always another dance or drink partner. Poor old Dad accepted it in the end. I sensed he was beginning to worry his marriage was going off the rails and I reckon that made him generally careless. He didn't seem to care about anything very much.' He sighed. 'I don't know if Mum actually had an affair, but I think Dad worried about it. He would never have had an accident like that under normal circumstances. He used to take me onto building sites when I was a nipper and he never stopped telling me to be careful of everything.' He paused. 'In the end he worked more and more and he got more and more tired. So that's why there's plenty for me to get depressed about, and why we were ending a week's unexpected holiday to cheer me up a bit when Sasha...' His voice tailed off.

After a short silence, Carol obviously thought it better to change the subject. 'So you definitely think that Clarke character is our man, Paul?'

Paul shrugged. 'He had it in for us after the thing with the grapnel and Leah. And I'm sure it was his face I saw when I briefly regained consciousness the night Sasha was killed. So it can't be anyone else really, can it? Frankly, it will be good to nail the bastard.' He felt a little embarrassed by how strongly this came out.

'So are you ready to tell the police we've got a name and address?'

'I certainly am.' Paul slid his mobile phone out of his pocket. 'In fact, I'm going to do it right now.'

— — ∞ — —

Paul agreed to meet DI Hughes at the new house, with Carol. They took the land train back to the car park and then Carol drove behind Paul's car to the house.

'Pretty impressive,' said Carol as she followed Paul up the staircase to the day level. 'It must feel really good to design your own home.'

'An architect's dream,' said Paul. He reached the landing as Leah appeared from the kitchen carrying a glass of orange juice. She was followed by Shep. 'Hello, Leah.'

'Hiya.' Leah looked curiously beyond her father to Carol,

who now joined them on the landing.

'Leah, this is Carol Davis.'

Shep gave a little bark and wagged his tail furiously when Carol held her hand out for him to sniff. She stroked him and he looked up at her with loving eyes.

'Carol Davis?' Leah looked hard at Carol as they shook hands. 'You're the actress?'

Carol nodded but gave her a rueful smile. 'Would-be actress,' she said. 'I'm sure my fame didn't reach you because of my acting ability, did it?'

Leah grimaced. 'I read about what happened to you in the Echo. It must have been awful.'

'You had an even more horrible experience in many ways,' replied Carol. Leah's mouth trembled and Carol's face crumpled in sympathy. She flapped hands for Leah to come closer. 'Come here. We both need a hug.'

While holding her glass of juice carefully out to one side, Leah allowed herself a short hug from Carol. They both pulled back, viewing each other with sympathy, although Paul saw Leah was a little taken aback.

Paul broke the uncertain silence. 'Carol contacted me at the office, this morning, Leah. We think the person who attacked her is probably the same person who attacked Mum. We're combining forces to try to come up with something that might help the police. And that Inspector Hughes is meeting us here in a few minutes. But there's something I need to tell you first, sweetheart. Come into the lounge for a minute and I'll explain.'

Leah looked from her father to Carol and held up her juice. 'Can I get you a drink, Carol? Juice or a coffee?'

Carol smiled. 'No thank you, Leah.' She turned to Paul. 'Look, would you like to talk to Leah alone for a few minutes? I could always wait in the car.'

'No, no, we're all in this together. Come on through, both of you.'

Paul took them to the lounge where he indicated an armchair for Carol to sit in. He sat in the other armchair and Leah sat on the sofa, Shep at her feet. Paul explained to Leah how he had recollected a brief spell of consciousness after his fight with the killer, during which he'd shone his torch and recognised the face. 'It was definitely the boy we had trouble with after he tossed that grapnel near you, Leah. We now know he's called Stevie Clarke. Some people apparently call him "The Sandman" because he's a beachcomber.'

Leah's mouth opened in surprise. She sat back, shocked. 'Are you sure, Dad? You really saw him that night?'

'I'm sure it was him. And I can now remember him coming over with a torch and shining it in my face. I think he must have kicked me in the head after that. The next thing I remember is waking up in the hospital, with you.'

Leah stared at him in disbelief. 'You mean you think this Stevie Clarke killed Mum because of that argument? To get his own back, or something?'

Paul shrugged. 'It doesn't make much sense, I know. If he had it in for anyone, you'd think it would be me. Unless he wanted me to suffer, of course.' Just then the doorbell rang and their conversation came to an abrupt halt. Paul stood. 'And that will be Hughes. So that's what I'm going to tell the police, Leah. Carol and I both believe it must be the same man involved.'

'But surely Carol didn't see him?' Leah looked at Carol. 'The newspaper said he was wearing a balaclava.'

Carol nodded. 'He was. No, I can't recognise him, Leah. But it seems unlikely there could be two people attacking women in the same area at around the same time. That's why your dad and I both think it must be he who attacked me as well.'

Paul headed for the stairs. 'I'll bring Hughes straight up. Let's hope the police can now make some progress.'

— — ∞ — —

Leah felt in a dream. Her body seemed heavy and lifeless in the chair. She listened wide-eyed while her father explained his suspicions to the police: that this Stevie character was probably Carol's masked rapist and her mother's killer. During this, the nice lady police sergeant, called Sam Gold, sat on the sofa next to her, frantically scribbling notes.

DI Hughes was doing all the talking on their behalf. He frowned when he spoke to her dad; Leah thought he looked rather fierce today. His face was hard. She wondered what terrible things he might have seen in his job. She thought of her mother lying dead on the road and wondered if there could be anything more terrible than that.

'So you can definitely identify the person you saw at the murder scene as Steven Clarke, sir? You could pick him out in an identification parade, for example?'

'No problem there,' said her father.

'Except that you might simply be picking out the person you had an argument with,' pointed out Hughes. 'How 'with-it' were you when you came-to at the murder scene and flashed your torch? How reliable is that memory, sir?'

'Very reliable. It was definitely Clarke's face in the torchlight.'

Murder scene. Murder scene. Leah clenched her teeth together, trembling slightly. Why did Hughes have to keep repeating it? Sam Gold must have noticed her tension for her hand touched hers again and she leaned across to whisper. 'Why don't you leave this to us, Leah? You don't need to be here if it's upsetting you.'

Leah liked Sam. She was kind. 'I'm all right. I want to be here. It was my mum who was murdered. It affects me, too.' She gave the sergeant a meaningful glance. Gold raised an eyebrow but nodded her understanding.

Hughes turned towards Carol. 'Miss Davis. Can you positively identify Steven Clarke as your attacker?'

Carol looked uncomfortable. 'Not positively, no.' She paused. 'But surely, with the same kind of attack in the same area, it has to be the same person responsible for both?'

Leah watched as the inspector's eyes gazed upward for a moment, in obvious exasperation. He focused them on Carol. 'I think you can safely leave us to draw conclusions like that, miss. Whatever you might think or expect, we can't assume two separate crimes are linked unless there is very good reason to do so. But, yes, because of the small time-window and the

113

same geographical location, I'm still inclined to believe these two crimes were probably committed by the same person. But they're being processed as two separate cases at the present.'

'Both by you?' asked Carol.

Hughes nodded. 'Yes, fortunately, both by me. So am I right that there's nothing concrete you can add to your earlier statement about your attack? Despite you telling me now you think Steven Clarke is responsible? You and Mr. Vincent are merely surmising?' He looked from one to the other of them.

'No, inspector. I suppose not,' said Carol.

'In that case, I would strongly advise you it's a very serious matter to accuse an individual of a crime unless you have some admissible evidence.'

Leah thought he now sounded quite cross and she felt sorry for Carol who looked both nervous and humiliated.

Hughes then turned his attention to her father. 'Mr. Vincent. Since I'm here. Why was it you went after your wife that evening, sir? Had you had some sort of disagreement earlier on?' His tone was brusque and Leah was amazed by this question.

Her dad looked surprised as well. 'No. Why do you say that? I told you at the hospital. I went after her because our dog came back to the hut in a panic. I followed Shep and he took me to her. He's a clever dog.'

'You didn't just decide to go after her, then?'

'No. I followed Shep.' Leah sensed her dad felt defensive, and she could understand it. It was as if the policeman doubted him.

'Hmm. A dog that clever?'

Hughes' obvious disbelief brought Leah to life. She pulled the hair back from her face to stare at the inspector. 'But it's true. I was there when Shep came back, all in a state. We both knew something was wrong at once.'

Hughes turned to face her. 'And your dad then followed Shep?'

'Yes. He told me to stay at the beach hut, and I did until Shep came back again. Shep was in an even worse state by then. That was why I followed him. I knew something bad must

114

have happened for Shep to come back without either Mum or Dad. That's when I found them both...' she tailed off. She could feel her eyes stinging.

'And what condition was your dad in when you got there, Leah?' Hughes was now using a more kindly tone than he had with her father.

'But I told Sam all this before.' Leah felt indignant and looked round at Sam Gold for support.

Hughes nodded. 'I know. But I need to hear it from you, personally, Leah.'

'I went to my mum first but she was all still and stiff.' Leah fought back the tears. 'I put my ear by her mouth but she didn't seem to be breathing. So then I went across to see how Dad was. He was breathing, but unconscious.'

'And you didn't see or hear anyone else there?' asked Gold. 'Is that right?'

'That's right.'

Hughes stared at her for a few moments and then went back to questioning her father. It allowed Leah to go back inside herself, although she made sure she listened to everything. She was quaking. Listening to her dad, she realized how sure he was that Stevie Clarke was the killer. He had seen him there, after all. Which meant Roger Lines wasn't the killer. What a fool she'd been sending the anonymous letter to the police. Was that the reason Hughes thought Dad might have had an argument with Mum? Because he thought Dad was mad with Mum about Roger Lines? And why hadn't she told her father she'd realised it had been Stevie Clarke who looked in their beach hut window that night? Was everything linked? Had she made things even worse with her stupid anonymous letter? Was she, herself, the centre of it all? Was Stevie Clarke trying to ruin *her* life?

— — ∞ — —

Leah and Marina met in Bournemouth town centre because Marina wanted to buy a new top, but Leah insisted they have coffee first. They went into Debenhams, got their coffee and claimed a window table overlooking The Square. Being Saturday, It was busy in town. Leah was bursting to tell her friend about the latest developments.

As usual, Marina was firstly sworn to absolute secrecy. Her eyes grew wider and wider as Leah told her about her father's recollections and that Stevie Clarke was almost certainly the killer. She also related how her father had told her about how he and Carol had spoken to the fisherman, Tom Blake, and that Stevie was also sometimes called "The Sandman".

'What a creepy character,' said Marina. Then, during a brief silence while they drank their coffee, some of the implications of all she had heard obviously began to dawn on Marina. Leah was watching her face, awaiting her reactions. 'So it wasn't Roger Lines?'

'Doesn't look like it, does it?'

'Oh, Leah! The letter.' Marina looked shocked.

'Have the police interviewed you yet?' asked Leah.

Marina stared at her. 'Der, no. You think I wouldn't have told you if they had?'

Leah sighed. 'I was wondering if they'd done any of the interviews with the people at the barbeque yet. And whether they'd interviewed Roger Lines.'

Marina shrugged. 'I told you not to send that letter, Leah.'

'I know, I know.' Leah had already beaten herself up about this. 'If only I'd listened to you, Marina. All that stuff about Mum and him needn't have come up.'

'So what do you think about this Stevie character? Did you get around to telling anyone he was the one at the window?' Her eyes widened when Leah shook her head forlornly. 'No?' Marina looked at her in disbelief. 'Why, exactly, are you digging a great big hole for yourself, Leah?'

Leah ignored this. 'Do you think Stevie is doing this stuff to get back at me, Marina?'

Marina looked astounded. 'You? Why would he do that? What have you done to him? From what you said, you gave him an easy time about that anchor thing.'

Leah shrugged. 'I don't know. But it all seems to revolve around me. He spied on me in the hut. He nearly clobbers me

116

with the anchor thing. He kills my mother and almost killed my father. Maybe he thought he'd even done that as well.'

Marina reached across the table and put her hand over Leah's. 'Of course it's not revolving around you. It was a coincidence the anchor thing happened after you saw him looking in the hut. You said yourself you were sure that was an accident.'

'Well, maybe he had it in for my parents after that. Mum spoke up to him as well as Dad.'

'I wouldn't try to figure out why. Look, Leah, this Stevie is obviously just a peeping pervert. If he attacked Carol as well as your mother, that shows he's after women in general.'

'And probably me as well,' said Leah in a small voice. 'Don't forget he's been spying on me.'

Chapter 12

While Leah was out with Marina that Saturday morning, Paul decided to check out Stevie Clarke's address at Stanpit. Spotting the odd house number as he drove slowly past the right area, Paul ascertained Clarke's house must be in a terrace of cottages that obviously backed onto the harbour. After parking at the first available space outside a shop, he walked back to find the number. Nothing distinguished the property from its neighbours other than its faded curtains. Having already noticed a way through to the harbour a little further back, Paul counted the houses along so he could identify the property from the rear.

He walked through to a harbourside path and then counted the houses along. At the bottom of what must be the Clarke's garden, in an area that sloped down to the adjoining public footpath, were sea-pinks dotted amongst an assortment of shells and twisted logs. These were arranged on a bed of pebbles and a thick blue rope ran through it in a fanciful form of decoration. A garden path of concrete paving slabs ran up the small slope and led straight to the back door across the lawn.

Behind the seafaring display was a wooden seat set in an area of gravel. Alongside this stood an old ivy-clad brick building with timber steps leading up to a wooden door. The building had small upright windows and looked to be in use since grimy yellow curtains were in evidence. Paul imagined it was some kind of workshop and guessed it was raised for flood protection: the cottages were not much above the water level.

So this was the lair of Stevie Clarke. It occurred to Paul it might be possible to waylay the youth here any time he wished; clearly Clarke would moor his boat on the sandy beach nearby. But Paul was not ready for that yet. He had a better plan in mind.

— — ∞ — —

It wasn't fair. Stevie knew the only person who saw him on the sandbank late that night was the murdered woman's husband: Vincent. And he also knew it was Vincent's word against his, so he was determined to stick to his story, no matter what. No torture would get more out of him. Not even pulling out his nails. He would be strong, like a captured prisoner-of-war. He'd only give his name and number.

Both the policewoman and the inspector were staring at him intently. It made him nervous.

'So you say you went out in your boat across to Mudeford Sandbank, that night, Steven. What for? Wasn't it late to be over there if you'd been there earlier the same day?'

Stevie shrugged. 'I go there lots. Often at night. I watch the sea and the stars from there. And foxes and owls. I like it over there. It's a free country.' Stevie looked sulky.

'The lad leads a simple life,' said Frank Clarke. 'He loves walkin' round that sandbank, like, collectin' driftwood and shells and stuff. And he likes nature, he does.'

'That's right,' added his mother. 'He doesn't do any 'arm.'

Stevie was grateful his parents seemed to be on his side, for once.

'So what time did you get back home, Steven?' asked Hughes.

Stevie scowled and shrugged. He knew it was late, maybe near to midnight, but that wouldn't do. 'I don't know. About half-past ten. Not any later.'

'I saw him going into his house in the garden about then,' said Mary. 'I was pulling the curtains at the time.'

'I see.' Now Hughes looked more satisfied and had risen from his seat on a front room armchair. 'I think that'll be all for now then, Steven.'

When Hughes and the detective sergeant had departed, his father marched angrily back into the room. 'Was that true, Stevie? Were you back here by half-past ten?' He glared at him.

'Yes.' Stevie looked defiant. 'I said so, didn't I?'

Frank turned to his wife. 'And you really saw him, Mary?'

'What ever's got into you, Frank?' She nodded firmly. 'Yes, I saw 'im. And that's an end to it. Go easy, Frank. Don't make 'im more upset.' She turned to Stevie. 'They weren't very nice to you, were they, Stevie? Makin' you all hot and bothered.'

Stevie looked from his father to his mother and then stormed out of the room, out of the house, and back to his own garden house. Once there, he flopped into his armchair, breathing deeply. Gradually his tortured expression turned to a little smile. One thing was good. Now it was more than his word. It was his mum's too.

— — ∞ — —

The following Thursday morning, feeling brave after steeling herself for it, Carol Davis rang Paul on his mobile phone and asked whether he would take her to the sandbank to maybe get a glimpse of Stevie Clarke. She thought a discreet sighting of him might help her to identify him, even if only through his build. But she voiced considerable concern about how she might react if Clarke spotted and recognised her.

'It would be his reaction to seeing you I'd be interested in,' said Paul. 'That could reveal his guilt. And I'll be there to watch over you. We must do it.'

'I wasn't really thinking about that. I only wanted a discreet sighting.'

'We'll play it by ear,' said Paul. 'Let's go on Saturday morning.' He wanted to see the youth close-up in order to observe his reaction to seeing them together. Unless Clarke was already locked up, of course. This he needed to know.

After talking to Carol, Paul phoned the Boscombe police station and asked to be put through to DI Hughes. Fortunately he was there.

'Have you arrested Stevie Clarke, yet?' he asked, getting straight to the point.

'We have interviewed Mr. Clarke,' Hughes replied. 'But there is no evidence to suggest he was involved, nor any reason to arrest him. He was at his home at the time.'

'But I saw him there, Inspector.' Paul was indignant. The

more he thought about it, the clearer the image of Clarke seemed to be in his head.

'So you said, sir.' Hughes sounded impatient. 'But his mother confirmed he was at home at the time.'

Paul paused while he took this in. 'She's lying. I saw him there, Inspector. I know I did.'

Apparently Hughes was not impressed and he reminded Paul that he'd suffered a severe blow to the head. Paul quickly hung up, feeling wretched.

Eventually Paul managed to get back to some design work and was thankful for it as a method of taking his mind away from all his problems: including his increasing concern about how depressed Leah seemed to have become. Just when he felt he was coping better, Leah seemed to be going downhill. Thankfully, she would be back at school the following Monday; like him, she had too much time to think, at present.

That evening, despite some qualms, Paul tentatively asked Leah if she wanted to go to the beach hut on Saturday. He explained he was taking Carol to the sandbank in the hope of her catching sight of Clarke and perhaps recognising something about him to confirm he was her attacker. He said he was also interested in Clarke's reactions to seeing them all together. At first Leah was very dubious about the idea, fearful it might provoke another fight, but, after considering the benefit of seeing Clarke's reaction herself, she agreed, provided Marina could come too. Paul said he was fine with this.

Carol met them all at the car park, and this time they all walked along the service road towards the sandbank. It was a bright day, the tide was high and the harbour glinted in the sunlight. While they walked, Paul found himself staring towards the distant harbourside houses, now very aware that one of them was Stevie Clarke's. He could almost feel hateful vibrations flowing out from him and across the placid water towards it.

When they came to the trees, Paul suggested they take the narrow footpath through the woods that lay parallel to the service road. Leah gave him a knowing glance and nodded firmly in agreement. They both knew this would avoid passing the spot where Sasha had been killed. After leading them a short way, Paul stood aside at a little wooden bridge to let Leah and Marina go ahead of him, gently touching Carol's back to signify she should also go ahead of him. He was startled by the effect of his touch: she bolted across the bridge like a startled horse. Once across, she stopped, turned, and gave him an embarrassed smile.

'I'm so sorry, Paul. I'm so jumpy since... well, you know what.'

'No, *I'm* sorry.' It was only then that Paul fully realised how fragile Carol was since the rape. Clearly she now abhorred the touch of any man. He must take special care with her.

The three of them trooped in single-file behind Leah until the path emerged again to join the road just before the beach huts.

They had only passed by a few huts when Paul heard his name being called out. Looking round he saw Russell Gartland striding towards him.

'Hey, Paul. Hang on a minute.'

'Yes?' Paul stopped abruptly. He was on a mission and the last thing he wanted right then was any diversion.

'Look, I'm so sorry about Sasha, Paul, but I've been wondering if Leah would like to carry on with her windsurfing lessons on her own. Or join another group, maybe?' He gave Paul a knowing glance, one eyebrow slightly raised. 'I think it would be therapeutic for her.'

Leah began to shake her head. 'No, I don't think so, thanks, Russell. Maybe some time in the future.'

'We have more important things on our minds, right now, Russell,' said Paul impatiently. 'And windsurfing is the least of them.'

Gartland took an uncertain step backward in the sand. 'Sorry, Paul.' He shrugged. 'Well just bear in mind you're both welcome to carry on at any time.' He flashed them a grin, dazzling white in contrast to his honey-coloured tan.

'I'll bear it in mind.' Paul strode on. A few yards out of Gartland's earshot he let his true opinion be known. 'Therapeutic! Talk about insensitivity.' He strode on ever faster, despite the others now lagging behind. Passing by their own beach hut he barely gave it a glance. It was the fisherman's hut he was heading for.

— — ∞ — —

Her father's impatient exchange with Russell worried Leah. She could tell he was in a dangerous mood. Suddenly afraid, she hurried up to him and pulled at his arm. 'This is madness, Dad. He tried to knife you before. We shouldn't go near him again. It's too risky.'

Her father shook his head but didn't even reduce his pace. 'That was all bluster and show, Leah. If you don't want to come, go back to our hut with Marina and we'll meet you there afterwards.'

Leah felt desperate. 'Look. If he is the killer, it's not just show, is it? We *know* he's really dangerous.' She wondered why she'd ever gone along with this idea. Now she was practically running to keep up with her father. She was aware her growing apprehension was beginning to rub off on the others and she hoped that between them they could stop him carrying this through. She feared he might be out for a confrontation rather than on a mission to allow Carol to see Stevie. There was little chance of halting him now, though, and he was marching way ahead of them by the time they passed the Beach House café. She exchanged a nervous glance with Marina but Marina grimaced and shrugged in return. Thankfully, when the rear of the fisherman's hut was in sight, her dad stopped and waited for everyone to catch up. Once again he told them this had to be done.

Feeling terrified, Leah looked from Marina to Carol. 'Carol, can't you stop him? Clarke's dangerous. Tell Dad you only need to get a distant look at him. Please, Carol. Why not just wander past on your own without Clarke realising.'

Carol hesitated. 'I don't know if I could do that, Leah.'

Leah turned back to her father, pulling the hair from her face to stare at him challengingly. 'You're out for a confrontation, aren't you, Dad?'

Carol stepped forward to put a restraining hand on her father's arm. 'Paul, let's leave it. I'm sorry I asked you to bring me here. You can't go tackling this man. Look, I'll casually wander past on my own, like Leah suggested.'

Paul shook his head. 'I'm not going to tackle him. But you really need to hear his voice, Carol. We need to get him to speak.' He waved his hand vaguely at some of the people passing nearby. 'There are plenty of people around. There's nothing he can do.' He jerked his head towards their destination. 'Come on, Carol, let's get this over. Leah, you stay here with Marina.'

'No way!'

Her dad shrugged. 'Let's go, then. Let me do the talking.'

Reluctantly, Leah, and a silent Marina, followed her father and Carol. Leah judged Carol was now becoming as apprehensive as herself. She was praying Stevie wouldn't be there, so it was a real shock when she rounded the hut and saw him sitting in the open doorway. He had part of a large net strewn over his knees and was using a wooden bobbin to thread twine through a fishing net that was pulled across a trestle in front of him. A strong smell of fish emanated from the hut. Stevie was just as she remembered him: the same unruly mass of blond hair, and the same antagonistic glare when he looked up and recognised her father.

'You!' The boy tossed the net from his knees and stood. He looked round at them, glaring at her in a moment of further recognition. Now she had no doubt. This was definitely the face she had seen looking through their beach hut window.

'You bastard.' Stevie's colour rose as he glared at her father.

'Hey, hey. What's all this?' Tom Blake emerged from the darkness of the hut and stood behind the youth. 'Don't get excited, Stevie, boy. These are the people I told you about the other day. That's the landscape gardener lady interested in yer wood. So be nice.'

Stevie glanced at Carol for a moment, then stared back at her father. 'You got me in trouble with the police, didn't you?' He shook his fist at her dad. 'I know it was you.'

'For doing what, Clarke? And why do you think it was me?'

'Because you're trouble, mister. And you want to get back at me.'

Her dad exchanged a querying glance with Carol, who seemed to give him a slight shrug. He turned to Stevie and wagged a finger at him. 'I saw you there that night, remember? Before you put the boot in? I bet you enjoyed doing that, didn't you?'

'No. I wasn't there.'

'You weren't where, exactly, Clarke? You know exactly where I'm talking about, don't you?'

It seemed to Leah her father must be right. Stevie had fallen into a trap. So he was guilty.

'I know where the police thought I was,' Stevie snapped back. 'Thanks to you settin' me up, you bastard.' He was getting red in the face now, shifting his weight from one foot to the other like he had before, never taking his eyes off her dad. Leah was grateful there was a trestle separating them. 'I promise I'm gonna get you for this.'

'Then you'd better watch out, because the police are keeping an eye on you,' said Carol. She took an involuntary step backward, looking surprised at her own boldness.

Stevie looked towards her. 'You keep out of this. I don't care what you want. I'm not dealin' with you if you're with him.' He spat in the direction of her dad. The glob of sputum landed on the net where Leah observed it clung like cuckoo spit.

Tom Blake came round the trestle to join them. 'Look, I don't know what this is about, but off with yer, getting Stevie all upset like this. He's a good lad. Leave him be.'

'He's a murderer. He killed my wife.'

Blake looked taken aback. 'What? Are you that poor teacher's husband?'

Her father nodded. 'And he threatened us after he nearly maimed my daughter. He threatened to kill me then.'

Blake looked uncertainly from her dad to Stevie. 'Is this right, Stevie?' He sounded astonished.

In his confusion, Stevie did a little shuffle. 'He was givin' me an earful, Tom. It was an accident. I didn't mean the grapnel to go near her.' He pointed at Leah and looked pleadingly at the burly fisherman.

'Look, you're all confused. Off with yer.' Blake began to push her father gently in the chest with the palm of his hand. 'Away from here or you'll get him even more worked up. Off, before I call the police.'

Thankfully, Dad took a step backward and now seemed ready to go: but not before a final volley at Stevie.

'I'm watching you, Clarke. I'll make sure you pay for this.'

'You bastard!' Stevie began to push around Blake, who managed to ward him off with his bulk. Stevie's angry red face glared round him. 'And you'll pay for what you've done. You'll see.'

As they walked back towards their beach hut, Marina whispered to Leah. 'That Stevie is so scary, Leah. You poor thing.'

'He's a killer, Marina, and the police won't listen to Dad.'

Marina caught her arm and they lagged behind. 'So Roger Lines is definitely innocent.'

Leah sighed. 'Since Dad remembers seeing Stevie's face, he must be. And he did look guilty, didn't he?'

'So we've really dropped Roger in it, Leah.'

Leah looked at her friend's shocked expression. 'It's still up to the police to find out who did it,' she protested. 'We can't be certain. That's one thing I've learned.'

'Your dad seems certain.'

''My dad is often certain, but he's too quick at deciding.'

'So were you,' pointed out Marina.

Leah gave her a playful shove and scurried after her father and Carol. As she drew level with them she heard Carol answering him.

'It might be him, and it might not. I was so frightened, I didn't take much in.'

'But it must be him.' Her father was clearly frustrated. 'Think hard, Carol. Surely that was the voice you heard?'

Carol shook her head in despair. 'It might be. I'm really not sure. I think he tried to change it.' She was clearly intimidated by Dad's look of utter disbelief. She stopped and turned to face him, blocking his way. 'I'm sorry, Paul, but I've got to be certain, haven't I?'

— — ∞ — —

Stevie had to strain his brain as he headed back across the harbour in his boat. He wanted to work out the man's name. He remembered he'd heard him called Paul after the grapnel incident. He'd made sure to remember that, but it was the surname he was after. He needed to know the name of all his targets. Then he remembered the newspaper article. What was the woman called? At last it came to him. Sasha Vincent. So now he had it: Paul Vincent. He would give Paul Vincent a hard time. And that daughter of his, too. What was her name? He knew he'd heard it when the man had been trying to make him apologise. Something unusual. Ah, yes. Leah, that was it. Leah Vincent. She had obviously dropped him in it about him looking through their hut window. She would pay as well.

And then there was Vincent's girlfriend. She was trouble as well. He felt uneasy at the way she'd been staring into his eyes.

When Stevie ran his boat aground and pulled in up onto the beach, he saw his mother waving to him from the garden seat. She was drinking a mug of tea.

'Hello, Stevie. Have a good mornin'? Any work from Tom?'

'Yes. Earned some money.' Stevie joined her on the seat, turning to smile at her gratefully. 'Thanks again for helpin' me out with that policeman the other day, Mum.'

Mary smiled back. 'That's all right, son. I could see he was gettin' you all flustered, like.'

'And for telling him I was home by half-past ten.'

'Well I saw your light on, Stevie, so I knew you were in the garden house by then. I thought you were home earlier than that, actually.' She patted his arm. 'Thought I'd say I saw you, mind, rather than just seein' your light. I know they're a suspicious lot, the police. I saw your light on from the kitchen.' She stood. 'Anyway, I must be gettin' on. I've the dinner to do.'

'Thanks Mum.'

Stevie gratefully watched her go up the garden path. Once the back door had closed, he went up the steps and into his garden house. Going into his bedroom he reached down to the plug and pulled out a time-switch that was connected to his bedside lamp. It might be better to hide it during the day. Pulling the carpet back a little, he exposed a trapdoor leading down to the net storage area below. He opened it up and jumped down. The little room below was only four feet high and he had to crouch in order to hide the time-switch under an old folded tarpaulin. Better safe than sorry. That Paul Vincent might get the police poking around again.

Chapter 13

The police car drew up by the road access to the shoreline at Stanpit. DI Hughes and DS Gold got out.

'Thanks a lot for doing this, guv,' said Sam Gold as they walked through to the path. 'I've got a gut-feeling his mother was lying last week.'

Hughes stopped to look across the water towards Hengistbury Head. 'Beautiful spot.' He turned to his sergeant. 'He's a nutter, that's for sure, Sam. And I think his mother might be lying as well, but she'll obviously keep it up.'

'Probably to protect him because he's a bit simple,' said Gold. She paused for a moment whilst also enjoying the view across the harbour. The heather on the Head gave its outline a vague purplish hue. 'So what's he got to hide, guv? He's admitted to being on the sandbank that night.'

Hughes shrugged. 'Maybe he doesn't want the risk of being associated with the proximity of the killing. A lot of people would think like that. Anyway, let's see if we can get a few answers without Mummy and Daddy hanging around our necks. And it would be good to bring up that earlier incident report about the quarrel. Thanks for finding that, Sam. It was a good bit of digging.'

Gold grinned. 'It's a link between them, even if it is tenuous. Are we taking him to the station, guv?'

'If he's in, we'll play it by ear, Sam. And get that swab, of course. But I don't think we've got enough to justify taking him in yet.'

On reaching the rear of the Clarke's house, Hughes saw a movement through the window of the outbuilding. 'Good. He's in there.' He climbed the wooden steps and knocked loudly on the door.

When Stevie Clarke opened it, his face fell. 'You.' His eyes flitted from one to the other of them. Hughes thought he looked particularly worried.

'Yes. Me. We want to chat with you a little bit more, Steven.' Hughes applied gentle pressure to the youth's chest, forcing him to step backward, so allowing him and his sergeant to enter the tiny kitchen. Gold closed the door behind them. It was crowded; everyone stood. Hughes could see a small bedroom through an open doorway.

'You've already questioned me,' the youth objected.

'And if I want to, I'll question you every day,' said Hughes. 'Answer up and I may leave you alone.'

'So what is it?' Clarke moved to pull the bedroom door shut and stood in front of it.

'I understand you had a little *contretemps* involving the Vincent family a couple of weeks ago. Am I right?'

'Contra... what?' Stevie's brow creased in bewilderment.

'A little trouble, Stevie. You had a spot of bother with Mr. Vincent, right? And his wife?'

The youth now looked sullen and suspicious. 'I suppose that bastard told you that.'

Gold exchanged a knowing glance with Hughes. 'What bastard would that be, Stevie?' she asked.

'Vincent. The man. He tried to tear me off a strip when that daughter of his nearly got hit by a grapnel 'cos she wasn't looking where she was going. It was only an accident. I suppose he told you different, did he?'

'Actually, a witness telephoned the police about the incident. The details are on record,' said Gold.

Hughes squared up to Clarke. 'But although it was only an accident, it did lead you to threaten Mr. Vincent with a knife and say you'd kill him. Isn't that so, Steven?' He held the lad's eyes in a beady stare.

Clarke shrugged. 'I was mad with him, that's all. He was tearing me off a strip. I never meant it.'

'And during this exchange, Mrs. Vincent got involved too, didn't she? Did you threaten to kill her as well?'

Clarke went bright red. 'No, I never. I never said nothing to her.'

'And the very next week, Mrs. Vincent is attacked and murdered.' Hughes paused. 'Funny that, eh? Were you pleased about it? Did it feel like you got your own back on the family?'

Clarke now became very agitated and raised his voice. 'I never had nothing to do with that. I told you. I was at home by half-past ten. Long before she was killed.'

'So, you know when she was killed, do you, Steven?' asked Gold. She and Hughes exchanged glances.

Clarke shrugged. 'Papers said something about it bein' late,' he said, sullenly.

Hughes took a step forward so he was only a foot away from Clarke. He stared into his face. 'So do you maintain you were home by ten-thirty that night?'

'Yes. I already told you.'

Hughes sighed. 'I'd advise you not to go around threatening people. It could land you in serious trouble. It's a good job Mr. Vincent didn't complain to us directly about that.' He nodded to Gold. 'Take the swab, Sam.'

'Yes, guv.' She produced a small container and a cheek swab from her bag. She stepped towards Clarke. 'Open your mouth, Steven. We need a DNA swab.' Clarke's eyes widened and he took a step backward. 'Open,' repeated Gold, more firmly. This time, Clarke meekly opened his mouth while Gold scraped the inside of his cheek with the swab.

Hughes smiled and nodded at Gold who was transferring the swab to the container, then turned and crossed to the door, which he opened. Turning back, he pointed to Clarke. 'Just behave yourself, lad. Remember. I'm watching you.'

— – ∞ — —

On the following Saturday evening Leah went to the cinema with Marina. As a result, Paul invited his friend Charlie over to the house for company. They sat on the balcony eating pizza and drinking beer while the sun went down. After discussing work in general, and their common interest in football, the conversation turned to the police investigation into Sasha's murder.

Paul admitted he was beginning to question what he'd seen when he came round. Had the fleeting image of Clarke's face been a dream or hallucination? 'Something the inspector said made me begin to doubt it. Can I be absolutely sure it was him after such a serious head injury? And it's important, Charlie, because if he wasn't the killer, it opens up at least two other avenues of suspicion.'

'Oh yes? Avenues of suspicion, eh?' said Charlie, gravely. 'What would those be, then, Paul?' He reached for another slice of pizza.

Paul could barely see his friend in the fading light. 'That Roger Lines I told you about, for one. He was cycling back down the service road shortly before Sasha went that way. What if they'd agreed to meet again or he waited for her? What if he went too far with her and Sasha protested? Maybe he was a bit drunk and got nasty.' Paul paused to let this scenario sink in.

'Have you told the police about you seeing this Lines fella messing with Sasha?' Even in a crisis, there was always something soothing about Charlie's slow drawl.

Paul shook his head. 'No. I don't want that coming out unless it has to, Charlie. I don't want people thinking Sasha was a…' The word he had in mind was 'tart', but he was unable to voice it out loud. 'And there's another mystery. Someone else who might be in the frame, for all I know.'

'Someone else?' Charlie sounded amazed. 'I can see why you might need a few beers before bed, now and then, Paul. Who else?'

Paul explained about the hang-up calls he'd taken from the person entered in Sasha's mobile phone's directory as Glenn.

Charlie gave an immediate response. 'Phone him up, then, Paul. Don't mess around. Find out. Threaten to tell the police if he doesn't talk to you? That'll produce results, I shouldn't wonder.'

'But he probably won't even speak to me, Charlie.'

'Threats of a police visit should lubricate his tongue well enough. Go on, Paul. You've nothing to lose. So why wait? Do it now.'

Paul looked across at the dark outline of his friend. He was grateful for his prompting. 'You're right, Charlie. Come into the lounge. Let's do it.'

They took their empties and the remains of their pizzas and deposited them on the dining table in the lounge. Paul fetched both Sasha's mobile phone and his own and joined Charlie at the table. He imagined this Glen had heard about Sasha's death. Figuring it would spook him if he used Sasha's mobile, he copied the number into his own phone and pressed the 'call' button.

'Hello. Glenn Mason.'

Paul felt pleased he at last knew the man's full name. 'This is Paul Vincent, Glenn. I need to talk to you.' After a long pause the line went dead. 'Damn!' Paul looked across at Charlie. 'He hung up again.'

Charlie gestured to the phone. 'Is it a mobile number?'

'Looks like it.'

'Then text him, Paul. Tell him he either picks up and talks to you now, or you get the police to talk to him instead. About Sasha's death.' When Paul looked hesitant, Charlie gestured again. 'Go on. Now. Strike while the iron's hot. I reckon he'd sooner speak to you than the police.'

Paul sent a short text message along the lines suggested by Charlie, cracked open another beer and waited a few minutes to give Glen the chance to read the text. Charlie asked if he had any ideas about who Glenn was, but Paul simply shook his head.

The next time he called, he did get an answer. 'Hello. This is Glenn. What exactly do you want, Paul?'

Paul felt an inward tightness. 'I take it you already know Sasha was murdered?'

'Yes, I saw it on the news. Look, I know I don't know you, but I am really sorry, mate.'

'Don't mate me. Let's face it, you've gone to great lengths *not* to speak to me, right? Always hanging up on me?'

'Yeah, I'm sorry about that.'

'So what was your relationship with Sasha? And why did you always hang up on me?'

'I didn't have any relationship with Sasha. We're previous school colleagues, that's all. I'm an art teacher. You've got

133

hold of the wrong end of the stick.'

'What's the right end, then? Because, if you don't satisfy me right now, I'll be asking the police to find out where you fit in... mate.'

Paul heard a loud sigh on the other end. 'It's quite simple, really. Sasha sometimes did life-modelling for my students at Bournemouth College. She told me you wouldn't like it and that she wanted to keep it secret from you.' He paused. 'She thought you might be against it. I only called her to discuss availability. That's all, honestly. I can prove it. I've got documentary evidence of college payments to her, with dates.'

Paul knew it sounded right. And Sasha had been right: he would have objected very strongly. The thought of people ogling her naked body made him feel sick.

'So you wouldn't mind repeating this to the police, then? If it crops up?'

'No reason not too. But I don't see why I need to be dragged into this.'

'Thanks.' Paul paused. 'Look, after we hang up, could you send me a text with your full name and address? And send copies of the documentation you mentioned, by post? I'll text you my new address. Could you do that tomorrow, please?'

'No problem, if it helps.'

'Thanks a lot. Convince me and you needn't get involved with the police. Oh, and sorry if I was a bit hard on you. I understand your difficulty in speaking to me now.'

'No worries, mate.'

Paul hung up.

Charlie looked at him expectantly. 'Well? What's his story? Does it sound plausible?'

Paul nodded. 'Oh, yes. Only too plausible.' He took a swig from his can. This was another red-herring resulting from his green-eyed monster. 'I'm sure he's nothing to do with it, Charlie. Apparently Sasha was doing some life-modelling work for the college and she didn't want me to know about it.'

Charlie raised an eyebrow. 'Is that right?' He paused. 'And can I guess why?'

Paul nodded, with a grimace. 'Sasha knew I wouldn't

approve.'

Charlie smiled. 'She knew you well enough, Paul. Mind you, not many husbands would approve, I reckon. So there you go then. One suspect down and only two remaining. I reckon you're getting closer.'

— — ∞ — —

Early evening the following day, Leah set out to walk to Marina's house in nearby Tuckton. It was their last day of freedom before returning to school. She told her dad she would take Shep with her to give him an extra walk. It was a pleasant evening and she walked through Wick village and took the path near the ferry that led to the riverside walk. Quite a few people were around, including numerous other dog walkers. A man often fed mealworms from a box in a wooded area, and she stopped to watch him for a short while, fascinated as a little robin dared to feed from his hand. She was looking to see where Shep was going when she saw a lad lurking beneath a nearby tree. She immediately knew it was Stevie Clarke and it was obvious he was watching her.

Startled and frightened, Leah called Shep and began to hurry along the path towards Tuckton Bridge and the tea gardens. It would be more populated there. She had no other option. To return home was out of the question for there were several lonely areas amongst the trees and even Wick Lane was too quiet. Nor did she want to show him where she lived. She knew that getting to Marina's house in Danesbury Avenue was her best bet. She really wanted to phone her dad for help, but if Stevie saw her on her mobile she thought that might provoke him into attacking her. When Shep began to hang back to exchange greetings with a friendly retriever she called him angrily to heel. Walking really fast, she was cross Shep was still lagging behind. She stopped to call him. As soon as he came to her, she clipped on his lead and began walking fast: almost at a run. A few glances back told her Stevie was definitely following; he was taking very large strides to keep up. It was frightening. How did he know where to find her in

135

the first place?

Leah rushed up to Wick Lane by the tea gardens, along to the roundabout, and through the shops of Tuckton to Marina's road. All the while he was behind her. He seemed to be making no attempt to catch her up, but simply maintained a constant separation of about twenty yards between them. Leah could see he was grinning, delighting in the fact she was scared. She was breathless and frightened when she repeatedly rang Marina's doorbell. When the door was opened by Jane, Marina's mother, she barged in, tugged Shep in after her, and pushed the door shut behind her, finally bursting into tears of relief.

'He's been following me all the way.'

Jane looked at her in concern. 'You poor dear. Who's been following you?'

Fortunately, Marina appeared, and Leah managed to explain. 'He must still be out there.'

'We should call the police at once,' said Jane, reaching for the nearby phone.

Marina put a comforting arm around her, obviously shocked by what had happened.

'I'll speak to them,' said Leah. 'But let me phone the Boscombe police station and speak to one of the people I know there. Please.'

Jane reluctantly relinquished the phone.

Leah was shaking as she took it. 'Just let me get my breath back first.' Shep was licking her hand madly, aware she was stressed. Bending down she hugged him. 'You would have looked after me, though, wouldn't you, Shep?'

— — ∞ — —

Paul was seeing a client right over at Sandbanks when he got Leah's call. She calmly explained how she'd been followed by Clarke from Wick to Marina's house, how she'd phoned the police, and how they had told her to wait there for them to come to see her. When Paul got to the house himself, forty minutes later, there was no sign of either the police or Clarke. Once inside, and after exchanging a long hug with his daughter,

136

Leah explained that Clarke had hung around for about twenty minutes and had then disappeared from sight, although she was worried he might still be hiding in a nearby service road behind some shops. Paul went outside to check, but there was no sign of Clarke. After that, Leah was only too glad to go home with him. Paul thanked Marina's parents for looking after her and asked them to explain to the police where they'd gone: if they ever got around to coming.

Sitting on the rear seat of the car, Shep was the only one who remained calm.

'How the heck did he know where to find me, Dad? I would have thought he only knew where to find us at the hut.'

'If that,' said Paul, negotiating the traffic on Tuckton Roundabout and heading down Wick Lane. 'He wouldn't even know which hut.'

'Actually, he does know which hut, Dad,' said Leah timidly.

'He does? How do you know that?' Paul glanced across at her in amazement.

'I'm sorry I didn't tell you before, Dad, but I didn't want the risk of you getting too mad at him. I knew he was dangerous.'

'Tell me what before?' Paul pulled the car into the side of the road near the little library under the trees. He read the guilt on her face. 'Come on, Leah. What do you know?'

'Promise you won't be cross, Dad. Please. I've had enough stress for one day.'

'What?'

'Promise.'

Paul shrugged. 'Okay, I promise. So what do you know?'

'That face that scared me at the hut window, one night.' She paused while he caught up. 'That was Stevie Clarke as well.'

— — ∞ — —

Stevie was really pleased with how easy it had been for him to find their new address. Now to make them pay. As he heaved himself over their rear garden fence from the path, he chuckled to himself. If Leah thought following her was frightening, let her just wait. Not that anyone would see him tonight in the

137

dark. He wanted to get home for the television that evening, anyway. He wanted to watch a late film. This was only a recce. He just wanted to see how the land lay for future reference.

He saw there was a light on in two of the upper rooms, the one with the big balcony and another one on the higher floor. There was even a ladder lying conveniently against the side of the house. How inviting. What a dream. He looked at his watch. Still plenty of time to get home on his motorbike. He even had a few minutes in hand. Perhaps he would take a quick peep now after all.

Chapter 14

Paul picked up Carol from her digs in Stour Road and drove to Christchurch where he parked near the Priory. He figured she needed some cheering up, and a short sightseeing tour of Christchurch seemed a good way to do it—after a brief look inside Christchurch Priory itself—which he explained was the longest parish church in England. Thankfully, he was now able to walk around it without getting too upset about his father's funeral. Then he showed her Christchurch Quay and explained the River Stour there was shortly joined by the River Avon, the merged waters then flowing out into Christchurch Harbour and so to the sea, alongside Mudeford Sandbank and their beach hut.

Carol smiled at him and pointed across the river. 'I think I'm beginning to get my bearings, Paul. Do you live somewhere across there?'

'That's right. Not very far behind the water-meadows.' He then turned to point to an old building next to grass covered by swans. 'Let's walk over there past the old mill. We can take a path between the River Avon and the millstream to get to the town centre. We could find somewhere there to have a drink. How does that sound?'

Carol beamed at him. 'Fantastic.' Wearing blue jeans and a pink blouse, he thought she looked really attractive: but young, some eight years his junior. She walked alongside him, admiring the river view with its Hengistbury Head backdrop. Paul found it good to be in the company of a woman again, but although there was nothing in this relationship but friendship, he felt slightly uncomfortable wondering what Leah was making of it. Leah had seemed fine when he'd explained Carol needed a bit of company after her frightening experience, but even as he justified it to her, he'd felt pangs of guilt. He was also nervous about leaving Leah alone, but she had homework to do and was fine about it. She said she felt quite safe in their new house. At least Clarke didn't know about that.

Carol was quite taken by Christchurch and its laid-back feel and she loved the river walk. As they looked down the river, Paul told her Christchurch's motto: "Where time is pleasant."

'I imagine it can be,' she smiled. 'If only all *our* time was as pleasant as this, though.' As they stood by the river near to the road bridge, she momentarily took hold of Paul's arm and looked up into his face. 'Thank you so much for this, Paul. I'm really grateful.'

Slightly embarrassed, Paul shrugged. 'For what?'

She tugged gently on his arm. 'For taking time-out for me. And for caring. For helping me realise there are still men I can trust in the world. I think I was going a bit mental.' Laughing self-consciously, she released his arm and went across to see some ducks on the mill stream. 'Aren't they gorgeous?'

Emerging on Bridge Street, a few minutes later, they turned left towards the town. Reaching the High Street, Paul asked whether Carol would like to go to a pub or a coffee bar; she chose the latter. He suggested they have a coffee in the Soho café-bar a little way to the left on the short road leading to the Priory. A few minutes later they were relaxing on a leather sofa in the window, their lattes on a coffee table before them. It was only then, after a few minutes of small talk, that Paul told her about Leah being stalked by Clarke the previous evening.

Carol was shocked. 'Gosh, you've kept that quiet, Paul.'

Paul gave her a wry smile. 'I'm sorry. I wanted us to have a bit of peace on our walk before reality struck back.'

'Poor Leah. She must have been scared witless. How did Clarke find her, for heaven's sake?'

'I can only assume he spotted her by chance. The riverside walk at Tuckton is popular. Maybe Clarke had his boat nearby. Anyway, I guess he took advantage of the opportunity to scare her. There's no way he could have known she would be there. She was bright not to head for home and show him where we live.'

'And is she alone tonight?' Carol sounded really concerned.

Paul felt a stab of guilt. 'Yes, but she's fine with that, Carol. Leah's a very mature girl, and she's very strong emotionally.

She's been stronger than me over her mother. Admittedly, Clarke shook her last night, though.'

'Shook?' Carol shivered. 'I would have gone to pieces.'

'She has lots of homework and she's not going out. I'm taking her everywhere in the car at the moment.' Paul looked at his watch. 'Anyway, I'll be going straight home after I drop you off. You said you didn't want to be late. Have you enjoyed your Christchurch tour, though, even if it was a bit speedy?'

'It was really nice to do something ordinary instead of sitting brooding in my room in the B & B. Thanks.' She briefly laid a hand on his arm. 'And you've been so kind to me, Paul. Thank you so much. I don't feel so alone here, any more.'

Paul smiled. 'We're both going through a traumatic time, Carol. I'm really glad you contacted me. It's good to have someone sympathetic to confide in.'

'Me to,' she smiled back.

'I don't know about you, but my head's all over the place. And so must Leah's be. I called Hughes today to tear him off a strip for the police not even following up on Leah's call. He shrugged it off as if it were of no significance and went on about higher priorities. Apparently no one went to Marina's house or even phoned back. How can they miss the obvious? Clarke is intimidating us and they should put a stop to it.'

'But what reason?'

Paul shrugged. 'To frighten us, I suppose. Probably retribution for me putting him in the frame with the police.' He sighed. 'And life is so complicated at the moment I can hardly concentrate on my work for longer than an hour or so.'

'At least you've got your work as a diversion. I wish I had.' Carol sipped her drink. 'What exactly keeps taking your mind away, Paul?'

Paul looked at her for a few moments, wondering how much to disclose. During their walk by the stream, Carol had confided how the rape had shattered her. Quite apart from the terror of the attack, and the questioning and intimate examination by the police, it was her new jumpiness and general fear of men that was wearing her down, plus the thought of how much worse it would be if her parents ever found out. Fortunately the news hadn't reached Canterbury.

Paul could tell that talking to him had relieved a little of her burden, and he now felt he could also use some release in return. As a result, he found himself telling her, in strict confidence, how he saw Sasha having sex with Roger Lines shortly before her murder. How he had wanted to break them apart, how he had longed to confront Sasha, how it had all unravelled when she was murdered so soon afterwards, and how mixed-up his emotions were in the wake of it all, with anger, hate and grief all vying for prominence, sometimes making his stomach feel like lead. It was fortunate their area of the bar was relatively quiet during these exchanges, for he heard his voice cracking at times.

'You poor thing.' Carol edged closer to him along the sofa and put her hand gently on his arm. 'You've got so much stress going on in your life and all I can think of is my own worries. Being attacked was really frightening, but at least it was over quickly. Your stress will never end. How awful for you, Paul. And for poor Leah.'

It did feel better to have shared it with her. 'Can you see why my head is all messed up, Carol? I really loved Sasha, and we were happy nearly all the time, but now I sometimes really hate her for what she did. How she was always flirting although she knew it upset me. She couldn't seem to help herself, but at least I imagined it was no more than that. But after seeing her with Roger Lines, I know different. I keep asking myself if there was anyone else. How long have I been living in a fool's paradise? She was beautiful and she knew it. She revelled in it, in fact. I've just discovered she even did life-modeling without telling me.' He shook his head. 'And I love her, miss her and hate her all at the same time, Carol, even though it doesn't make much sense.'

'Of course it makes sense, Paul. As an actress, I've learned that emotions often pull you in several different directions at once. Let alone in your circumstances.'

Paul was aware he was near to breaking point. 'Excuse me, I need the gents.' He hurriedly left her to go to the toilets. Locked in a cubicle, he regained his composure and wiped his eyes. He was about to return to Carol when his mobile phone rang. It was Leah: in a panic.

Paul practically ran out of the pub after briefly explaining to Carol there was an emergency involving Leah. He'd never run as fast as he did then to collect his car from the car park.

— — ∞ — —

Her world seemed to implode. Her desk was in the window of her bedroom on the top floor of the house: alongside the bedroom that should have been shared by her mother and father. It was high, and the view was tremendous, although darkness had by now descended. After finishing her homework, she had looked up to savour the view of the twinkling lights of Mudeford one last time before drawing the curtains. It was then she saw the face.

Leah screamed. His face. Again! And she was on the *second floor*: with no balcony outside. She tore the curtains across to obliterate him so fiercely that one partly ripped from its runner. Her mobile phone was on the desk at her side. She was shaking so much she could hardly select her dad's entry. Please God he was not far away.

— — ∞ — —

Leah was downstairs, still shaking, when she heard her father's key in the door. The wait had seemed like an age but, in reality, it was no more than about fifteen minutes. After briefly hugging her dad and telling him what had happened, she nervously waited while he went out into the back garden to look for Clarke. Two minutes later he was back.

'He found the ladder at the side of the house and used that, Leah. It's still propped up under your window, sweetheart. I'll get Charlie to take it away tomorrow.'

Leah watched her father close the back door and lock it. She went across to him for another hug. 'Oh, Dad. He's so scary. Why won't the police arrest him?'

Her father took his mobile phone from his pocket and

143

selected a number from the phonebook. 'I'm calling Hughes now. I'll make sure he listens this time.' He put an arm around her. 'Don't worry. I promise not to leave you alone again until Clarke's arrested.'

— — ∞ — —

DI Hughes arrived an hour later with a uniformed male police officer he introduced as Constable Harding. Meanwhile, Paul and Leah had been sitting in the lounge, drinking tea.

Judging by his impatient and brusque manner, Leah guessed the inspector was none too pleased at being called out so late. The first thing her father did was to take them through into the garden to show them the ladder. Leah waited in the hall. When they all came back into the house her dad asked Hughes why Clarke had not been arrested. The inspector seemed totally uninterested in this and brushed him aside to approach her. He had scary, penetrating eyes.

'I want to hear your story, young lady.' He turned to her father. 'We need to interview your daughter somewhere alone, sir.'

Her father shrugged. 'I'll go up to my bedroom and you can use the lounge.'

'No, we'll talk to Leah in her bedroom, if you don't mind. She can show me where she was sitting when she saw Clarke. All right?'

Dad shrugged and Leah nodded. 'All right,' she said, turning to the stairs. 'I couldn't believe it when I saw his face at my window. It's two floors up. Follow me.'

When the reached her bedroom, Leah explained what had happened. She looked at Hughes pleadingly. 'Please arrest him, Inspector. He's freaking me out.'

'Where were you sitting when you saw him, Leah?'

Leah pointed to her desk by the window. 'Right there. I was doing my homework. I looked up and there was his face at the window. I screamed and pulled the curtain across. Look.' She pointed to where a small section of the yellow curtain had been ripped from its securing tape. 'I did that, I was in such a hurry.'

'Hmm. And what did you do then?'

'I phoned Dad. To get him to come home straight away.' She noticed the other police officer was taking notes.

'Why not call the police first, if you were so frightened?'

Leah pulled hair from her face and glared at him. 'What would be the point? I did that yesterday, after Clarke followed me to my friend's house, but the police never came, even though they said they would. You didn't even contact us afterwards.' She paused significantly. 'My dad came straight away.'

Hughes grimaced. 'I'm sorry about that, Leah, but there were other priorities that night. Now. How long is it since you moved in here?'

'Just under two weeks.'

'And how do you imagine Clarke knows where you live? Did you tell him?'

Leah was incredulous. 'Of course not. I don't talk to him. I don't see him. I've no idea. Dad thinks it might have been chance he saw me by the river yesterday. Maybe he's followed me ever since.'

Hughes looked at her sternly. 'Look, Leah. Did your dad ask you to say all this to us? About the ladder and everything? Did you really see Clarke out there?' He paused. 'Be absolutely honest, young lady, because we'll find out the truth eventually. You'll be in big trouble if you lie to us.'

Leah was astonished. She raised her voice in indignation. 'Lie? Why would I lie?'

At that moment the door burst open and her dad came in. She was mightily relieved to see him.

'What's going on?' he demanded. He looked at her in concern. 'Are you all right, Leah?'

'I was, until he accused me of lying,' said Leah through clenched teeth, pointing at Hughes.

Her father drew himself up. 'Look, Leah's had enough to cope with recently, without you accusing her of lying, Inspector. She always tells the truth. Now leave her alone, she's been upset enough. You can ask me anything you want to know.'

Hughes surveyed him briefly and nodded. 'Do you know, I think that's an excellent idea, sir. If you'd like to come along with me now we'll have a little chat back at the police station.'

Her father was indignant. 'I can't leave Leah here alone after this. Talk to me here.'

Hughes shook his head. 'No, you need to come with us. Is there a relation you could ask to come over to be with Leah? Constable Harding will stay with her until someone else arrives.'

'I suppose I could ask my mother to come over.'

'I suggest you do that right away, sir. It might be a while before you return.'

Leah could not believe it. From Hughes' tone it sounded like Dad was in serious trouble. She felt desperately responsible because of her wretched letter. Her world was crumbling.

— — ∞ — —

It was unbelievable. He was being treated like a criminal and it made him really nervous. Even during the ride to Boscombe police station, the police inspector had been unusually curt. It was now well past midnight, Paul felt tired, and Hughes was glowering at him across the plain table. A pink folder lay between them. A police officer sat nearby with a pad. Hughes informed him they were going to tape the interview, and he made a preliminary announcement about this for the tape before glaring at Paul.

'Right. There are a lot of things we need to know from you, sir.'

Paul was only too aware from the other's tone that the 'sir' was pure sarcasm. There no longer seemed to be any respect for him. Why were they turning on him like this? 'I've already told you everything I know. Have you been looking for my wife's murderer? Have you interviewed people who were on the sandbank that night?'

Hughes wagged a finger at him. 'I'm the one asking the questions here. But I will tell you this. We have now interviewed most of the people who attended your barbeque.'

'With any results? Did anyone see anything suspicious?'

Hughes sighed. 'More to the point, did *you* see anything suspicious that evening?'

'No. You've already asked me. Don't you think I would have told you if I had? Sasha went off running to clear her head after the party. She took our dog with her. When Shep came back in a panic, I followed him. By the time I reached Sasha she was being attacked. I tried to help her but I was hit over the head by her attacker. I came to for a moment and that's when I saw Clarke with a torch. He was examining Sasha's body. What more evidence do you need to arrest him?'

'It was dark. How did you know it was Clarke?'

'I told you. I had a pocket torch. I got it out and flashed it in his face when he came over to look at me. I think he kicked me in the head then. That's all I remember... until I woke up in hospital.'

'Hmm.'

'So Clarke was there that night, whatever he says.'

'Apparently he was well tucked up at home by then,' said Hughes. His mother corroborated that.' He raised an eyebrow. 'So it's just your word against his, sir.' He raised a finger. 'No, actually it's his and his mother's word against yours, isn't it?'

'Then she's lying for him.' Although Paul might once have had momentary doubts about whether he really saw Clarke that night, now he was perfectly certain. He'd thought a lot about it since confiding his doubts to Charlie, but the image of flashing his torch onto Clarke's face kept coming back to him. How could Hughes possibly doubt his word against that crazy youth's?

'You seem to have it in for Clarke, don't you? Is it something to do with that incident involving your daughter and a grapnel?'

Paul's heart sank. They had clearly been digging and that argument did look bad for him. 'It doesn't help. That was why he is so antagonistic towards us,' said Paul. 'He threatened to kill me after that, and all I did was try to get him to apologise to Leah. He could have killed her with his carelessness.'

'The fact is you got pretty angry during that altercation

didn't you, sir? So much so that someone called the police. They were worried when Clarke threatened you with a knife.' He paused. 'That made you pretty angry, didn't it?'

Paul felt his anger rising again but he held it in check. 'How would you feel, Inspector? He could have killed or maimed Leah. I only asked him to apologise to her but he refused. He had no idea how dangerous his carelessness was. He needed that to sink in. And pulling a knife shows how aggressive Clarke really is. He threatened to kill me when no one was around.'

'And that made you very angry, right?'

'I guess so.'

'It doesn't do to get very angry, Mr. Vincent.'

'Look, Clarke killed my wife, Inspector. Why don't you concentrate on asking him the questions?'

'But why kill your wife instead of you? You said it was you he threatened. Do you think he killed her out of spite? Is that your theory?'

'I'll leave the theories to you. Ask him. All I know is that he was there, at the scene. Why would anyone other than the killer be there and not report it?'

'But you were there, sir. And we have no evidence he was there.' Hughes leaned forward to scour Paul's face. 'I repeat. Did you have an argument with your wife that evening?'

'Argument? No. It was a good evening. A successful party.'

'Much of which you missed. Where were you between the time you were cooking on the barbeque and when your guests were leaving? No one seems to have seen you for most of the evening. That seems a bit odd for the host of a party.'

Paul swallowed hard. This was getting very uncomfortable. 'I wasn't feeling well, Inspector. I had a bad headache.' He was making it up on the fly now. 'I went for a walk to clear my head. I sat down by the Black House for a while. The time went by quicker than I realised. When I checked my watch and saw how late it was I hurried back. Most of the guests were leaving by then to catch the late ferry we'd organised to get them back to their cars on Mudeford Quay.'

'And you did nothing else during that time, sir? Did you see your wife at all during that period?'

'No. I knew she was busy entertaining our guests. That's why I felt I could take some time-out. She was good at that.'

'Let's talk about Roger Lines,' said Hughes. Paul's heart sank. What did they know? 'Did you see him with your wife during the period you were away from the party?'

Paul shook his head. 'No.'

'Are you perfectly sure about that, sir?' After a pause, Hughes leaned forwards across the desk. 'Didn't you see Roger Lines having sex with your wife between some beach huts? Wasn't that why you took your little walk afterwards? Wasn't that why you needed some time-out? When you realised your wife had been unfaithful?' He seemed to spit the words out.

'No.' Paul tried to look surprised, but knew he was unconvincing. 'I don't know what you're talking about.'

Hughes opened the folder in front of him and took out a piece of paper. He turned it around and placed in on the table between them in such a way that Paul could read what was printed on it. He read it with growing disbelief. It stated that Roger Lines had sex with Sasha that evening.

'Did you send us this anonymous letter, sir? So we would suspect Roger Lines?'

Thoughts of a solicitor began to run through Paul's head. Wasn't this the point where he needed one?

'No, I didn't send the letter. I've never seen it before.'

'Well, I suggest you did, Mr. Vincent. And that you made sure there weren't any fingerprints on it.' He leaned across the table to shout at him. 'And, I also suggest, that while you were missing from the party, you did see Roger Lines having sex with your wife. That incensed you, didn't it? So much so that you followed her when she went on her run and you argued with her. It ended up in fight, didn't it? One in which she hit out at you to defend herself. Hence your lump on the head. Did things get out of hand because of your anger?'

Paul could hardly believe what he was hearing. 'How could I have killed her when I was knocked out?'

'When people get knocked on the head they don't always pass out immediately. As in your case, consciousness can sometimes come and go. Unlike life, Mr. Vincent.' After a pause for Paul to take this in, Hughes fixed Paul's stare. 'We've got DNA evidence that your wife definitely had intercourse with Roger Lines that evening.' He nodded. 'Yes. But you knew that, didn't you? You saw it. And Lines admitted to it when we told him about the DNA evidence. He had little choice. And that was the reason you went missing from the party, wasn't it? To think about what to do about Lines?'

Paul realised there was no point in further denying it. 'Okay, okay. Yes I did see them together. And that was why I went away to cool off. But I didn't want to do anything about Lines. I was worried about my marriage. I loved Sasha, you see. I didn't know how to handle the situation. I didn't tell you about this before because I didn't want anyone to know Sasha had done such a thing.'

Hughes smiled. 'At last we're getting somewhere. So did you send the letter implicating Lines?'

'No. I don't know anything about the letter.'

Hughes stood and came round the table. He sat on the edge of it next to Paul, gathered his collar in his grip and hissed in his face. 'So go on then. Admit the whole thing. You challenged your wife about it when you caught up with her on her run, had a row, and killed her in a jealous rage. Isn't that right?' He roughly let go his collar and spoke more calmly. 'I can understand you being angry. Sasha was a pretty woman, after all. If you admit it now, you'll probably get off with manslaughter: by reason of provocation. It was an accident, right? And, if she accidentally fell during your struggle, and struck her head as a result, it might well be judged to be accidental death. So, various opportunities are open to you, Mr. Vincent, all probably leading to virtual freedom in this lenient age. Better than a life-stretch for murder, surely? So tell me what happened. This is your last chance before things get tough.'

Paul reflected things were already pretty tough.

Chapter 15

Stevie was busy. He'd dragged lots of junk out from the storage area beneath his garden house. To avoid taking it through the main house, he was transferring it to his dad's red van by wheelbarrow, via the harbourside path. It was all going to the tip. He'd decided to move it while his dad was out at work rather than be pestered with too many questions.

His mother, however, was curious. 'So what's this all about then, Stevie? I reckon I've never seen you so busy.' She accosted him at the end of the garden when he returned for a new load. Stevie stopped to wipe his brow with the back of his hand. She, meanwhile, absently picked dark cobwebs off his T-shirt.

'Just gettin' rid of old junk under the garden house, Mum.' He nodded towards the kitchen. 'Makin' some tea soon?' Unfortunately this attempt to change the subject fell flat.

'But why ever bother with that, Stevie? Forget about it, that's what I say. It's been there for years and it can stay there for years to come.' She peered into the storage area to see what was left.

'And what about rats? Don't want them moving in underneath me, do I? Saw one on the shoreline the other day.' He was especially pleased with this line; he'd thought it up the night before. 'Anyway, I need more space to store my own stuff,' he added sulkily. 'Waste of space all bunged up with rubbish. I'm makin' more room for the bike and tools. And boat stuff. Anyway, got to get on.' He began pulling more items out, including an old pram that had last carried him, and two broken chairs that were older than he was. He was greatly relieved when his mother shook her head, clicked her tongue, and headed off back to the house.

Stevie peered through the double doors with pride. It looked far more spacious now. He would sweep out every last cobweb, get some chipboard to line the floor and fit a nice secure padlock on the doors. He needed it to be really secure.

— — ∞ — —

To Paul's amazement, uniformed police officers arrived at his office on Wednesday morning with a search warrant. They rifled through his filing cabinet and demanded to take away all the company's printers, computers and disks.

'But this is our work,' objected Paul to the sergeant in charge. 'We need the design data on these computers to function as a business. It could ruin us if something happened to it. We would sue.' Even as he said it, Paul regretted sounding quite so hysterical. They had independent backup data stored elsewhere in any case. He moderated his approach. 'Anyway, I insist on talking to DI Hughes first.'

Jackie was watching from the doorway and looking aghast. The sergeant, meanwhile, seemed worried at the strength of Paul's resistance. He left a constable in the room with Paul and retreated to consult his superiors by radio, well out of earshot. A few minutes later he returned with a reprieve. 'DI Hughes says he will send a computer expert out here right away to take a copy of all your computer hard disks. That way you can keep the machines here. But you can't touch them until that's been done. But he does insist on removing all the printers.'

By this time Paul's partner, Tom Bellamy, had joined the group and he now began posing angry questions to the sergeant. 'What's all this about, sergeant? How can a modern business function without printers?'

'Damn it,' said Paul turning to Tom before the sergeant could answer. 'Look, I'll go over to PC World and buy a cheap printer to keep us going.' He caught his partner's eye. 'Tom. Please stay here and make sure our PCs aren't removed, or all work will grind to a halt.'

Tom was equally determined. 'Don't you worry about that. I will do.' He was glaring from the inspector to Paul, without discrimination.

Paul worked out what the police wanted while driving to the computer shop. Since they obviously thought he'd sent them the anonymous letter implicating Roger Lines, they now hoped to find the original file on one of the work computers, or match a printer to the printout.

This became even more apparent when, at the computer shop, he took a call on his mobile phone from his mother. She told him uniformed police had turned up at the house with a search warrant. She had let them in and watched as they searched all the papers in the house and removed his printer, disks, and both his and Leah's laptops. Things were looking serious.

The hand of the police was now getting far too heavy for his liking and it was clear where their suspicions lay. Paul realised he needed to take urgent action while he could. Even Tom was getting more distant with him. Paul dreaded to think what his suspicions might be.

On his way back with the new printer, Paul analysed the situation. He urgently needed to question Stevie Clarke. By now he was far beyond being scared of the youth and felt he would take any risk in order to prove Clarke was a killer and rapist. He'd gone through hell at the police station on Monday evening, but they obviously had no evidence to support their suspicion he killed Sasha. The absence of any questions in relation to Carol's rape did, at least, suggest they realised he was not involved in that. If the police thought he was a killer, did they really imagine there was also a separate rapist on the loose? That was hardly logical. By the same token, it suggested Lines was not involved in Sasha's murder if he wasn't involved in Carol's rape.

Paul could not understand why Hughes would not respond to his request to check out any forensic evidence found in connection with Sasha's murder against Clarke's DNA. According to Hughes, Stevie Clarke was a simpleton incapable of murder. Yet it had been Clarke he'd seen that night looking at Sasha's body. But although he didn't have much conviction Lines was anything to do with Sasha's death, this diversion was welcome, given he now seemed to be the prime suspect himself.

Paul mulled over the fact that those closest to a murdered

person were automatically the first suspects for the police; so their jealous rage argument was a particularly dangerous one for him. In these circumstances he felt lucky to be free and he intended to make the most of it. The harsh reality was that he might not have his freedom much longer unless he could spoon-feed the police with some evidence to help them. Either Clarke or Lines must have the answers and he planned to visit them both: starting with his primary suspect.

On impulse, Paul decided there was a more important matter than getting the printer back to the office. At Christchurch, he turned back and headed for Stanpit. He intended to go straight to Clarke's house, no matter what the implications. There was no time to be lost. Ideally he would like to catch Clarke by surprise, but he would take whatever opportunity arose. He now even carried a leather-sheathed fruit-knife in his pocket for defence.

He was certainly not going to knock on Clarke's front door, so he decided to take a look at the rear again. On reaching it, there was no sign of Clarke's boat on the shore, suggesting he was out. Surveying the garden, Paul noted he might be able to hide at the back of the brick workshop and surprise Clarke when he returned. He was still trying to plan this out when a crackly voice called out to him from the next-door garden.

'Hello. Are you looking for someone?'

Paul turned to see an old lady watching him. She had a quivering head and a pleasant smile on her face. 'Is this the house where Stevie Clarke lives?' He hoped he didn't look too suspicious.

'That's right.' The old lady came through a gate from her garden to join him on the path. 'But he's out in his boat, as usual. He lives in that little building.' She pointed to the brick building Paul had taken to be a workshop.

Paul could hardly believe it. 'He lives in there?'

The old lady laughed, picking up on his surprise. 'Yes. It's better inside than it looks. He's made it quite comfortable and it suits his needs.' She chuckled. 'He likes to get out of his parent's hair, I think.' She paused. 'Do you want to leave a note for him? You could push it under his door. I've got some paper.'

Unsure what to say, Paul decided it was best to leave. 'No, no, I'll be in touch with him later.'

'He's a nice lad. Always ready to help.' She gestured towards her own garden. 'He always cuts my grass. He's called me 'Aunty Hilda' since he was a 'young-en', you know.' She looked at him inquisitively. 'What was it about? Should I tell him you were looking for him? I could give him your name, if you like.'

Paul was thankful when his mobile phone rang. He took it from his pocket, glanced to see who it was, then answered the old lady first. 'No, no. I'll catch him later, thanks. Excuse me, I must go now.' Turning on his heel he spoke into the phone as he headed back down the path to the road. 'Hello Tom... Yes, I've chosen a printer, but there was a bit of delay while they found it in the storeroom. I'll be as quick as I can.'

— — ∞ — —

After his abrupt departure from the rear of Clarke's house, Paul returned to his car and drove to a nearby car park where he stopped to think. Sasha's body had recently been released and the funeral was due the following day at Christchurch Priory. It would be a difficult day for them all and he was thankful his mother was staying at the house for a short while. Right now there needed to be somebody in the house when Leah got back from school, and Connie's presence did mean he could come and go without worrying about Leah's safety.

He knew Leah was distraught about Clarke still being on the loose, and the police doubting her word about him stalking her and climbing the ladder to look in at her bedroom window. He could still hear her indignant words ringing in his head. 'How can they possibly doubt me?' she had demanded. 'What would my motive be to lie, Dad? And how can they even think you would want me to make that up?' Sadly he had no answer he was prepared to give her on that.

Sighing, Paul headed back to work with the printer, still deep in thought. It was a tricky situation with Leah in many ways. He was determined to conceal the fact the police suspected him of Sasha's murder: it would make Leah desolate. The situation had also provoked countless awkward questions from his mother. Paul knew that getting to the truth independently of the police was his only answer.

That afternoon he was unable to function properly at work, so he made an excuse to Jackie about visiting a client and headed for home. Surprised to see him back so early, his mother made them both a cup of tea, glad of the unexpected opportunity to talk. They told each other about their day.

'So are these policemen all idiots?' Connie asked after they were both up-to-date.

Paul sat facing her. He nodded gravely. 'That's about the size of it, Mum. They think Clarke is a simpleton, incapable of murder, but Leah and I saw how unbalanced he was after the grapnel incident, when he pulled a knife on me. Let's face it, he threatened to kill me for just trying to get him to apologise to Leah. He's been on our case ever since.'

'And it sounds as though you've been on his.' Connie looked at him critically. 'Can you be sure it was him, Paul? Is that what's making him so mad? Are you stirring up a hornet's nest for yourself?'

'There's only one hornet, and it's mad. I told you. I'm sure I saw Clarke looking at Sasha's body when I came to for a few moments. It's the last thing I remember before coming round in the hospital.'

'And does seeing him there make him guilty of murder?'

Paul sighed. 'Whose side are you on, Mum? You're worse than the police. Why else would he be at the scene of the crime? It was late, dark and isolated. Then he kicked me in the head. Why would he do that if he wasn't guilty?'

'If he did. If it was him. Can you really be sure you saw him under those circumstances, Paul? After those blows to the head?'

Not again. Please, no more doubts about his memory. In his mind's eye, Paul saw the flash of light that illuminated the face of Stevie Clarke. And, before that, the light from Clarke's torch illuminating Sasha's body. How could there be any doubt?

Why did his own mother seem to question him?

With the light about to fail, there were not many people around on the beach. Mandy Jones was jogging steadily. Most evenings she ran from Boscombe Pier to Southbourne and back, along a familiar promenade used by many other joggers. It was therefore quite normal to hear footsteps padding behind her. Now, half-way back to the pier and enjoying, as ever, the sight and sound of crashing waves breaking on the beach, she glanced periodically across to watch the fast-setting sun. With no wish for an iPod to distract her from the beauties of Nature, she clearly heard the person behind her speeding up and, as the footfalls drew near to her, she expected to see someone fly past—with the expectation of admiring their stamina and speed—but it did not happen that way.

An arm suddenly caught her around her waist. Before she realised what was happening, Mandy was roughly dragged between two beach huts. Trapped in a narrow space with a tall stone wall in front of her and a beach hut close by on either side, she turned to see a man pulling down a black balaclava. He was blocking her way and was clearly pleased with his own cunning. His evil grin was framed by ragged edges of wool. Distracted, as he tore roughly at her jogging bottoms, Mandy brought her knee up sharply into his groin causing him to double over, groaning with pain. She pushed his shoulders and sent him reeling backward. Taking advantage of his agony while he scrabbled to get up, supported only by one hand on the ground behind him, Mandy lunged forward and wrenched the woolen cover from his head. His eyes grew wide with shock as he looked up at her. She almost thought she saw fear in his eyes. Bracing herself against the beach huts on either side, Mandy stamped her right foot out. It caught him a glancing blow on the side of his head. The flat of her foot slipped to engage sharply with his shoulder blade. This sent him flying backward onto the ground again, cursing loudly. Mandy pulled up her jogging bottoms.

'That'll teach you to pick on me, you pervert.' Her lips curled into a satisfied smile, but she knew there was no time to waste; he was much stronger than her. Aware of a gap between the beach huts and the stone wall at their rear, Mandy scrabbled behind them and, a few moments later, emerged on the promenade a couple of huts farther along. She sprinted in the direction of the pier and was far away before her attacker could gather either his strength or wits.

Mandy frequently glanced back, but there was little chance he could catch her now. She finally saw him appear from between the huts and lope off in the opposite direction. With no one else near to help, she decided to run up the nearest zig-zag slope up to the relative safety of the cliff top. Once at the top of the slope, she looked down to check her attacker was not following. It was too dark to spot him now, but she could see that no one else was on the zig-zag. Shaking a little, but at the same time feeling very triumphant—if a little more breathless than usual—Mandy took out her mobile phone and dialled 999.

— — ∞ — —

Despite its size, Christchurch Priory was crowded for Sasha's funeral: it seemed as if her entire school was attending. It made it feel more like an ordinary church service until the coffin arrived. Paul felt choked with emotion. He clutched Leah's hand, unable to take his eyes from it as it was carried and set down so near to them. Could Sasha really be inside that polished box? Only too recently he remembered the same incomprehension at his father's funeral, with the coffin resting on the same spot. Looking at his daughter, he saw she was only just holding it together, despite a trembling lower lip. Connie was on Leah's far side, patting her hand. Beyond Connie sat Sasha's parents, who had rushed over for the funeral from Australia.

Leah had helped choose the hymns that were sung, knowing what her mother liked, and the vicar spoke of Sasha's sterling work for schoolchildren and of the love for her shared by colleagues and pupils alike. He knew her personally and was deeply affected by her loss. Yes, Paul thought, it was a tragic loss for all, but it almost seemed she had no private life. 'What about her family?' Paul felt like shouting. His emotions had hit extreme highs and lows since his wife's death—missing her, loving her, hating her—but now he could only think of the good times, and there had been so many of those. At one point he shook with emotion and Leah was the one to squeeze his hand and give him the extra strength he needed to get through the service. Thank God he still had Leah.

After filing out of the church behind the coffin, now heading for the crematorium for a small family service, he was amazed to see there were throngs of people lining the pathway to the iron gates.

'A lot are parents,' Leah explained to him, recognising a few faces. 'Mum knew so many people, Dad.'

Paul then saw a face he did not expect: Stevie Clarke's. The youth was closely watching the progress of the coffin back to the hearse. Paul froze at the sight of him and, sensing it, he saw Leah follow his gaze. She too looked shocked. For a moment Paul thought of going across to Clarke and telling him he had no right to be there, but one of the funeral director's caught his arm and pointed towards the car that would take them to the crematorium. Paul satisfied himself with glaring at Clarke, allowing himself to be led to the car. Perhaps to go on feeling like a zombie was the best way to get through the rest of the day.

— — ∞ — —

Paul agreed to meet Carol in the bar at the Riverside Inn, near Tuckton, late the following afternoon. It was only a short walk from her B & B in Stour Road and a short drive for him from work. As usual the pub was buzzing with people, but they were able to find a pleasant table in the garden, overlooking the river.

'I've got some good news.' Carol seemed jubilant about something.

'What? Have the police got somewhere at last?'

Carol staged a grimace. 'Nothing like that. We should be so

159

lucky. No.' She beamed at him. 'I've got a job.'

'Do you mean in a play?'

'No, no. Not acting. As a shop assistant, actually.' She screwed up her lips, waggled her head from side-to-side and smiled again. 'I know. But it's work. It's money. I'll be selling perfume at Debenhams, in Bournemouth. I'm standing in for someone on maternity leave. So now I can escape from the B & B, rent a little flat and smell good at the same time.'

They both laughed. Paul was pleased. 'That's really good news, Carol.'

'Isn't it?' She beamed. 'It doesn't mean I'm giving up on acting for good, but I figure dealing with the public will be good for me, right now. I can act on the job. I need to get my confidence back, Paul. And it means I won't be running home and getting a load of hassle from my parents. I'll never tell them what happened here. That's all in the past, now. Although I still want the bugger caught, of course,' she grinned. 'And it also means... I can see more of you?' There was a definite question mark at the end of this statement.

Paul looked at her searchingly. She was coyly hiding her face behind her glass, but still grinning. For the first time he realised how important she was becoming to him: and it was nothing to do with their shared interest in putting Stevie Clarke away.

'Which would be very nice indeed.' He suddenly realised how much he enjoyed her company—and empathy—and it was a joy to have such an uncomplicated relationship with a woman after all the baggage that went with Sasha: especially one interested in him. But the shadow of guilt passed over him again. It was so close to Sasha's death: and burial. How would Leah react if he saw a lot of Carol? More significantly, how would his mother react?

Carol put her drink down and placed her hand gently over his. 'Sound a bit more enthusiastic, then, if you want to convince me, Paul.'

Paul laughed and put his other hand on top of hers. 'No, I mean it, Carol. It really is good news. I was wondering how Leah might take it if I see a lot more of you; if there's more in it than chasing Clarke, that is. With her mother, and everything.' Feeling rather self-conscious himself, he removed his hand and picked up his beer.

'Well, Paul, we're only talking friends here, right?'

Paul nodded uncertainly. 'I suppose.' He now realised he wanted more than that.

'And she's cool with me, I can tell. I like her. I don't anticipate any problems.'

'That's female intuition, I suppose?'

Carol laughed. 'You could call it that. We've got a lot in common. Both afraid of the same guy. And both liking the same guy.' She grinned. 'You, in the latter case. You're a wonderful dad, Paul, and anyone can see she loves you to bits. You've gone through so much together over this. The affair thing her mother was having must have been a real shock to her, as well.'

Paul nodded. 'And there's even more to shock her, if it ever comes out. And I'll need all the support I can get if that happens.'

'If what comes out?' Carol looked concerned. 'Is there something you haven't told me, Paul?'

'Just a little.' Paul explained about his unpleasant interview with Hughes and how near he probably came to arrest—and how near that still might be.

Carol was shocked. 'No! How can he possibly suspect you of that?' Her eyes grew wide in astonishment.

Paul looked round to make sure no one else was in earshot and dropped his voice. 'He thinks the motive is jealousy after me seeing Sasha having sex with Lines. He thinks I chased after Sasha, had a fight with her over it, and that she fought me off with a branch and knocked me out.'

'In which case you couldn't possibly have killed her.' Carol held up her hands in disbelief. 'That doesn't make any sense, Paul.'

'Hughes suggested that Sasha hit me with a branch and then fell back and hit her head on the road, which was what killed her.' Paul paused while Carol took this in. 'Anyway, I googled 'concussion' afterwards. Apparently any violent blow to the

161

head that causes even brief unconsciousness can lead to concussion. Which is why Hughes tried to get me to agree to a scenario with me unconscious when she finally fell. He suggested I could get away with manslaughter with provocation if I admitted to attacking her; or that the verdict might even be accidental death because it resulted from her fall.' He shrugged. 'But why should I admit to attacking her when it's not true? Anyway, I want the killer caught and brought to justice. He's very devious, is Hughes. I thought about it afterwards. I reckon he figured that if I admitted I picked a fight with Sasha he could wrap the case up.'

Carol looked at him in concern. 'You poor thing, Paul. And what you remember is seeing Sasha fighting someone off when you arrived, her going down, and then him attacking you. Right?'

'Yes. Precisely. I've said that over and over to the police. But Hughes refuses to believe it.'

'And Leah doesn't know you went through all this at the police station?'

'No. I couldn't let her know the police suspect me, could I? It would knock her for six. But that's the reason they think we're making it all up about Clarke pestering us. To shift the blame. Hughes thinks I got Leah to make stuff up and she can't understand why he would think that.' Paul briefly swigged his beer. With foam on his lips, he added, 'It's such a mess, Carol. Such a rotten mess.'

'I want to see Leah, Paul. Can I come back with you for a short while?'

'Why?'

'To let her know we're a team and that we'll get Clarke put away, whatever it takes. I want to.'

'My mother's staying at the house for a while to make sure there's always someone there for Leah.'

'Oh.' Carol hesitated for a moment but then tapped her hand on the table. 'Never mind. I'm not scared of your mother. I still want to come.'

Paul raised an eyebrow. 'You might be scared once you meet her. But if you can take her on, customers at Debenhams will seem small-fry. It will be an education for you. Are you still up for it?'

Carol nodded and grinned. 'I'm jolly well up for it.'

Paul drained his glass and stood. 'Right. Come along then, fair lady. Into the fray.'

Chapter 16

Paul opened the front door and let Carol in behind him. He called out as he headed up the stairs in front of her. 'Anyone home?'

'Yes.' It was his mother's voice, and it snapped.

'Oh dear,' said Paul, softly. He stopped for a moment to grin round at Carol. 'I did warn you. She doesn't sound amused. Still game?'

Carol pursed her lips, nodded, and hissed back at him. 'Go forth. I'm game.'

'Hello guys,' said Paul, smiling as he entered the room, closely followed by Carol. 'I've brought Carol to see you, Leah.'

No one seemed interested in meeting Carol. Paul was instantly aware of the frosty atmosphere. Connie was sitting grim-faced on the sofa. Leah was sitting in an armchair and looked as though she'd been crying. Both their faces were pale. Was this the aftermath of the police invasion or something more? Both seemed to look at him reproachfully.

'What's happened now?'

'The police took our laptops and DVDs away, Dad,' said Leah. 'Even the printer.'

Paul looked at her, surprised by how distraught this seemed to have left her.

'And they took Sasha's mobile phone away, too,' added his mother. 'But that's not the worst of it.' Connie pointed towards the table. Take a look at today's Echo. Leah saw those headlines on a billboard after school and bought a copy. What a dreadful way for us to both find out, Paul.'

Dry mouthed, Paul went to the table. Carol hung back uncertainly. Paul picked up the paper. The headline shocked him: 'MAN QUESTIONED BY POLICE OVER WIFE'S MURDER'. The short front page piece said the husband of schoolteacher, Sasha Vincent, was interviewed by police on

Monday evening in connection with her murder. It also stated that a source had disclosed Mrs. Vincent had been having an affair with a former colleague. It referred to page five for further information. Paul was about to turn to this when Connie came over and snatched the paper away from him.

'Where do they get all this stuff from?' muttered Paul.

'There are always leaks connected with the police: if they want there to be,' snapped Connie, no doubt from her great experience of reading mystery thrillers. 'To pile on the pressure. Anyway, the rest doesn't do much more than report the murder all over again. But the implication is there for all to see, Paul. And on the front page. That you murdered Sasha because she was having an affair.' Her tone suggested she would have liked to have added: 'The shame.'

Paul gaped at her and gestured towards Leah. 'Please.'

'It's a bit too late to worry about Leah's sensibilities when it's all over the papers.'

'Actually, I did know about Mum having an affair, Gran,' said Leah, getting up.

'You did?' Connie looked at her in amazement. 'You never told me. And when did you learn that, young lady?'

'I overheard Dad telling his friend about it.'

'Oh, I see.' Connie drew herself up very straight and turned back to Paul. 'So no one gets to learn anything around here directly, Paul. I'm sure you wouldn't have told me anything about this unless you had to.' She gestured towards Carol. 'And who is this, exactly, learning our private business?'

'I'm Carol Davis, Mrs. Vincent. Paul and I got together to try to bring that Clarke lad to justice.' She looked down. 'I was attacked and raped by someone on Hengistbury Head. We think it was the same man.'

'I see.' Connie moderated her tone.

'So do the police think you were involved, Dad?' asked Leah, bringing the discussion back on course. 'The paper implies you would have a reason for killing Mum. Do the police actually think that?'

'Oh, darling.' Paul went to her and put his arm around her. He sighed. 'You know what the police are like. They always suspect nearest and dearest.'

'And it usually is the nearest and dearest,' said Connie.

'Meaning?' snapped Paul, glaring at her.

'I hope you're not suggesting—' began Carol, but Connie cut her down.

'I certainly would not suggest my own son killed his wife. But the plain facts are that everyone reading this paper *will* assume it. And the least you could have done, Paul, is to give me some inkling of this instead of keeping it to yourself.'

'I didn't want to worry anyone with it,' said Paul. 'I imagined the police suspicions would blow over. Things were bad enough for Leah already.'

'So you couldn't even get round to telling your own mother the police suspected you of murder?' Connie tossed the paper onto the table and marched towards the door, where she stopped and turned. 'I'm getting my things together and I'm going home. If you can't trust me, I'm not staying here.' She flapped her hand at Leah. 'Leah, darling. Get your things and your school work together and come to stay with me for a while.'

'No.' Leah moved to stand by Paul. 'I'm not leaving Dad now, Gran. I found them *both* after the attack, remember. The murderer attacked them *both*, for heaven's sake. And Mum— my mum—deceived Dad with that other man.' Her voice was shaking as she clung to Paul's waist. 'I'm staying with Dad. He's been through too much. He needs me now. And I don't care if I do have to be alone here sometimes,' she added defiantly, seeing Connie about to raise an objection.

Connie hesitated and lifted her chin high. 'Fine. I'll pack my things and go then. I know when I'm not wanted.' Her tone was brittle.

'I'll drive you home,' said Paul.

'No need. I've got my mobile phone in the bedroom. I'll call a taxi. I'm quite capable.' With that she stormed out of the room.

Paul kissed his daughter on the forehead. 'Thank you so much, sweetheart. I really want you to stay. I'll look after you, I promise.'

166

'Don't worry, Dad. I'm okay. I love you. We'll get through this.'

'I love you too. I couldn't do without you.' They hugged and Paul went across to the table to look at the paper again. Carol joined him, and he waited for her to read the front page before turning to the rest of the article. Leah joined them to read it again. As Connie had said, it mainly recapped on the murder, but there was a definite slant that the murder, Sasha's affair, and Paul being questioned were all linked.

Paul looked ashen after reading it. 'What ever will your school friends and my clients think?'

'I know. It was a shock seeing it outside the shop.'

'You poor thing.' Carol put one arm around Leah and the other around Paul. 'You guys don't deserve this.'

'I see. Very cosy,' said Connie, suddenly behind them. 'I've phoned for a taxi. It should be here any minute. Clearly I'm not needed here.'

Sighing with exasperation, Paul turned to her. 'I'll carry your case down, if you really do insist on taking a taxi, Mum.'

'Thank you. A taxi will be just fine.' Connie gave Carol a withering look and glared at Paul. 'I wouldn't want to interrupt you while you're entertaining.'

— — ∞ — —

Everything was going round and round in Leah's head. It was a living nightmare. She was upset by the way her grandmother had gone off in such a huff, but she understood why her dad had tried to protect her from the knowledge of his troubles and she respected him for it. Now she knew why the police didn't believe Stevie was stalking her. Unbelievably, they thought Dad had killed Mum and that she was helping to divert the blame. Her anonymous letter had actually suggested a motive as to why her father might have killed her mother. Having found her dad lying unconscious on the road at the scene of the murder, it had never occurred to her that he might become a suspect himself. It was total disaster and she realised her involvement in sending the letter to the police was a secret she

167

must take to her grave: and one her best friend must also take to hers. What if Dad ever found out? She shivered with apprehension.

It had been absolute torture waiting for Dad to return after bringing the newspaper home. But she knew he had to be made aware of it. Gran knew there was something wrong the moment she had entered the house, but Gran was a complication they were better off without right then; a problem less. While they had waited for Dad to come home, Gran had obviously been seething with anger.

Leah had discussed the murder many times with Marina and they were both completely unsure as to whether the murderer was Roger, Stevie, or someone else. If only she'd listened to Marina and not sent the letter. Whatever happened now, the least she could do was to be there for her dad. Yet could she cope on her own? She realised Dad must feel desperate at being suspected. Thank goodness they at least had new neighbours who didn't really know them yet. Leah snapped out of her dark thoughts when Carol spoke.

'It must have been a dreadful shock for you, Leah, seeing those headlines.'

'Tell me about it. I would have bought up all the copies if I'd had enough money.' She smiled at Carol. 'It must have been bad for you to read about your attack in the papers.'

'At least it only portrayed me as a victim.' Carol turned to her father. 'Anyway, Paul. I think we could all use some food. Point me to the kitchen and I'll rustle something up.'

'No, no, I can do something,' objected Leah. The way she felt, it would be good to do something—anything—although she appreciated Carol's offer.

'I'll do it. Or we could get a take-away,' said her father.

'No,' insisted Carol strongly. 'I'll do it while you two gather your wits. I insist.' She pointed to the landing door. 'Did I spot the kitchen across the way? Would something simple like omelettes do?'

Paul gave her a grateful smile. 'There are plenty of eggs, and mushrooms, too, if you want to add those to the mix.'

'Sounds just the job.' Carol pointed to the balcony. 'Go. Sit.

Enjoy the view you worked so hard for, Paul. And you, too, Leah. I'll call you both when it's ready.'

Leah smiled gratefully at her. She was nice, and it was good to have someone to help keep her dad afloat. She marvelled at how cheerful he'd managed to appear since the police interrogation, probably to mask it from her. What an effort he must have made.

Carol produced the meal quite quickly, and chatting over it was made much easier by her taking the lead to reduce tension. Her dad had been very quiet since reading the newspaper article. Carol told Leah about her temporary job and staying on in Bournemouth, and how she was going to look for a flat to rent because the B & B was too expensive long-term; which led to Leah's idea. It seemed stupid for Carol to stay on at the B & B when they had a spare bedroom. Leah knew she should discuss it with her dad first, but it was good having Carol around and so she just blurted it out. 'Why don't you stay in our spare room until you find somewhere else, Carol?'

Carol was taken aback, and her dad also sat upright as if shocked by the suddenness of this suggestion.

'Er, Leah, I don't think your Gran would be too pleased if I just moved in when she moved out,' said Carol with raised eyebrows, looking across to her father.

Leah shrugged. 'It's only until you find somewhere. Gran will understand.'

'I don't think so,' said Carol in a sing-song voice. She looked at her father, obviously prompting his reaction.

Leah gave her dad a barely perceptible nod when he glanced across at her. Then he looked at Carol. 'You know, I really don't care what my mother thinks. I think it's a great idea.' He smiled at Carol. 'Consider the room taken, if that would be a help.'

'And meanwhile, we can help you look around for a flat,' said Leah, pleased with herself. Carol seemed nice enough, but best to leave a loophole.

— — ∞ — —

No sooner had he agreed than Paul became very dubious about Carol moving in. He had left her clearing up with Leah on the pretext of having to make an important business call, but in reality he'd gone up to his bedroom and was sitting on his bed, deep in thought and feeling even deeper in guilt.

At a personal level, he would be very happy to have Carol around because they had become good friends and their mutual support and understanding seemed to be working well. Leah was wonderfully strong and supportive, but it would be good for him to have adult empathy. Also, it might help to make him stronger for Leah, and Leah would feel less afraid having someone else around the house. And, he had to admit, a certain something did seem to be developing between Carol and him such that her touch, no matter how light, sparked excitement and an undeniable sexual chemistry: albeit tainted by guilt. He was beginning to really look forward to her company and ready smile. The idea of her staying was an appealing development, especially since it was inspired by Leah.

Yet there were many negative aspects to nag him. With his murdered wife only buried the previous day, agreeing to allow another woman to move in was hard to rationalise. Most people would regard it as scandalous. He knew it would appall his mother: although, come to think of it, she'd hardly waited any time after Dad's death before she got on with her own hedonistic lifestyle. He also had Sasha's parents to consider. What if they got to hear of it or visited unexpectedly? What if the press discovered and reported it? What if their new neighbours figured out who he was? And it would certainly look suspicious to the police. Would it spur them to take it as yet another motive to further implicate him in Sasha's murder? The more he thought about it, the more he became certain he would have to retract, much as he hated the idea of upsetting Carol. Yet he was confident she would understand.

As he glanced out of the window and it registered how beautiful the view was across the harbour, Paul reflected how life seemed to be so unfair to him. How happy the three of them could have been there if only Sasha had not cheated on him: and if Clarke had not been so unbalanced. Since Sasha's death, he had many times regretted pushing Clarke so far over the grapnel incident. He felt compelled to admit this might be the root cause of their current situation. Indirectly, it might have caused Sasha's death, and that was hard to live with. He directed anger at himself, anger at Sasha for cheating, anger at Clarke for killing her, anger at the police for failing to see it. Now he was angry with himself for so readily agreeing to let Carol stay. He got up from the bed. This was something he must correct at once.

Feeling determined, Paul hurried down the stairs, where he met Leah and Carol heading from the kitchen to the lounge. 'Look, I've been thinking, I'm not so sure this is such a good idea after all.'

'What idea?' asked Leah.

'Carol staying here.' Paul looked sheepishly at Carol. 'I'd love her to, but I'm worried about what people might think in the circumstances. Particularly the police.'

'Think?' Leah was indignant.

'I quite understand,' said Carol. 'Of course I do. You're right. It's mad. And your mother would go ballistic.'

'I don't particularly care about that, after the way she acted earlier,' said Paul. 'I'm more concerned about Sasha's parents finding out, and what the police might make of it.'

'Why does anyone need to know?' asked Leah, simply.

Paul spread his hands. 'Let's get real, sweetheart. People *will* find out.'

'But I only suggested it until Carol found a place to stay,' said Leah. 'And it would be good to have more people around here, with Stevie Clarke still on the loose. But it's up to you two.' With a shrug, she went out of the kitchen and padded up the stairs to her bedroom.

'Oh dear,' said Carol. She lowered her voice. 'Do you think she mainly wants me here for additional protection, Paul?'

Paul jerked his head towards the lounge and Carol followed him in: and then out onto the balcony. They both leaned on the railings, quietly surveying the view.

Carol was the first to speak. 'I'll stay for a few days if you think it will help Leah with the Clarke situation. Or I'll stay at the B & B a bit longer if you think moving in will create too many problems.' She put a tentative arm on his shoulder, looking up into his face. 'I don't mind. It's your call, Paul. It's your house.'

Paul looked down into the soft eyes, the warm face, and felt his heart melting. 'Damn it, why should I live my life for others? To tell the truth, much of the problem is to do with guilt so soon after Sasha, but let's face it, she was cheating on me. And for how long? How many times? That's been tearing me to bits.'

'Oh, Paul.' Carol put an arm around him. 'You're in such turmoil, aren't you? And I hardly help.'

Paul pulled away from her, turned to face her, placed his two hands on her waist and looked deeply into her eyes. ''But you do.' Carol looked at him quizzically. 'You do help,' he clarified. 'You understand and... you're special.' He gently touched her cheek and was relieved when she did not flinch away. 'And, I need you.'

Slowly, gradually, almost imperceptibly, their faces drew nearer, tentatively at first, as they exchanged glances, interpreted and then allowed their lips to meet in something much deeper than impulse. The kiss lingered long enough to send an exciting shiver of emotion through his body.

Paul drew back. 'Do you think Leah knows?'

Carol raised an eyebrow. 'That there might be something between us?'

'Yes. Which there hasn't been, of course, until now,' he grinned.

'I think she might have figured it was coming. And now it has come, wouldn't you say?' Carol laughed softly.

Paul chuckled. 'And if there is something, she's definitely encouraged it.'

Carol gave him a second brief kiss. 'And my female intuition tells me she would approve... but eventually. I don't think she's quite ready to see any of this yet, Paul. I'm not sure if either of us is quite ready for that, either.'

'True.' Paul winked at her, held her hand and turned to look out across to the distant harbour. 'Still, let's hope we'll all be ready for it before too long.'

—— ∞ ——

Stevie parked his dad's faded red van in a side road at Wick village and took a walk back to the cul-de-sac in which they lived. Carefully watching out for them, he walked a little way down the road but, on seeing Vincent's car in the garage, he hurriedly returned to the van. It was too conspicuous for him to be out in the open.

He turned the van around and drove to the end of the Vincent's road, where he parked. If they went out together, he could follow them. If Vincent went out alone, the girl would probably be alone in the house. If she went out alone, he could follow her. The plan was brilliant. So many possibilities: all good.

Reaching for his Sainsbury's shopping bag he took out his new magazine and a flask. Who knew how long this might take? He also had sandwiches, but he'd save those for later.

The only danger was that if he became too engrossed in the magazine he might miss something. Still, he could keep looking up. He would concentrate on the pictures. The pictures were the best part, anyway. Such pretty girls.

—— ∞ ——

The plan was for Paul to bring Carol's things over from her B & B the following evening: Friday. Leah asked him if she could spend the weekend at Marina's, so he said he would drive her there before going on to collect Carol. He didn't want Leah cycling alone after the riverside incident.

As they pulled out into Wick Lane and headed towards Tuckton, Paul was vaguely aware of an old van with fading red paintwork that pulled out and followed them to Tuckton Roundabout. After heading past some shops, he turned into Marina's road, parking outside her house. Carrying Leah's small bag, he went to Marina's front door with her, kissed her goodbye when Marina opened the door to their ring, handed

173

Leah the bag and returned to his car. To save turning around, he drove on round the block, barely more than subconsciously noticing the same red van parked a little further up the road.

Despite himself, Paul felt very excited at the latest development concerning Carol, although he was uncertain about Leah's motives. Was Leah glad to get away from the house after her scare with Clarke or was she actually setting him up with Carol and giving them some space? Maybe she even considered it right for him to get a new life after discovering how Sasha had deceived him. Two things were for sure: Leah was a very mature girl now, and she had told him, in private, how much she liked Carol. All the same, it seemed odd for her to want to push them together quite so quickly. Yet he did sense Leah bore a lot of bitterness towards her mother for cheating on him. He, after all, had always been very conscious of Sasha's flirting and her liking for other men's company, and Leah must also have noticed it. His ongoing jealousy probably stemmed from the fear such an eventuality might occur.

As for the difficult aspects of people disapproving of Carol moving in—albeit, on the surface, a temporary arrangement— at least his mother was not in a particularly good position to complain, given her own behaviour after Dad's death. He would remind her of that if she made trouble. Connie had made no secret of the fact she used other men as dance partners and to enliven her evenings when Dad was too busy or tired to go out with her. It had been an arrangement that had suited them both for a while, but when she continued to dance with her men friends a week after his father's funeral, much of his respect for his mother had evaporated. Now he found himself on a parallel track, but with one significant difference: his partner had cheated on him and had maybe done so before. Relieving his conscience with such thoughts, Paul excitedly collected Carol and moved her things into the spare bedroom of the new house. Deep within himself he knew he hoped this would be far more than merely a kind deed.

They ate out at the nearby Riverside Inn and later returned to the house to enjoy an evening drink on the balcony. It was a hot and sultry night and it was inevitable their previous kiss would be repeated: this time more relaxed, more lingering, more sensuous, more meaningful.

'Do you know, Mr. Vincent, I think you've actually cured my new-found fear of men.' Carol smiled at him and they exchanged a further kiss.

'You'd better reserve that judgement until later, Miss Davis.'

'It was very convenient of Leah to sleep-over with Marina this weekend, wasn't it?'

'It certainly was. She's a good girl.'

'You don't think she was actually setting us up, here, do you?'

'What? My little daughter? Surely not? Why would you think that?'

After exchanging grins, they kissed again.

'I think she's very perceptive. And mature,' said Carol.

'In that case, we should both thank her for foreshortening the inevitable.'

'Inevitable, Paul? Foreshorten what inevitable?'

'You know what inevitable, very well,' he laughed, hugging her. Her cheek felt good against his. At least life could be good again after Sasha. 'So are we ready to foreshorten things even further?' His fingers fumbled uncertainly with her blouse.

She pulled at his shirt. 'I'm not sure foreshortening is the best phrase to use, Paul.'

Paul laughed. 'You noticed?' He took her wandering hand in his and gently led her to the stairs. 'I'm sorry your bedroom only has a view over the front, Carol. But did I show you the view from mine?'

'No you didn't, but I can hardly wait to see.'

— — ∞ — —

Sitting on the end of Marina's bed, Leah was near to tears. Her friend was seated at her computer desk with the chair turned around to face her, an anxious expression on her face. This was the one place Leah allowed herself to drop her guard. She had told Marina everything, but she now needed her to really

175

understand how things had built up for her.

'First it was Mum's funeral on Wednesday, with Stevie Clarke there, staring at us. Dad was seething. Then, yesterday, the police took Dad and my laptops away—and our printer, by the way—plus the Echo article came out about Dad being questioned by the police. Which probably makes everyone believe the police think Dad killed Mum. Then Dad had that almighty row with Gran, when she went off in a huff.' Leah looked at Marina. 'And I can't imagine what Dad feels like about Mum now. I can't even come to terms with Mum myself. I'm, like, sad and mad at once? Do you know what I mean?'

'You poor thing.' Marina shot across to sit on the bed next to her friend and to put a comforting arm around her.

'Yes, I know Mum led men on for a laugh, I know that, but how terrible for Dad to see her *at it* with Roger Lines. Then, a short while later, he sees her being murdered. I mean... what? How must he feel about her after all that? ' She threw her hands out, palm upwards. 'His head must be spinning. He loved her, but he must hate her now, as well, Marina.' She continued in a more confiding tone. 'He was a bit possessive, at times, actually. But poor Dad. Poor Mum. Poor Carol.' She began to sob softly while Marina did her best to comfort her.

'And poor you, caught in the middle, Leah. And knowing Stevie's stalking you.' Marina reached for a box of tissues and passed it to Leah.

Taking it, Leah pulled a couple out and blotted away at the tears that now streamed down her cheeks. The thought of Stevie watching and following her was the last straw. She didn't need reminding of that.

'Go on, let it all out, Leah.' Moving to sit beside her on the bed, Marina cuddled her as Leah let her tears flow freely.

'I can't let go with Dad around, you see,' sobbed Leah. 'Not that we haven't had a little cry together. We have. But I've got to keep strong most of the time or he'll go to pieces. I know he will. But worse of all.' She turned to Marina, now finding it difficult to speak. 'The worst thing of all is that it's all my fault the police think Dad killed Mum out of jealousy. Because of that stupid letter we sent.'

'*We?*' Marina said it softly, but there was no disguising the fact she did not feel responsible.

Leah took this onboard immediately. 'All right, all right. It was *me*, Marina. I sent it. I was the one. You told me not to. I know, I know. Why didn't I listen? I know. That's why it's so dreadful. And even though I've now told Dad about seeing Stevie's face through the hut window that night, I can *never* tell him I sent that letter to the police to implicate Roger. Never!' She looked intently at her friend. 'On your life, Marina, you must *never* tell anyone I did that. Do you promise? Solemnly? Never?'

Marina squeezed her hand. 'Of course. Don't worry. I never will. But you did it with the best of intentions. To help the police find the killer. You really thought it must be Roger at the time. I did too, Leah.'

'Yeah, well.' Leah paused to wipe her cheeks. 'It's taught me not to interfere. And if Dad's happy with this Carol, I'm happy with that. She's really nice, anyway, thank God. And they seem to be good for each other.'

'What do you mean, 'happy with Carol', Leah? Are they more than friends?'

Leah looked at her and nodded. 'Yep. I'm pretty certain.'

'More than just good friends?' Marina held her gaze.

A little laugh broke through sobs as she nodded again. 'I think so. And if not, I guess they soon will be. Which is why I figured they needed some space now she's moved in.'

'And you really don't mind? So soon after your mum?'

Leah shrugged. 'Yeah, well, my head is all over the place about Mum, too. But life has to go on, right? And Carol's good for Dad. Thoughtful. And they've both been through the mill, and they're both working to get Stevie locked up.' She shrugged again. 'No, I don't mind. Although Gran will probably be livid about it, right after the funeral. Especially with Carol moving in. My fault again. But if Gran's mad, it'll be about what people might think, nothing to do with Mum.'

Marina grinned. 'She is a one, your Gran.'

Leah grinned back. 'Yep,' she nodded. 'But I don't care. I like Carol. That's why I suggested she stay on for a while. It was my way of saying I'm okay about their relationship. And that's really why I'm sleeping over tonight.' She looked at her friend and smiled. 'You sure you don't mind? I'm so sorry to be such a load on you. I didn't dare go to Gran's because Dad would feel I was being disloyal after their row.'

'A load on me? Rubbish. You're not a load. You're my best friend, Leah, you know that. We're always there for each other, right? What are best friends for?' Marina got up off the bed. 'And, like you said, we've all got to move on.' She pointed to the computer. 'And I've got this great new computer game. Come and check it out.'

A new computer game was the last thing Leah was really interested in but she forced a smile and went across the room to bring a spare chair over to the computer. Thank goodness she had Marina.

Chapter 17

It only took five minutes for Leah to walk from Marina's house to the convenience store in Tuckton. It was only round the corner and it was a nice light evening. She told Marina it was important for her to do this alone. She persuaded herself it was no big deal. She went to buy her favourite magazine and was confidently browsing through it while she walked back. Engrossed, she was only vaguely aware of the red van parked in the alleyway behind the shops; it had its rear doors open adjacent to the pavement. She didn't even look up until a figure stepped out from behind the van door and blocked her path. She barely had the chance to recognise Stevie Clarke's grinning face before he somehow managed to slap sticky tape across her mouth and roughly push her into the rear of the van, grazing her leg as he did so.

While she struggled hard, he was much too strong for her and soon had her hands and feet bound with cord. After checking in her pockets, he slammed the van doors shut, hurried round to the driver's door, jumped in and started the engine. The van sped off, bumping down the lane, leaving Leah rolling around in the back.

Eventually she managed to haul herself up into a more comfortable position that avoided her from being flung from side-to-side. She was bound so tightly it hurt to wriggle either her hands or ankles. Lying in silent shock, she wondered what he intended to do with her. Would he rape and then kill her, just like he did to her mother?

— — ∞ — —

Success! Finally he had her. Stevie grinned to himself as he drove back to Stanpit. He thought she looked even prettier than he remembered. Now that bastard would worry. No doubt the girl's friend would soon phone her dad to say she was missing.

Serve Vincent right for getting him all tied up with the police. He'd already frisked Leah to check she didn't have a mobile phone on her. It had been a good grab. A perfect snatch mission: over in seconds.

Stevie parked under the trees in the car park near his home and fumbled in his pocket to locate a new strip of chewing gum. He waited until no one was to be seen before going round to the back of the van, opening the doors and jumping in with the girl. He let the door fall closed and grinned at her. There was just enough light from the front to see her eyes were wide with fear.

'Now don't panic. Leah, isn't it?'

Leah gave a minute nod.

Now it was his turn to nod. 'Thought so. I remembered it, see. From when that bastard dad of yours argued on the beach. Made me look a fool, he did. You knew I never meant to hurt you, didn't you?' Leah nodded again, more vigorously this time. 'Yeah. Obvious. Stupid bastard. Wouldn't hurt a pretty girl like you.' He reached out to stroke her cheek with the back of his hand but she jerked away from his touch. 'Don't be afraid of old Stevie,' he laughed. He moved closer to her but the girl trembled and tried to wriggle further away. 'Don't panic, girl. I'm takin' the tape off. If you promise not to scream or shout, that is.' He looked at her sharply. 'You do, don't you? Otherwise you're in real trouble. I've got a knife, remember. Get it?'

Leah nodded again. Stevie leaned forward and pulled the tape from her mouth. She emitted a thankful sigh.

'Where are we? What do you want with me?' Leah glared at him, her voice trembling.

'I want to give your dad a good scare.' Stevie laughed. 'So be a good girl and you won't get hurt. I'll probably let you go if you promise not to tell where you've been.' He stared into her eyes. 'Would you do that? Would you promise me that, Leah?'

'It depends. If you don't hurt me. Why are we here in this van?'

'Just waitin' till it gets dark. Then we can go. But we can talk till then.' He smiled at her. 'Nice name you've got, Leah.'

He jerked his head. 'Not my van, this, you know. I've got a fast motorbike. And a boat. Which do you like best, Leah? A fast boat or a fast motorbike? When this is over I could take you for a ride, if you like.'

'When what's over?'

Stevie shrugged. 'This kidnapping bit.' He laughed again. 'S'pose I could ask your dad for money, if I wanted. I need some money, see. I'm going to America.' His eyes gleamed at the thought. 'Land of the free. Home of the brave.' He reached out and this time managed to rub his fingers against her cheek. He was amazed by the smoothness of her skin. 'Are you brave, Leah?'

Leah nodded.

'Yep, thought so. Want to come, Leah? Ride Route 66 together?'

He was startled by her reply.

'Well maybe, Stevie. If you're very nice and don't upset me.'

— — ∞ — —

Paul lay awake thinking how wonderful it was to have a stress-free relationship with a woman who was not preoccupied with her appearance. It was not that Carol didn't use make-up or look nice—she did—but this was not her primary concern. How different to Sasha. He grinned at the thought of how Carol had nodded off, now apparently well over her fear of men, thanks to his services. But these ponderings were halted abruptly by the sound of the doorbell. He looked at the clock radio. At gone eleven, this was an unwanted surprise. It was far too late for casual callers. Shep started barking in the distance. Could it be his mother feeling guilty about her sudden departure? He immediately thought of the awkwardness of Carol being in his bed. Now she was stirring.

'Paul. Is that the bell?'

'Stay here, Carol. I'll get rid of them.' Paul sat up in bed.

Carol opened her eyes and smiled sleepily up at him. She put her hand on his arm. 'Let it ring, Paul. Whoever it is will go away.' She looked at the bedside clock. 'It's too late to answer the door, anyway.'

'No, I must answer it in case it's an emergency.'

Carol sighed. 'Emergency? What have our lives turned into, Paul?'

'Quite.' Paul got out of the bed naked, but quickly grabbed a toweling robe. 'You stay here and I'll get rid of whoever it is.' He looked at her pleadingly. 'Please stay quiet to keep things uncomplicated.'

'You think I would do anything else?' She tilted her head and beamed at him with such an endearing smile he had to force himself to leave.

He flicked a switch which flooded the atrium area in soft-blue lighting and then padded down the stairs barefooted. Shep was already waiting, and agitated, by the front door. Opening it revealed DI Hughes and the somewhat nicer DS Sam Gold. The sight of the inspector at that hour filled Paul with trepidation, but this was somewhat mitigated by the fact he was accompanied by Gold. Previously Hughes had always seemed less intimidating when accompanied by Gold.

'What now? I just went to bed.'

Hughes looked him up and down as if he almost knew he'd not been alone there. 'So I can see, sir. This won't take long. Just a few more questions that won't wait. May we come in?'

Shep looked warily at Hughes, probably because of his somewhat aggressive tone, but he approached Sam Gold with a wagging tail when she held out her hand to be sniffed. Gold smiled when Shep licked it. 'Good boy,' she said enthusiastically. Paul realised she must be a dog-lover.

'Come in, then.' Paul stood aside for them to enter the hall, closed the door and took them up to the lounge. Shep brushed past them all to lead the way. Indicating the sofa, Paul refrained from offering them a drink. He wanted this exchange to be as short as possible after the way Hughes had interrogated him at the police station. He was now very wary of the man. He was also nervous at the thought of Carol waiting quietly above. He didn't want police minds working in overdrive at this new development. He fervently hoped she would not make a noise.

Once the two were seated, Paul sat in an armchair facing them. Gold took out her notebook and pencil to take notes, but she gave him a reassuring smile.

'I've got a few general questions, Mr. Vincent,' said Hughes. 'Can you tell me where you were last Wednesday evening?'

Paul looked at him in surprise. This was something new. 'What time?'

Hughes tilted his head slightly but continued to focus on Paul. 'You tell me, sir. All evening?'

Paul thought back. 'I was here.' Gold started to scribble.

'Alone?'

Paul paused to think. Wednesday had been the day before Connie's sudden departure. 'No, my daughter and mother were here too. My mother stayed the night.'

Hughes asked for her contact details, which Paul gave. These were duly noted by Gold. 'So your mother will be able to confirm you didn't go out all night, sir?' asked Hughes.

'Yes.' Then Paul remembered something. 'Oh, I did walk the dog that evening, but I was only gone for about an hour.'

Hughes' eyes gleamed. 'Oh, really? And what time did you leave, sir?'

Paul pondered. 'I'm not absolutely sure. About eight, I suppose.'

'And where did you go?'

'Through the field at the end of the road, along the footpath to the barn at Hengistbury Head, around the Barn Field and back by the sea, while the sun was setting.'

'On foot? No bike or car involved?'

'Yes, on foot.'

'And did you meet anyone on that walk, sir?' asked Gold.

Paul shrugged. 'I saw a few walkers, mostly with dogs, but no one I can name.'

'What a pity. Right. Thank you.' Hughes stood, and Gold did likewise. He gave Paul a piercing gaze when he also rose from his chair. 'And have you remembered anything more about the night you followed your wife, Mr. Vincent? The night she was murdered? Anything else that might help us?' He paused. 'You do want to help us, don't you?'

'You know I do,' said Paul, standing indignantly. 'And I didn't *follow* Sasha that evening, as you well know, Inspector. Shep took me to her.'

'Ah, yes. Shep.' Hughes glanced down for a moment at the dog. Shep was eyeing him warily. 'Clever little Shep. Almost human, eh, Mr. Vincent? Not only does he fetch you to the scene of the crime, he then goes back to fetch your daughter. I thought dogs only fetched sticks and balls, not people. I suppose your dog is super-intelligent, though.' The statement was heavy with sarcasm.

'He is an intelligent dog. He's part border collie.' Paul nearly added they round things up better than the police, but he bit his tongue on that one.

Looking down at Shep, Hughes addressed him in sarcastic tones. 'You're just so clever, aren't you, Shep?' He paused while Shep, puzzled, looked up at him with his head on one side. 'What? Nothing to say, Shep? You mean a clever dog like you can't talk?'

'Not funny,' said Paul. Even Gold gave her superior an impatient look. Shep whined softly and put his head on the other side.

'It's a pity that dog can't talk, given it's such an important part of your alibi, sir,' said Hughes. 'You don't deny feeling angry after seeing your wife having intercourse with Mr. Lines, I suppose?'

'How can I deny it?' snapped Paul. 'How would you feel if it was your wife? But to suggest I would want to kill her because of it is ridiculous. I loved her.'

'But you do have rather a quick temper, don't you, sir? Like that incident with Clarke on the beach? About your daughter? That was a real ding-dong, wasn't it?'

'He could have killed her with that grapnel, the stupid fool. And, remember, he pulled a knife on me.' Paul felt angry now, but he held it in check. 'Anyway, back to Sasha. Anyone will tell you how happy our marriage was. I would never harm a hair on her head. No matter what she did. I loved her too much.' He glared at Hughes. 'And I expect you to find out who did kill her, if you're so certain it wasn't Clarke. Although I'm sure it was. How convenient his mother was the only witness he was at home that night.'

'And how convenient your mother is your best witness you were mainly at home on Wednesday evening, sir?'

'Leah was here, too. Why do you keep going on about Wednesday evening?'

Hughes paused before replying. 'I wondered when you'd ask. Another girl was raped that evening, sir. One who got a really good look at her attacker. Yes.' He smiled triumphantly at Paul. 'Happened about the time you say you were out walking the dog. And she says she can identify her attacker.'

Paul was shocked by his tone and glare. 'I don't like your inference, Inspector. And where was Clarke at the time? Have you asked him?'

Hughes stared at him disdainfully. 'I think that's my business, don't you, sir?' He walked towards the landing but stopped, turned and looked back. 'Oh, and by the way. I expect we'll be asking you to attend an identity parade quite soon. You won't mind doing that, will you, sir?'

Paul returned his stare. 'Not at all, Inspector. I'd be pleased to, if it would ease your mind. Provided you can guarantee Clarke will be there as well, of course.'

'I believe I can decide who will be there, Mr. Vincent.'

'And our laptop and data disks? Your lot took them from here on Wednesday. We need them. Leah has school work on hers and I need mine to work at home. When can we have them back?'

'When we're good and ready, sir. Probably in a few days.' Hughes glared at him, paused and thankfully descended the stairs. Paul stood aside for Gold who gave him a glance that seemed momentarily sympathetic: maybe even apologetic.

'I just want my wife's killer caught, sergeant,' Paul said to her. 'Don't you understand that?'

'I know you do, sir. So do we. It's our highest priority, I can assure you.'

— — ∞ — —

Leah had been alone in the back of the van for some while. Stevie had returned to the driving seat long ago. She tried to calm herself with the thought that if he wanted to harm or rape her he would have done so by now. She was particularly cross she'd left her mobile phone in Marina's bedroom. By the time the van doors opened again it was quite dark and she desperately needed the toilet.

Stevie climbed into the van, this time leaving the door ajar. The light from a nearby street lamp provided a little illumination. She drew back in fear when she saw a cloth coming towards her.

'Don't worry. It's only a blindfold. I'm going to lead you a little way after movin' the van. The tape's got to go back on your mouth, mind.'

Two minutes later her mouth was taped again and now she was also blindfolded. He drove for a couple of minutes before stopping. After a few moments she heard the rear doors being opened. He untied her ankles and helped her out of the back. After slamming the van's doors, he led her slowly by the arm.

Firstly she was aware of crossing a hard surface, then grass, then gravel. She was trying to work out where they were. She was conscious of the vague smell of seaweed, of dampness in the air and the slop of gently breaking water nearby. After a slight incline he stopped her, warned her of four steep steps to climb and pulled her on again. She heard the hollow sound of wooden runners beneath her feet as she hesitantly ascended the steps. After being warned to step over a threshold, she heard him close a door behind her, pull some curtains and click on a light; its brilliance was visible beneath the blindfold on either side of her nose. She thought the room she was in smelled of burnt toast and fish.

After taking her blindfold off, Stevie painfully ripped the tape from her mouth, stinging her lips. Leah blinked against the bright light. She was standing next to an open doorway leading to a bedroom.

The room she was in contained a tiny aluminium sink unit with cupboards, an armchair, a small pine table and chair, and a television. Turning to look through the door into the bedroom, she saw it contained a single bed, a chest-of-drawers and a curtained area she guessed served as a wardrobe. Everything looked very basic. The television appeared to be lined up so it could be viewed either from the sitting area or directly through the door, from the bed. A further small door led off from the bedroom to what she assumed was a bathroom. It looked like a tiny flatlet.

'How did you find out where we live?' Leah stared defiantly at him. This had been bothering her as she lay in the back of the van. Moving house should have made them difficult to find: unless he'd followed her or Dad from Hengistbury Head, which hardly seemed likely.

Stevie smiled and winked. 'I was clever, Leah. Looked up your dad in the phone book; went to your old address; asked them for a forwardin' address.' He laughed. 'Easy-peasy.'

Too easy, thought Leah. Then practicality called. 'I need the toilet.' She looked at him challengingly. He was just as she remembered him: blond unruly hair, thick lips, insolent, dangerous blue eyes: eyes that now seemed to be flitting around the flatlet, no doubt looking for problems in her connection.

He went through to the bedroom and opened the little door near the bed-head. 'In here. Toilet and shower. You're stayin' the night, see, so you might want a shower. The water's hot. There's a towel you can use.' He actually smiled at her.

Leah was aghast. 'You must be joking. Do you think I'd take any clothes off with you around?' She turned her back to him, waggling her arms. 'Well come on. Get this stuff off me, Stevie. My wrists hurt.' She looked back over her shoulder at him.

Stevie looked taken aback by her dominant tone but he obeyed and fetched some scissors from a drawer in the table to cut the tape around her wrists. He pointed to the bathroom. 'Make sure you use the toilet, 'cos you won't get another chance 'till mornin'.'

Stevie allowed her to close the bathroom door and, after using the toilet, she looked around for a weapon. There was nothing of use. She washed her hands, preferring to leave them

187

wet rather than touch his grubby towel. When she nervously went back into the bedroom, she was alarmed when Stevie approached her. The peculiar set smile on his face, combined with his wide and staring eyes, completely unnerved her. She was about to dodge back into the bathroom when he lunged around her to catch hold of the door.

'I don't think so.' Grabbing her arm he jerked her away from it.

'Don't touch me, Stevie.' Leah tore her arm from his grasp and glared at him. He almost seemed mesmerised by her stare. If necessary she could jump on and over the bed to the far side: not that this would help very much.

Stevie blinked and shook his head as if trying to shake off her influence. He nodded towards the bed. 'Lie on the bed, Leah. It's really comfortable, honest. A bit small but it'll do.' He winked at her. 'You're really pretty, Leah. Nice figure.'

Leah was trembling, her heart fluttering, but she knew she needed to appear calm and strong. 'You're joking. Let me out of here now, Stevie, or you'll be in serous trouble. And I mean *now*!'

Stevie grinned at what he no doubt considered to be futile threats. He reached forward and somehow flipped her onto the bed using both his arms and a leg. The front part of her body crashed onto the bed, her feet flailing, and his hands seemed everywhere, pulling at her legs, turning her over onto her back. She struck out with bunched fists, making contact at one point with his face. Finally she pulled her legs up to her stomach, rolling into a ball, and he let go. Had it been like this for Mum when he attacked her? He waited until she eventually put her legs down and lay still.

Leah was fearful of the evil grin on his face as he slowly undid the buckle of his belt. 'The bed's not very big, Leah, but we can manage, can't we?'

As he undid the top button of his jeans, Leah scrambled off the far side of the bed. 'Don't even think of touching me, you monster.' She ran round the bed to get back into the kitchen, but he quickly moved towards the door to cut her off. She backed up into the corner by the bed, getting as far away from him as possible, letting out a shrill cry for help.

'Quiet, Leah! Any more noise and you'll get hurt, for sure. There's no need to be scared. Okay, okay, I'll leave you now.' He did up his jean's button and belt while she watched from her cornered position by the bed. 'You'll get to like me if you give it a chance. You'll see.'

'Nothing is ever going to happen between us, Stevie. Just understand that. There is no chance.' Leah's voice was firm. 'You'd have to kill me first.' She was surprised by the firmness her own voice had taken. 'Like you did to my mum.'

'Don't say that. Don't ever say that! It's not true.'

There was a long pause while they sized each other up, his eyes running up and down her figure, his tongue briefly licking his lips like a lizard. Inwardly, Leah was petrified by what seemed certain to come.

Stevie shook his head as if pitying her lack of understanding. 'Don't worry. I won't hurt you, Leah. You're nice.' The strange grin returned and he stepped closer, stretched out his arm and stroked her cheek gently with the back of his fingers, one arm now around her waist. Leaning forward he tried to kiss her but she managed to jerk her head aside to prevent his hateful lips contacting her flesh.

Leah's hands were shaking. Hating the close contact as his body pressed against hers, she managed to slowly push around him. Then, tearing herself free from his grasp, she ran through to the kitchen, screaming for help again as loudly as she could. Stevie was swift in his pursuit, only a second or so behind her, twisting her around and pulling her hand from the doorknob. The door was locked and there was no key in the lock.

'That's enough of the noise. I warned you.' He spat the words out and waved a warning finger at her. 'I'm going to have to tape you again. It's your own fault, Leah.'

Stevie stepped towards the bedroom and bent to jerk a rug aside. This revealed a trapdoor, to which he pointed. 'Your room's down there. It's a bit cramped. You'll have to duck.' He pulled on a ring to open the trapdoor and switched on a nearby socket from which there trailed a lead. Light flooded a shallow room beneath the floor.

'You've got a sleepin' bag and a light down there, Leah. I'll be up here all the time. If you make any noise—especially if you hear anyone come—or if you try anything on, it's big trouble for you, girl. I'm only leavin' the tape off your face now 'cos I'm kind, but if you make the slightest noise the tape goes back on for good. And if you misbehave, you get cut. Get it, Leah? Cut.'

Leah was scared when the horrible knife she'd seen him threaten her dad with appeared in his hand in an almost magical way. He waved it menacingly.

Leah nodded to show her understanding, but tried not to reveal her fear, even though she felt herself trembling again. 'Why are you doing this to me, Stevie?'

'Your dad, of course.' Stevie looked incredulous she did not realise. 'Time for him to worry a bit, see. That bastard shopped me to the police over your mother's murder.' He smiled. 'Time for him to suffer now, Leah. By worrying about you.'

'Dad will come looking for me. And the police. You'll be in serious trouble when they find me.'

Stevie shrugged. 'But they won't ever find you, Leah,' he grinned. 'I'm not tellin' them, see. And neither are you.' He winked. 'And there's plenty of time for us to get to know each other. I'm lookin' forward to that.'

Stevie laughed, lay his knife down on the kitchen work surface and picked up a roll of tape. He unwound a strip, nicked it with his teeth, tore it and wrapped it tightly around her wrists. He allowed her to keep her arms in front of her this time. Tossing the tape aside he waved at the trapdoor. 'Now, down you go. Be careful to step on that crate as you go down. There's some ginger biscuits and a mug of water down there. And a bedside lamp. I reckon you can still pick up a biscuit or the mug if you're careful. If you make any sound I'll tape your mouth and switch off your light. And you won't like it down there in the dark, Leah, I promise. Only a light will keep the rats away.' He laughed at the horror she knew must show on her face. 'Get some sleep. See you in the mornin', babe.'

— — ∞ — —

190

Paul saw Carol flitting into the spare bedroom as he began to climb the second flight of stairs. By the time he reached the top she had re-emerged wearing a shortie nightie. It looked very appealing: a nice antidote to the police.

'I suppose you gathered that was Hughes and Co.,' he said as he reached the top of the stairs.

She nodded. 'I could hear Hughes' voice from the bedroom. What's it about now, Paul?'

'Another girl was attacked on Wednesday night. Another attempted rape. He was keen to point out it happened while I was out walking Shep.' He grimaced at her. 'And they want to put me in an identity parade. Apparently this girl saw her attacker's face.'

Carol looked at him aghast. 'You poor thing. Still, it might help show them you're nothing to do with it.'

Paul shrugged. 'Trouble is, I reckon there's always a chance someone could pick the wrong person in a line-up. They pick people for the line-ups who look quite similar, after all. Imagine my problems if she picked me.'

Carol tugged at his hand. 'It's no use worrying about that. Come back to bed, Paul. This is good news. There's every chance they'll catch him now. I presume they're putting Clarke in the parade as well?'

Paul sighed. 'That's what I'm demanding.' As they entered the bedroom his mobile phone rang. 'What now?' He gave her an eyes-up sign and went across to it.

He expected some further irritation from the police and was mildly surprised when it turned out to be Marina's mother. He could hardly believe his ears when she spoke. 'You're sure about this, Jane? How long ago?' Paul weakly sank onto the bed. As if things were not bad enough already. Missing. He could only imagine the worst, and that definitely involved Clarke. 'Thank you for telling me, Jane.' Paul terminated the call, tossed his mobile phone onto the bed and held his head in his hands.

'What?' Carol pulled on his arm. 'What's happened now, Paul?'

'Leah's gone missing. I should have kept her here. That was Marina's mother. She would have called earlier but she and Marina have been making a statement to the police. Apparently Leah popped down to the shop for a magazine and never came back. She even left her mobile phone in Marina's bedroom.'

'Clarke?' Carol stared at him. 'It's got to be Clarke.'

Paul looked at her with a glazed expression. 'It really can't be anyone else, can it?'

'Where would he take her, Paul? Is he totally crazy?'

'Pretty much.' Paul sighed. 'But I know where to look first.'

'In the dark?' Carol shook her head. 'This isn't a job for you, Paul. You must tell the police what you think.'

'Do you think I trust them any more?' Paul shrugged off his robe and began to dress. 'I know where that monster holds up and I'm going there right now. I let Leah down before and I'm not doing it again now. She needs me. Who knows what Clarke might do to her.'

Carol caught his arm. 'You mustn't go alone, Paul. He's a killer. He could stab you... or Leah. Leave it to the police.' She seemed desperate. 'Please. Leave it to the police.'

'I can't, Carol. I just can't.'

— — ∞ — —

Paul drove to Stanpit like a madman. Skidding to a halt at the end of the harbourside path and parking next to a faded red van that looked vaguely familiar, he jumped out of his car and hurried quietly along the path to the little brick building the old lady had told him was Clarke's strange home. There was a light on in the building and the curtains were drawn. He was about to creep into the garden, concerned about making a noise crossing the gravel, when a light went on in a rear window of the house and the back door opened. Paul hesitated, watching intently. Several policemen emerged with flashlights. Not sure whether to be pleased or annoyed, Paul ducked back onto the path.

Alarmed, he saw lights moving around at the end of the path. He realised the police were about to come around the back as well, trapping him between them. Not wanting to tangle with them, he quickly jumped over the nearby wall into the old lady's garden.

From his crouched position close to the wall, Paul heard several policemen pass by. A few moments later they were banging on the door of Clarke's outbuilding. Several of them called out: 'Police. Open the door.'

This was immediately followed by a woman's shrill voice. 'Open the door, there's a good lad, Stevie. Don't worry. Mum's here.'

The door was obviously opened after a few moments, for he then heard the raised voices of the police and that of Clarke himself. It was too much for him. Standing, Paul vaulted over the wall and went round to join them in the Clarke's garden. A policeman caught his arm and flashed a torch in his face; another grabbed his arms and forced them high up behind his back. 'Who are you?'

'Let me go. I'm Paul Vincent. Clarke's got my daughter in there.'

The policemen were not interested in his protests. Held tightly, Paul was force-marched up the path to the nearest police vehicle which was parked behind his own car. After listening to his explanation, a uniformed policeman told him to wait in the police car while matters were resolved. Now somewhat more understanding, they said they would tell him if they found Leah with Clarke. Fifteen minutes later they informed him there was no trace of Leah in the house or the outbuilding.

Paul was held in the car for a further ten minutes, after which Hughes appeared and glared in at him. 'I don't know what you think you're doing here, Mr. Vincent. You should have contacted us yourself the moment your daughter went missing. And she's definitely not here. We've thoroughly searched the house and the outbuilding. Now go home. Stay away from here or I'll arrest you for causing a nuisance. You say Clarke is hounding you? From where I'm standing, I'd say you're hounding him.'

Paul sighed in despair. 'Look, I want my daughter back, Inspector. He must have done something with her.' Paul could hardly believe what he was hearing. He'd been so certain Leah would be there. 'Aren't you even going to question him? She'll be tied up somewhere if he's not already killed her.'

Hughes looked at him impatiently. 'There's no reason to suppose something like that, sir. Or that Clarke has anything to do with this. Finding your daughter is our job, and she's not even been missing for long. Officially she's not even a missing person. There's no evidence she's been taken anywhere against her will. Perhaps she decided to go to see another friend.'

'After telling her best friend she was only popping down to the shops? Without taking her mobile? She always takes that with her.'

'Please, go back to your car and go home. We'll be in touch as soon as there's any development. We're checking with all the friends listed on her mobile phone.' He seemed to be hovering somewhere between anger and compassion. 'Meanwhile, don't worry. We'll find her. So just go. Please, sir.'

— — ∞ — —

Back at the house, Carol was very sheepish. 'I'm so sorry, Paul, but I had to tell the police you were going there. I was afraid Clarke would kill you. Or both of you.' She looked at him earnestly. 'Have a brandy, or something. You look done in. There's nothing else you can do now if you say the police are contacting all her friends. And the police have searched Clarke's place, so you know she's not there. The fact is, I really can't be certain Clarke was the person who attacked me. Maybe we've been wrong all along.'

'So now the police know we were together.'

Carol shrugged. 'We did approach them together in the first place, so I don't really think it matters.'

Paul kissed her briefly on the cheek. 'Don't worry, Carol, I'm not really annoyed about you telling them. I would have probably contacted them myself, given more time. All I could think of was getting there fast.' He headed for the drinks cabinet and, as she suggested, poured himself a neat brandy.

After a swig he put the glass down and turned to her. 'Carol, I know it's him. Look. He's been stalking Leah, remember. And he's crazy.'

Carol went across to him and took both his hands, holding them tenderly as they gazed into each other's worried eyes.

'You know I'm as worried about Leah as you are, Paul. She's such a lovely girl, and you're such a wonderful dad. Of course your first thought was for her safety. And I'm not surprised you didn't rely on the police after their performance so far.' She shook his hands gently. 'You've got so much to be proud of with Leah as a daughter. I know she's strong, Paul. She'll get through this.'

'She might be strong, Carol, but the trauma of this could affect her for life. Think what he might do to her.' Paul had to cling to the assumption she was still alive: although desperately in need of his help. 'What if he rapes her?'

Carol squeezed his hands. 'Don't think like that. She'll get through this, Paul. We must stay strong. At least the police will realise things are much more complicated than they imagined now.'

Chapter 18

Leah heard several voices calling out Stevie's name. Obviously it was this which prompted him to open the trapdoor and jump down, his eyes scarily wild. She could see a naked light bulb in the room above. She'd been dozing, but clearly it was still night time. He rapidly forced some white material into her mouth and slapped tape across her lips. She was fearful of choking while he hurriedly tied her hands and feet tightly together in such a way she felt like a strapped turkey. Then he lashed the end of the rope to a central post to ensure she was fixed in one position. He worked with precision and a practiced knowledge of knots. It only took him a minute or so and then he was gone. The trapdoor closed and the table lamp then went out. It was horrible in the darkness, but she clearly heard the word 'police' shouted above her. All the while the voices continued to call out. A few moments later, the sound of several footfalls in the room above gave her a growing sense of relief. At last she would be rescued.

When she heard her father's voice a few moments later, her heart leapt for joy. The hubbub of voices made her tremble with excitement at the thought of imminent release. She prayed they would find the trapdoor quickly. If only she could move to make a noise that would attract their attention, but Stevie had been far too shrewd for that. She was bound so tightly that the more she struggled, the more it hurt. In the end she stopped struggling in order to concentrate on breathing and not choking. What had Stevie put in her mouth? It clamped her tongue down hard and prevented even the slightest chance of her squealing; instead, she had to concentrate on trying not to swallow, her natural reaction.

After a while it sounded as though the people above had left the building. Leah was dismayed when a long silence followed: a terrifying silence that confirmed Stevie's prediction: she would not be found. Now they would never know she was down there. Her father would never find her. Had they taken Stevie away? If so, she knew she would die there in the darkness, her body gnawed by rats.

Once again she desperately tried to cry out but it proved impossible. Earlier, Stevie had thankfully left her with light from a table lamp, although even that had mixed blessings: she got no more than a couple of hour's of fretful sleep, despite being cocooned in a snug sleeping bag. Now she longed for the light. She knew she was near an old motorbike. If Stevie really was gone, she might be able to use its horn to attract attention. If he came back, her best plan was to try to persuade him to leave her untied down there so she could try that.

Leah finally heard him moving above her, again. It was strange to feel grateful he was around. It seemed ages before the trapdoor opened and he jumped down to remove her bindings. As the tape was removed from her mouth she spat out what looked to be part of a torn and dirty handkerchief. It made her want to retch. By the time she was allowed to stand on the crate and heave herself up into his bedroom, Stevie was sitting on the edge of the trapdoor in the kitchen doorway, grinning wickedly.

'What about that, then? The police an' all? Did you hear them?'

Leah nodded as she stood rubbing sore wrists. 'Of course I did.' She glared at him and pulled the hair from her eyes. She felt dirty and horrible and her mouth tasted foul. She remembered the vow she'd made to herself in her dungeon during the long night and moderated her tone. 'And I heard my dad.'

Stevie laughed. 'That was the best bit. He looked right through the door. And no one ever guessed I was standin' right on top of you. Is that cool, or what?' His laugher grew stronger, creasing his face. 'Daddy will never find you here, will he, babe? Eh?' He stood up, blocking the doorway. 'Now we can have some real fun.' She ducked back as he reached out to stroke her cheek again.

'Don't touch me, Stevie. I'll talk to you, but I won't let you touch me.'

Stevie shook his head as if not comprehending why she should object. 'He'll be going ape, your dad. And serve him right for persecutin' me.' He slowly undid his belt, looking at her lasciviously. 'Don't worry. I won't hurt you, if you're good. I can't wait for ever.'

Leah felt her heart beating faster. 'Persecuting you? What do you mean?'

'Tellin' the police I killed his wife. The bastard.'

Leah looked at his dangerously changed expression and pointed to the bathroom door. 'I really need to use the bathroom, Stevie. And I need some privacy in there. Okay?' She looked at him with steely determination.

Stevie smiled and winked. 'I like a feisty girl. Go on then. Help yourself. Make yourself pretty for me.' He did up his belt. 'We've got all the time in the world. What do you want for breakfast? Cornflakes and toast okay?'

Leah looked at him uncertainly and nodded. 'Thanks.'

She went through to the tiny bathroom. Before she could close the door, Stevie called out to her.

'You can use my toothbrush if you like, darlin'.'

Before closing the door she glowered out at him. 'I'd sooner brush my teeth with a slug.'

— — ∞ — —

He let her sit on his only upright chair at a tiny table in the living area. He gave her the promised cornflakes and toast, plus a hot cup of tea. Previously starving, Leah felt a lot better afterwards, even asking for another round of toast, which he eagerly provided from his ancient-looking toaster.

'You see, I want you to be comfortable here, Leah. I like you. You're pretty.' He tilted his head on one side. 'I'm not so bad either, am I? If you're honest.' Leah scraped margarine and marmalade onto her toast and looked up at him. He was leaning against the sink, watching for her reaction. 'I said... I'm not so bad looking, am I?' This time he sounded impatient.

'No. Very handsome,' said Leah, munching apprehensively. He clearly didn't know how to take this, for he stared back uncertainly. After a few moments she spoke again, quite softly. 'Why did you do it, Stevie? Why did you kill my mother? What did she do to you? She even tried to make the peace when you had that argument with Dad, outside the café.' Leah watched his face closely for any tell-tale signs.

'I never! I never killed her.' He seemed genuinely indignant and his eyes were wide. 'Leah, don't you say that.' The pitch of his voice rose. 'Don't you ever say that. She was a pretty woman, your mother.'

Leah put down her toast and stared at him. 'But Dad saw you there, Stevie. Didn't he?'

Stevie fidgeted with his hands, rubbing them together. 'All right. So I was there. He saw me. But I didn't kill your mother. Honest.'

'You expect me to believe that? When you kicked my dad in the head?'

'He deserved it, the bastard.'

'He did not deserve it, Stevie.' Leah's voice wavered slightly as she pulled back her hair, now staring hard at the boy. 'Nor did my mother.'

'I told you. I didn't kill her.'

'Then who did?'

'Someone else. A surfin' guy from the sandbank. Not me.'

Leah's eyes widened as she stared at him. He seemed really earnest. 'You mean you saw it?'

Stevie nodded, lips pursed, head down, shamefaced. He didn't answer.

'Well why haven't you told the police this?' Leah almost felt she believed him.

'Because they wouldn't listen to me, would they?' He held out his hands imploringly. 'Well, would they? If I said I was there then I'd be in jail fast, wouldn't I?' He angrily kicked the baseboard beneath the sink behind him, knocking the panel loose. He looked down at it disgustedly, kicking it aside.

'But they have DNA to prove who did things these days, Stevie. It would rule you out.'

'DNA?' He looked at her questioningly. 'Don't understand DNA.'

'It can prove whether someone was involved in a murder, Stevie. Look. Tell me exactly what happened.' Leah tried to keep her voice calm.

Stevie shrugged. 'First I watched the party on the beach, see. You were there. Nice bikini, by the way. And your mum's.'

'Never mind the damn bikinis, Stevie. Go on.'

Stevie sighed. 'I saw your mum go off runnin' in the dark. Thought she was silly. Then I saw the other guy runnin' after her, a while later.' He shrugged. 'I worried for her. So I followed them. I wondered what was going on.'

'Which other guy, Stevie?'

'I told you already. The surfin' guy.'

'Why do you keep calling him the surfing guy?'

'He hangs out at one of the beach huts on the sandbank. Always surfin'. Or runnin'. Always on the go.'

'You mean you can identify him?'

'If I wanted to.'

Leah swallowed. He still sounded convincing. 'Okay. So what did you see?'

'I kept real quite. Like the SAS. When I caught up he was strugglin' with your mum.'

'So why didn't you help her?'

Stevie shrugged. 'I never knew he was going to kill her, did I? I mean, I thought he was just going to have sex with her.'

'Just?' shrieked Leah.

Stevie flapped both his hands. 'Keep the noise down or you'll be gagged again. Understand?' Leah nodded. Stevie continued. 'She'd had sex with some other bloke earlier. I saw it. Didn't bother her then. She liked it, your mum.'

'You saw that, as well?' He nodded in response. 'And you actually saw this surfer kill my mum?'

Stevie nodded. 'He forced her to have sex with him. I was hidin' in the bushes. They didn't know I was there. Your dog ran away, but it came back later with your dad. When the surfer guy looked round to see your dad comin' and shoutin', your mum grabbed a fallen branch and hit out, but he got it off her. They struggled and your mum fell backward. Your dad

200

attacked him.'

'And?'

'I 'spect she hit her head on the road. She didn't move after that. The guy hit your dad with the branch and he went down. It was all so fast. The guy went to look at your mum, dropped the branch and ran off towards the huts. It's a wonder you didn't see him when you came on. Still, he was probably back at his hut by then. It's' near the Head end.'

'And you never tried to stop any of this, Stevie?' Leah was aghast.

Stevie shrugged again. 'I didn't want no trouble, did I? Why should I get involved in a murder? Anyway, why should I save your dad when he's accused me to the police? It was too late for your mum. I was checkin' to see if she was all right when your dad shone his torch at me. So I went over and gave him a little kick. Didn't want him seeing me there, like. Knew he'd be trouble again.'

There was a long silence.

'Is this the honest truth, Stevie?'

'Course it is. I never killed no one. Never.'

'But you attacked that girl on the Head. And that girl on the prom.'

'I never. Don't know nothing about that. Leah, believe me.'

'If you tell the police all this, you'll be off the hook, Stevie. Then they can catch the real killer.'

'But they would never believe me.' He seemed near to tears. 'You and your dad wouldn't believe me. I've told you 'cos it was your mum, but I'm not tellin' no one else. I'll deny it. They'd never believe me, Leah. Never.'

Leah got up from her seat, went round the table and put a comforting hand on his arm. She spoke softly. 'They've believed you so far or they would have arrested you already. And I believe you, Stevie. And I'll help you make them believe all this, if you don't hurt me. Promise me you'll tell the police what you saw.'

Stevie met her eye. 'All right, I'll call the police. If you want.'

'Please, please do, Stevie. Thank you so much.'

Stevie looked into her eyes and dissolved into a crying heap, his head over the sink, loud tears plopping onto the aluminium. Putting her hand comfortingly on his shoulder, Leah spoke softly to him. 'It's all right, Stevie. I understand. And I'll explain to the police it makes sense and that I believe you. It'll be all right, I promise. Just call them now.'

— — ∞ — —

'What do you think you're doing there?' The old lady's quavery voice made Paul jump. It was eight o'clock the following morning and he was caught in the embarrassing position of squatting down between a large shrub and the wall at the bottom of her garden. She was pointing a long-handled garden fork at him, her eyes wide: but more in surprise than fear, he suspected. He felt stiff—he'd been there for an hour and a half—and his back and legs were hurting as he straightened up. He stepped out onto the grass. She took a step backward to keep her distance.

'I'm sorry I'm in your garden. I don't mean you any harm, I promise.' He saw her do a double-take in recognition.

'Wait a minute.' She pointed at him with her free hand. 'I saw you here before, didn't I? You were looking for Stevie?'

Paul nodded. 'Yes.' He held out his hands in supplicatory fashion. 'Look, please don't be afraid. I'll tell you the truth. Clarke's been stalking my daughter, Leah. He's been frightening her for days. Now she's gone missing. I think he's kidnapped her.' He saw her disbelieving look. 'Didn't you hear the police last night? They were looking for her.'

The old lady nodded. 'I heard the commotion and looked out the window and saw them. They had their flashing blue lights at the front and torches at the back.' She gave a nervous laugh. 'It gave me quite a scare.' Amusement at her own fear changed to concern. 'But Stevie? It can't be true.' The old lady lowered the fork and stuck it into the grass. 'He's a good lad.'

'No, it's true. Leah recognised him when he followed her. And he's threatened me, too. With a knife. We know it's him. And we're pretty sure he murdered my wife on Hengistbury

Head. Sasha Vincent? It was in the papers.' Now the old lady looked shocked and had a hand to her mouth. 'The police also think Clarke's involved in that. That's why they were here last night.' He saw she was now beginning to believe him. 'They've not found Leah yet, but I'm still sure he's got her hidden somewhere. I'm desperately worried about her safety. I was hiding in your garden because I need to find out what he's done with her. Look.' Paul reached for the wallet in his back pocket, took it out and opened it to show her the picture of Leah in its transparent panel. 'That's Leah. Have you seen her around here?' He waved the wallet towards her. 'I'm Paul Vincent, her father.'

She took a step nearer to look at the picture more closely. 'What a pretty girl,' she said, at length. 'No. I've not seen her, I'm afraid. I know Stevie's a bit odd sometimes, a bit shy, but he's always been lovely and kind to me.' She lowered her voice. 'Some might say a bit simple, but I can't believe he'd do something like that. I've known him all his life.' Paul noticed the gentle bobbing of her head and sensed the sincerity of her words. She smiled at him. 'I'm Hilda, by the way. Stevie's been a wonderful person to me. Cuts my grass regularly. You must be mistaken.'

Paul lowered his voice. 'There must be a side of Stevie you haven't seen, Hilda.' He gestured towards Clarke's little building. 'Do you know if he's in there now?'

Hilda walked slowly down to her wall and peered across at the water. 'His boat's not there, so he must have gone out in it.'

'His boat's pulled up next to the building. I've seen it there this morning.'

'Really? Well! That is unusual.' She frowned. 'I suppose he must be there, then. Unless he's out on his motorbike or jogging. He goes jogging some mornings, you know. He's always saying he likes to keep fit.'

'I can't wait any longer, Hilda. I'm going to see if he's there. If there's any trouble, please phone the police.'

Hilda put a trembling hand to her mouth again. 'Oh dear.' As Paul headed for the gate leading out onto the harbourside path she called after him. 'Be careful.'

Climbing the wooden steps, Paul banged on Clarke's door.

'What? Who's there?' Paul recognised the lad's muffled voice.

'Paul Vincent. Open the door. Have you got Leah in there?'

'Dad!' Her shriek was unmistakable. Paul's heart leapt a grateful beat.

'Is that her?' Hilda was right behind him.

Paul looked round at her. She had also heard Leah call out. He nodded. 'That's her. Phone the police, Hilda. Please. Now!'

'Oh dear, oh dear.' The old lady took a couple of timid steps backward.

A window opened next to the door and Stevie's head poked out. He glared furiously at Paul. 'Yeah, I've got her. And this.' He waved a knife out of the window. 'And she'll get cut up if you don't back off and go away. You know I mean it.'

Paul heard Leah's voice inside. 'Dad! Don't do anything. Call the police.'

Clarke banged the window shut and silence followed. Paul looked round at Hilda. 'Well, go on then, Hilda. You saw the knife, didn't you? That's my daughter in there. Phone for the police now. Dial 999.'

Hilda flapped her hands around wildly. 'Oh dear, oh dear.' She hurried off back towards her house.

Paul decided backing off was the best thing to do. He called out to Clarke. 'Okay, I'm going now.' He went round to stand by Hilda's garden wall, well out of Clarke's view. Two tense minutes later Clarke appeared. He was holding Leah with one arm twisted around her back, a knife at her front. He spotted Paul immediately.

'I told you to clear off,' he shouted angrily.

'Let her go, Clarke.' Paul caught Leah's eye. 'Are you all right, Leah? Has he done anything to you?'

'No, no,' said Leah. 'He's not hurt me. *Please* stay back, Dad.' She looked really scared.

Clarke jerked his head towards the garden. 'You. Pull my boat into the water.'

'What?'

Clarke waved the knife around dangerously, firstly pointing

it at Paul and then turning it to point at Leah. 'You heard. Do what I say, or Leah gets hurt.'

Paul went to the boat and tried heaving it from its position. It was well bedded into the gravel and seemed far too heavy to move, but spurred on by Clarke's shouts and the waving knife so near to his daughter's throat, he found the right grip and an inner strength that allowed him to finally drag the boat out of the gravel and down the sandy beach to the water.

Paul watched breathlessly as Clarke forced Leah into the boat, pushed it out into deeper water and climbed in himself. He started the engine and threw it into reverse to take the boat away from the shoreline. Paul looked around desperately. Another motor boat moored to a short wooden jetty nearby caught his eye. He ran to it, jumped in, and was relieved to see the key was already in place. As Clarke's boat spurted away into the distance, Paul pulled on the starter cord. As the outboard motor burst into life, a huge, rounded man in baggy blue shorts and a grey T-shirt came hurrying out of a nearby garden gateway and waddled towards the jetty, shouting furiously at him and waving his fist.

'Sorry. I'll bring it back soon,' Paul called back to him. 'It's an emergency.' He turned his back on the expletives and concentrated on following Clarke. The other's boat was already way ahead and it would be difficult to catch up. Paul wished he had a better knowledge of the hidden sandbanks in that part of the harbour, but he knew enough: go too far out of the marked channels and he might run aground; the water was low. As he followed Clarke's boat down the channel towards the harbour mouth, he shivered at the thought of how Leah must be feeling. What could the youth's intentions be? And why go off by boat?

— — ∞ — —

Hilda sat in the little chair by her telephone, her hand outstretched and shaking. Something prevented her from picking up the handset. Tears of confusion poured from her eyes and she crumpled in the chair. The man must be wrong. Stevie was a good boy. Maybe the man was intimidating him and he was taking the girl for protection. There had to be some other explanation. Stevie must be really scared to be waving a knife around like that. It wasn't like him. It must be the man who was scaring Stevie. He was a suspicious man, hiding in her garden like that. She'd never seen the poor lad look so wretched. Poor Stevie.

— — ∞ — —

Leah was scared, worrying about Stevie's intentions, but she guessed the boat was probably the easiest way for Stevie to escape. Sitting nervously in the bow, she watched as her dad ran to a nearby jetty. A short while later, by then well distant, she saw another motorboat start out from the same area of the shoreline that was also following their course. Hopefully it was her dad. She realised she must introduce some delaying tactics so he could catch up.

Being a good swimmer, thoughts of tumbling into the water held no fears for her. And she knew there was a central sandbank that must be quite close to the channel they were in. If she could swim to that she could perhaps wade away from where Stevie's boat could get: giving her dad a chance to catch up and rescue her. When Stevie was looking over his shoulder at the following boat, Leah tumbled overboard. The water was cold, but the contrast was like a tonic to her system that counteracted her previous feeling of sluggishness. She swam at a fast crawl away from the boat.

Stevie brought the boat around so the bows pointed towards her. 'You stupid girl,' he shrieked, cutting the throttle. 'Get back in the boat *now*, or I'll drive it at you. Do you hear me?' Leah was treading water, uncertainly. As if to illustrate his point, Stevie opened the throttle and headed fast towards her, only cutting the throttle back and swerving a few feet away. The wash hit her in a giant wave.

Leah was crying by the time he pulled alongside, and she let him heave her back into the boat, shaking with fear.

'Promise you won't try that again, or I'll get you. No more chances. Promise!'

206

Leah nodded vigorously. Soaking, she scrambled back to her original seat in the bow, anxious to keep as much distance between them as possible. At least she had achieved one thing. Now the other boat was much closer; now she could actually see her dad in it.

— — ∞ — —

Stevie Clarke's boat was heading towards the harbour entrance. Although Paul followed at full throttle, he didn't seem to be closing on the other boat at all; a constant, tantalising distance was maintained between them: until he saw it swerving around for some reason and then stop. Staring, with a hand to his brow to shield against strong sunlight, he could no longer see Leah; but as he drew closer, he saw Clarke pulling her back into the boat. Thankfully he was now getting much closer. Clarke's boat sped off again at full throttle, with Leah in the bows.

Paul was alarmed when he realised Clarke was actually intending to head out to sea, but both boats slowed considerably when they became caught up in the powerful waters of The Run, at the harbour mouth. There was a strong incoming tide; sea water was flowing fast into the harbour. As they entered the narrow opening between Mudeford Quay and the Black House, Paul thankfully found his boat was at last gaining on Clarke's. Leah was sitting in the bow, watching him intently.

Paul's boat gradually drew half-broadside to Clarke's, which allowed him to nudge his bow into the other, turning it slightly towards the hidden sandbank. This induced Clarke to leap forward in order to reach out to push Paul's bows away, swearing angrily as he did so. Grabbing the loose mooring rope, and timing the movement between the two boats very carefully, Paul leapt across into the stern of Clarke's boat, managing to twist his rope a couple of times around a rowlock before Clarke could react. Paul hoped tying his boat on gave Leah and him a good chance of escape. Clearly surprised by Paul's initiative, Clarke turned back to face him, pulling a knife from its hidden sheath. Glaringly, he stepped towards Paul, waving it menacingly. Paul experienced a dangerous sense of déjà vu. The boats, meanwhile, floundered randomly as the motors argued with the fast tidal waters.

'You bugger,' said Clarke. 'I warned you not to tangle with me.'

'Come on then, big man.' Paul gave him a two-handed come-on gesture, taunting him to divert attention from the fact that Leah had picked up an oar behind Clarke's back. The boat rocked wildly as Clarke lunged towards Paul. As he did so, Leah rose and brought the edge of the oar blade sharply down onto Clarke's extended arm. The knife shot from his grip, bounced onto the edge of the boat and fell harmlessly into the water. Paul shuddered with relief when Clarke turned to swear at Leah while clutching his arm in pain; it gave him the opportunity to move in closer.

When the youth turned back to face him, Paul managed to deliver a crashing punch to Clarke's jaw, one that sent him reeling to the floor of the boat. Bending to quickly take advantage of the situation, sure in the knowledge the fit youth could almost certainly out-fight him in an even match, Paul simultaneously grabbed him by the collar and the waistband of his jeans and violently heaved him overboard into the swirling water. Surging adrenalin seemed to have given him powerful strength that morning: although it did little to alleviate the pain in his fist. Only then, while triumphantly panting from his exertions, did Paul become aware of the amazed spectators on Mudeford Quay: one of whom punched the air and cheered gleefully.

Leah shot across the boat to give him a damp bear-hug, but she quickly sat down again when the boat began rocking wildly. They both knew how dangerous the fast flowing waters were right there. 'Oh, thank you so much Dad.' Leah was beaming with relief.

Paul quickly unravelled the mooring rope from his commandeered boat and gave it a shove towards the sandbank which extended out below the water from the spit beyond the Black House. He reduced the throttle of Clarke's outboard and turned the bow to mid-channel, keeping an eye on Clarke as he swam towards the other boat. There was little space to manoeuvre in the narrow waters, but Paul managed to turn Clarke's boat around, narrowly missing the concrete harbour wall as he did so. As they caught the helping hand of the incoming tide, Paul saw Clarke trying to scramble aboard the other boat as it struck the sandbank. When it juddered to a halt it caused Clarke to loose his grip and fall back into the water, but with the boat aground, he would obviously soon be able to get onboard.

Pointing at Clarke for Leah's benefit, they both laughed at the sight of him standing knee-deep in the water by the boat, angrily shaking his fist at them. As she turned back to face him, Paul looked at her thankfully. Not surprisingly, she looked shattered.

'Thank you for that oar manoeuvre, Leah. That was a brilliant move.'

Leah grinned. 'No problem. Do we make a good team, or what?'

Paul laughed heartily. 'We have to now, sweetheart.' After a little while of silent thought for them both while they sped towards safety, he spoke again. 'Did he really not hurt you, Leah? Didn't he do anything to you at all?' He figured they both knew what he meant by that.

Leah shook her head and blew air out through her lips in noisy relief. She smiled broadly. 'No, Dad. Honestly. He didn't touch me other than to tie me up. But wait till I tell you what I found out from him.'

'What?' Paul looked at her expectantly.

Leah raised her voice. 'Stevie didn't kill Mum.'

Paul throttled back to listen more closely. 'What? How can you know that?'

Leah shrugged. 'He talked, Dad, and I believed him. Honestly. He didn't kill Mum. He's all bluster. He's not the way he looks.'

'That knife didn't look like bluster.'

Leah shrugged. 'But I think it was. I don't think he could kill anyone. And he told me he saw who killed Mum.'

Paul stared at her in amazement and patted the seat next to him. 'Come and sit here. Explain.' She joined him on the rear seat. He fully opened the throttle, pointing to Clarke in the other boat which was now heading after them, although fortunately well in the distance. 'But we must get back to Stanpit before he catches up. The car's there. I've had enough of clashing with him.'

Leah shook her head in exasperation and raised her voice. 'I can't possibly tell you over all this noise, Dad. It's much too complicated. Wait till we get to the car.'

Paul nodded. 'Okay. But first we drive. I'm not giving that monster a chance of catching up with us.'

— — ∞ — —

Clarke was still way in the distance when Paul beached the youth's boat as near as possible to where the car was parked. They ran from the waterside path to the car. After grabbing a jacket from the rear seat which he placed around Leah's shoulders to keep her warm, Paul drove off. Only when they were well away from Stanpit and Paul was sure Stevie could not find them did he park the car, turn off the engine, and take out his mobile phone.

'Who are you calling, Dad?'

'I'm going to call Carol and Gran, in a minute, to tell them both you're okay, but first I'm calling the police. I asked the old lady next to Clarke's house to do that, but there's no sign of them. They need to get there quickly to arrest Clarke. They should catch him at his house if they move fast. Then we must get you home and out of those wet clothes.'

Leah put a restraining hand on his arm. 'Never mind the clothes, Dad. It's not a cold day. Please wait until I've explained about Stevie. I need to explain everything before you talk to the police.'

Paul sighed. 'But it's their best chance to catch him if I phone now.'

Leah was firm. 'No, Dad. You must listen to me first.'

— — ∞ — —

She was so earnest, Paul was persuaded to listen to her against his better judgement: although he kept noting the passing time on his watch.

'He's like a scared little schoolboy, Dad,' explained Leah. 'He's only full of bravado when he's got a knife to wave around. He's only confident when he thinks he's got the upper-hand. Look, I grant you he's a bit simple, but I'm sure he could never kill anyone. He was actually quite gentle with me. He even tried to be nice some of the time. Apart from tying me up a bit tightly, and keeping me gagged and down in a cellar place below the floor of his hut—'

'You mean you were there all night?'

Leah nodded. 'Yes. I heard you with the police, but I was bound and gagged so tightly I couldn't make a sound. He told me he'd pulled his boat up next to the hut to hide some doors that led to the cellar. But there was this trapdoor from above. He put me down through that.'

Paul shook his head. 'And you expect me to take it easy on him? Remember he threatened me with a knife again, Leah.'

'I told you about the knife, Dad. It's just a prop.'

'A darned dangerous prop.'

Leah shrugged. 'Whatever. He's only a silly Peeping-Tom with a big chip on his shoulder. He just watches people. He was watching our party on the beach that night. He saw Mum with Roger Lines.' She grimaced and hurriedly continued. 'He watched Mum go off on her run afterwards, and he saw the man who murdered Mum run off down the road a bit after her. Stevie reckons this man saw her pass his hut and then followed her. Stevie says he followed them because he was worried about Mum.'

Paul scoffed. 'A likely story.' He paused. 'So you say this person has one of the huts?'

Leah shrugged. 'He uses one of the huts. Anyway, Stevie followed them both very quietly. He says he's good at that.'

'That I'll believe.'

'Then he saw it all. The man attacked Mum, who tried to fight him off, and Shep ran off to get us.'

'So why didn't he help Mum?'

'He says he was scared and stayed out of sight. He saw you arrive and fight with the man. He doesn't know his name, but he knows his hut.'

Paul still felt completely sceptical. 'If this is true, why didn't he tell the police, Leah?'

'Because he thought they'd never believe he stood by and watched. He thought he'd get done for murder if anyone knew he was there. Says he'd get blamed for everything else, too. Like we blamed him for everything.' She looked guilty.

'So why did he harass us? And stalk you?'

'To get his own back on us, Dad. On you, mainly. Don't you see?'

'So, although he wouldn't tell the police any of this, he told you?'

Leah gave him a brief smile. 'People talk to me because I listen, Dad.'

'And when I saw him, he kicked me in the head. Did he happen to mention that?'

Leah nodded. 'Well, yes, he admitted doing that. After the murderer ran off, he was checking to see how you and Mum were. He figured Mum was dead, but when you shone your torch on him he panicked at being seen there. He ran off home after that.' Leah hesitated. 'And there's something else I never dared tell you at the time.'

Paul looked wary. 'Go on.'

'It was Stevie who scared me by looking in at the hut window that night.' She looked bashful when Paul stared at her in disbelief. 'But I only realised who it was when the anchor thing happened on the beach, Dad, and you were far too angry for me to tell you then. It was too late after that. You'd have killed him if you knew then.'

'Pity I didn't.'

'So do you understand what he's really like? He's only a peeper, Dad. That's what he does. Okay, he's a nut-case as well, but he's not a murderer. And he can identify who is. That's what's important and why you've got to treat him right. He knows who this other man is, and he's the only one who can get you off the hook with the police. Don't you see?'

Paul stared at her earnest expression. 'And you honestly believe all this poppycock, Leah?'

Leah held his gaze. 'Let's be logical about this, Dad. You can see he's a nut-case, can't you?' When Paul nodded in response she looked triumphant. 'Well there you are. He's not clever enough to make all this stuff up. And the fact of the matter is that he reckons you've been hounding him and giving him more agro than he's ever given you. That's why he kidnapped me. Just to worry you for a bit.' She nodded. 'Honestly. He told me that from the start and I believe him. Was it a proper kidnapping? Well, was it? Did he ask you for any money?'

'But he must have realised there was no way out for him after kidnapping you, Leah.'

Leah shook his head. 'He doesn't think that far ahead. As we agreed, he's not the sharpest knife in the drawer.'

'Bad simile, Leah.'

She laughed and grinned at him. 'The best bit is that he's promised me he's going to tell the police what he saw.'

'And you believed that?'

Leah shrugged. 'He's not as bad as you think. He's kind underneath. You've hounded each other and that's why you've only seen the worst of each other. Why would he want to help you, Dad? The plain fact is that you've both been bull-headed. And that's the truth of it.'

'Well, thank you for that, Leah.'

Leah raised an eyebrow. 'Any time, Dad. You need someone to keep you on the straight-and-narrow now Mum's not around.'

— — ∞ — —

When he saw them both running to the road, Stevie knew it was too late. Spotting Fat Joe waving to him from his jetty, he drew alongside, cut the motor, grabbed the mooring rope, and handed it to Joe as he jumped out.

'Here's your boat back, Joe.'

'Jees, thanks Stevie. Thought I'd seen the last of it. What's

213

going on?'

Stevie shrugged. 'Stuff.'

Stevie hurried down the jetty and along the path towards his garden, waving briefly to Hilda who was staring over her wall at him.

'What's going on, Stevie? Tell me. Why was that man chasing you?'

'He's just a nutter, Auntie Hilda.' She'd already seen far too much and he wasn't about to explain anything to her. She was a nosy old bat when she got going.

Stevie unlocked the basement doors of his garden house. He rolled and tied up the sleeping bag Leah had used the previous night. Next he took out a jerry can full of petrol. Leaving these things by the steps, he went up and into his garden house to quickly pack a backpack with spare clothes, food and water. A few minutes later, wearing the backpack and carrying the other items, he headed for his own boat. No one saw him except Hilda. She was still watching from the bottom of her garden.

'Where are you going, Stevie? Just being quizzy,' her voice quavered as he passed by.

'Nowhere special. Just for a little trip. See you soon.' He smiled as best he could: his casual smile. After heaving all the stuff into his boat, he pushed it out into deeper water, jumped in and started the engine. He headed off back down the channel again towards Mudeford Sandbank.

— — ∞ — —

Paul arranged for DI Hughes and DS Sam Gold to come to the house later that morning: while Carol made herself strategically absent. The four of them sat in the lounge.

Hughes firstly told them Stevie Clarke was missing. Apparently no one knew where he was. He asked Leah for full details of her kidnapping, which she related, with Gold taking notes. Leah finished by putting forward a convincing case for Clarke not being the killer or the person responsible for the other local attacks on women.

Hughes was taken aback. 'You seem to be remarkably

forgiving of the man who kidnapped you and threatened you with a knife, young lady. How do you explain that?'

'I'm a Christian,' she said, proudly. 'Forgiving is what life should be about. I had enough time to get to understand him better. He's just a scared lad, really. A bit... simple-thinking, shall we say.' She smiled from Hughes to Sam Gold, who seemed to be looking at her with admiration. 'But it's not fair to charge him with murder. Please check out what he has to say about this surfer. If he won't tell you anything, let him know what you know about him following my mum and watching what happened. Explain that admitting what he saw that night might save him from a murder charge.'

'My word. Telling me my job now.' Hughes looked from Leah to Gold, and on to Paul, who actually observed the glimmering of a smile playing on his lips. Perhaps Hughes did have a human side after all. The inspector smiled at Leah. 'Thinking about a job in the force, by any chance?'

Leah was taken aback. 'No way.'

Hughes and Gold both laughed, then Hughes turned to Paul. 'I can tell you now, sir, that Clarke will not be going on a murder charge. Or rape. DNA evidence excludes Clarke on both counts.' He looked sternly at Paul. 'Which is why we've not had him inside, like you kept asking us to do.'

'You could have told me this before,' said Paul, indignantly.

'With all due respect, sir, it's down to us what we tell people. And when. Anyway, we are trying to find Clarke now, and we'll certainly question him about what he saw that night, Leah. Not to mention the little matter of his kidnapping you.'

'He should definitely answer for that,' said Paul. 'He's put my daughter through hell, lately.'

Leah shrugged. 'It could have been worse.'

— — ∞ — —

Stevie dropped the grapnel from his boat a little way from the harbour shoreline, near to the water-meadows, then stepped out in shallow water. Lifting out his sleeping bag and backpack he carried them above his head as he waded ashore: just like the

215

SAS.

When he eventually reached the familiar old beach hut he sat down with his load and waited until no one was near. This hut was almost derelict, no one seemed to use it, and he often hid underneath it where it was dry, enclosed and secret. He pulled aside a loose panel and scooted into his secret den. There he spread out the sleeping bag on the piece of groundsheet already in place, unpacked some things and made himself comfortable. He was not quite sure of his next move – or how long he would be there. Slipping into the sleeping bag her could smell Leah's perfume all around him. Drinking it in, he closed his eyes and imagined her there with him. He'd never let Mum wash the sleeping bag again.

After an hour or so he'd made up his mind what to do. Gingerly emerging from beneath the hut, making sure he was not observed, he replaced the panel and walked a little way along the beach. Pulling out his mobile phone he checked in its directory for the number the police inspector had given him in case he thought of anything further that might help them. He pressed the call button.

As soon as he heard Hughes' voice he said all he'd rehearsed. 'I've got something important to tell you about Sasha Vincent's murder,' he began. He didn't listen to the voice on the other end and just talked over it. He had decided the clever thing to do was to 'mitigate the circumstances.' He couldn't remember quite where he'd heard that phrase, but it had stayed with him. Yes. It was time for him to 'mitigate the circumstances'.

He told the inspector how he saw Paul Vincent killing his wife.

Chapter 19

It was Leah's idea to go to the beach hut that Sunday: the day after Paul had rescued her from Stevie's clutches. 'I want to get back to a normal life right away,' she said at breakfast, that morning. 'We've got to move on, Dad. And we've got the hut, so we must use it. Mum wouldn't want us to waste it and nor would Granny and Gramps.' This was a reference to Sasha's parents in Australia. 'It was their "Brief Respite", and now it's ours. Let's all go to the hut for a day of respite.' She looked from Paul to Carol with a hopeful smile. 'Please.'

Shep made a delighted bark and his tail began to wag wildly.

Paul laughed, pointing to Shep for Carol's benefit. 'Shep always gets excited when he hears the word "go". Almost as excited as when he hears the word "walk".'

Shep barked again to confirm this, now excitedly bouncing around all over the kitchen.

Carol looked uncertainly from Paul to Leah. 'I'm not so sure it would be a good idea for people to see me lounging around at your beach hut, so soon after your mum's death, Leah.'

'I don't see what that's got to do with anything,' said Leah. She had a very determined look and Paul guessed she also had ambiguous feelings about Sasha.

Carol looked back at Paul. 'What do you think, Paul? You don't want anyone getting the wrong idea, do you?'

Paul was feeling rebellious in any case. Why shouldn't they openly enjoy Carol's company? In any case, he was beginning to think he never really knew Sasha. Perhaps her work as a life-model for Glenn Mason, and her affair with Roger Lines, were only two of many secrets. Since the funeral, the thought had sometimes spooked him that there might have been more than one of her ex-lovers among the mourners: although, thankfully, he had not spotted Lines. Yes, he had loved Sasha—and he still

217

had an underlying love for her—but given her unfaithfulness, he was somehow glad he could move on. Hopefully, Leah had now persuaded Clarke to tell the police all he saw when they finally caught up with him.

Carol was such a refreshing contrast to his turbulent life with Sasha and it was a wonderful bonus that Leah seemed to like her so much. As for his mother, and other people... well, it was his life.

'Paul!' Carol finally regained his attention. 'Are you okay about me coming to the hut? What about your friends on the sandbank? What will they think?'

Paul smiled at her. 'I would hope they'll think how lucky I am to come out of this with a new life.'

'Not if I'm any judge of human nature, Paul,' said Carol. 'You surely can't be that naïve.'

'But I don't particularly care what anyone thinks. You come.' Paul smiled at Leah. 'It's a great idea, Leah. Yes, we do need to get back to normality. A new normality. But one which includes Carol. Wouldn't you say, Leah?'

Leah grinned at them both. 'That's fine by me.'

— — ∞ — —

Stevie had been sitting on his thinking seat on top of Hengistbury Head for at least an hour. He'd been staring out to sea and feeling bad and guilty about what he'd said to the policeman. He liked Leah. She was nice. She'd put a hand on his shoulder. She'd comforted him and seemed to understand him. He'd promised her but then let her down. He felt really bad about it.

Stevie sat with his mobile phone in his hand, willing himself to call again. He should put things right. But was there any point? Would they believe him if he changed his story? Would they think it was because he loved Leah? And Leah's dad had been a bastard towards him. Just thinking about that scene on the beach in front of those two lovely girls at the café still made him go hot with anger. He'd been getting on so well with them. One of them might have gone for a ride with him on his motorbike. Why should he help Vincent? Then he thought of Leah, again. What a beauty. And so nice: even after all he'd put her through.

— — ∞ — —

Leah was secretly—almost guiltily—pleased Carol had come to their beach hut. She was so good for her dad. She made him happy again and he really deserved that. The looks that passed between them were so clear; she'd guessed it was right all along. She could never forgive her mother for what she'd done to Dad. All Mum's little flirty things might just have been for fun, but how it must have upset Dad. The shock he must have had at seeing her having drunken sex with Roger Lines, only yards away from them all at the party, was too awful to contemplate. No wonder he'd disappeared for so long that night. Of course she'd loved her mum, but her feelings for her would never be quite the same again. Sometimes she wondered if there had been other men, so she guessed Dad would think the same.

Leah was sitting in a director's chair on the hut's wooden veranda, reading a book. Her dad was sitting alongside, reading his architectural review magazine. Shep lay contentedly between their chairs and Carol was busy inside preparing some lunch. It was almost like having a mum again.

Leah became aware of someone approaching and she looked up at the same time as her dad.

'Hey.' Stevie was standing there, looking sheepish. He looked very nervous.

'Hiya.' Leah's eyes widened with surprise and she glanced apprehensively towards her dad.

'Clarke.' Dad was obviously astonished Stevie had dared to approach them.

'I've told the police,' Stevie said to Leah, but he was also periodically glancing across at her dad.

'You mean you've told them about the surfing chap? The one you saw killing my mum?'

Stevie nodded. 'And attackin' *him*.' He embarrassingly

gestured towards her dad.

Leah looked really pleased. 'Well that's wonderful, Stevie. Thank you so much.'

'Not before time,' grunted Paul. He was staring at Stevie. 'I don't know how you can show yourself here after what you did to Leah.'

Stevie thrust his arms out, palm upwards. 'Look, man, I'm sorry, right. But you told the police it was me. They were on my back. It was murder. How would you like it? Think about it, man.' He shuffled his feet uneasily in the sand as he looked up at them.

Eventually Paul sighed. 'Okay. And I'm sorry I felt so sure it was you. I guess everything built up for both of us.'

'I was really mad with you, see. I only took Leah to give you a scare. I didn't hurt her, I promise.' He looked at her. 'No way, man. Tell him, Leah. I didn't hurt you, did I?'

'No, Stevie. You didn't hurt me.'

Leah thought she detected uneasy guilt in her father's expression, and it must be true, given how calmly he was now talking to Stevie.

'And you've really told the police you saw the person who killed my wife?'

At that moment, Carol came out of the hut onto the veranda, clearly amazed to see Stevie there. 'You!'

Stevie glanced up at her but took no further notice of her. He looked back at Paul. 'Look, Mr. Vincent, I'm here to say I'm sorry, right. Peace, yeah?' He took a couple of steps forward and stuck his right hand out awkwardly.

Her dad stood and then pointed to Carol for Stevie's benefit. 'And you never attacked this lady?'

Stevie took a step backward. 'No way, man. I never attacked no one. Never saw her 'till you came round to the hut pretending she was a gardener, or somethin'.' He glared at her. 'Why did you do that?'

Leah watched Carol hold Stevie's gaze. 'To see if I could recognise you as the man who attacked me.'

'And now you know I wasn't, right?'

Carol looked at Paul. 'He's about the same build, Paul, but

the voice doesn't sound right.'

'I see.' Leah watched with amazement as her dad stepped down off the veranda and held his hand out to Stevie. 'I'm sorry for telling the police I thought it was you, Stevie. But you can imagine what I thought when I saw you looking at Sasha with your torch.' They briefly shook hands, quickly letting go afterwards as if it were painful for them both. Leah expected a qualifier from her dad, and she was not wrong. 'Not that anything excuses you not telling the police right away, of course. Or kicking me. Or hanging around spying on people and looking into hut windows at night.'

Stevie shrugged again. 'Sorry. I didn't tell the police before because they wouldn't believe me. They'd think I did it. But now Leah says it'll be okay because of DNA. Is that right?'

Paul nodded. 'That's right, Stevie. And I know what it's like to have the police breathing down your neck. So it's peace, right? We were both in error?'

Stevie nodded gravely but then grinned. 'Right then.' He smiled at Leah. 'If you ever want a proper ride in my boat, just shout, Leah. Yeah?'

Leah smiled. 'Thanks, Stevie.'

Stevie grinned back at her, took a final look at the others and turned to wander off towards the end of the spit: with a kind of swagger, Leah thought. Another ride in his boat? No, she'd definitely pass up on that one.

Leah sank back into her chair feeling a burden had been lifted from her shoulders. Now the police only needed to catch the real murderer for Dad to get off the hook. She might also be off the hook, despite sending that stupid letter. One day she'd perhaps get around to telling Dad about it. Some time in the very distant future. Maybe.

— — ∞ — —

Hilda was surprised and nervous when she opened her front door to find a tall uniformed policeman standing outside. She'd seen enough of them the previous day.

'Sorry to trouble you, madam, but I need to have a little

word.'

'Oh dear. What's it about, then?'

'May I step inside for a moment, to explain, madam?'

'Oh, yes, yes.' Hilda opened the door wider and stood aside. When the policeman had stepped into her little hall she closed the door behind him.

'It's about your neighbour, young Steven Clarke, madam. Have you seen him today?'

'No, I haven't.' Hilda looked at him warily. 'Why? What's the matter now?'

'We urgently need to talk to him, madam. He's given us some information. You're Mrs...?' He now had his notebook out.

'Hilda Redland. He's a nice boy, officer. I'm sure he wouldn't mean to do anything wrong.'

'What do you mean by that, madam?'

Hilda felt confused. 'Well, he's just a little bit...' She hesitated. 'Slow on the uptake.' She gave a nervous laugh. 'But he's a good lad. Always cutting my grass, he is. He's a kind boy.'

'But not entirely harmless, madam. I believe officers talked to you yesterday. About the girl he abducted?'

'Oh dear, oh dear. I talked to her father yesterday, you know. I saw them go off in boats. Are they all right?'

'Now don't you worry. The young girl is safely back home with her father, and she wasn't hurt in any way. But we do need to find Steven Clarke in connection with that abduction. So may I ask you if you'd be good enough to phone us at the station the moment you see him around here again? Would you do that for us, madam? It's very important.'

'Oh dear.' She nodded glumly. 'Yes, I suppose so. Is he in serious trouble, officer?'

The constable cleared his throat. 'Well, madam, that remains to be seen.'

— — ∞ — —

After Carol got home from work the following Monday, Paul

greeted her with the surprising news they had all been invited to go to his mother's for a meal that evening. From her expression, this news clearly put a blight on what had otherwise been an enjoyable day in her new job.

'And you needn't try to hide the fact that Carol woman is staying with you,' Connie had announced after inviting Paul and Leah. 'I suppose I need to get to know her since she's obviously such an important part of your life now, Paul. So bring her along too.'

Paul could only assume Leah had carried out some gentle preparations behind the scenes. 'And maybe you should invite Barney, too, given he's such an important part of yours since Dad died,' Paul had retorted. His mother had just snorted at this and said, 'I'll see you all later then.'

Quite unexpectedly the dinner proved to be quite a success. Somehow Carol managed to flatter Connie sufficiently about her choice of furnishings and décor to make herself popular. The truth was that Connie had often bickered with Sasha, so this was a promising development. They got home quite early in order that Leah could tackle some lengthy homework. Alone in the lounge, Paul and Carol snuggled together on a sofa facing the open balcony doors. The view of the harbour and across to Hengistbury Head had a faintly blue haze to it. A light breeze wafted the scent of freshly cut grass into the room. They were drinking a delightfully crisp Pinot Chardonnay in tall wine glasses, unwinding from the stress of dining with Connie. Paul gave Carol a lingering kiss. It was official now. Leah had already caught them kissing and had been totally un-phased.

'You've really made a hit with my mother,' Paul grinned. 'And that's not an easy thing to do.'

Carol laughed. 'Maybe that's because we're both actresses.'

This sent Paul into fits of laughter. 'Too true. You've got her number.'

They were kissing again when Carol's mobile phone rang. 'Oh dear.'

'Let it ring.'

'And what if it's a call from an important television director? Or Hollywood calling?'

Paul shrugged. 'I don't think I'll let you go to Hollywood alone, young lady.'

Laughing, Carol pulled away from him and went to the table where she exchanged her wine glass for her mobile phone. After a short conversation she put the phone back onto the table and returned to the sofa, glass in hand again. 'That was Hughes. He wants me to attend an identification parade tomorrow afternoon. Says they've caught someone. He says the other girl who was attacked recently will also be attending. Apparently she managed to pull off her attacker's balaclava. When I reminded him it would be a waste of time for me because I hardly saw the attacker, he said I could ask them to say something. "Listen to his voice", he said. She sat down, put her hand on Paul's knee and beamed at him. 'Do you realise, Paul, this could be the end of the nightmare, at last?'

'There'll still be a court case to attend, even if they've caught him. And Sasha's inquest.'

'But we won't have to worry about Hughes bullying you any more, Paul. That's what matters.' She kissed him.

Paul was enjoying returning the soft pressure of her lips when his own mobile phone rang in his pocket. 'Damn. Why can't people leave us alone for five minutes?'

Paul was surprised to hear Hughes was now calling him. Again it was about the forthcoming identity parade: except, this time, Paul was required to be in the line-up. When he had finished the call and told Carol, he wagged his finger at her. 'Now don't you go picking me out in a balaclava. I've enough problems. I'll wink so you know it's me,' he grinned.

Carol looked at him in mock horror. 'But Paul, don't you realise? I'd always choose you from any line-up of men.'

— — ∞ — —

DI Hughes burst into the office with a look of triumph on his face. He placed a photocopy of a sketch on the desk in front of his sergeant. 'We've got him, Sam.'

'What?' Gold looked up at him enquiringly. 'Got who, guv?' She looked down at the mugshot drawn from Mandy

Jones's description of her attacker.

'Our man. I recognised him. We interviewed him. He was at the Vincent's barbeque. Thought he looked vaguely familiar all along. Don't you remember him?' Gold still looked blank. Hughes went to his desk and grabbed the phone. 'You will. But first I must make a little change to the identity parade.' His grin was wider than Gold had even seen it before.

Chapter 20

DS Susie Gold stayed in the room with Carol while DI Hughes took the other girl through to the identity parade. He was smiling widely when he returned with her a few minutes later. She departed after he thanked her profusely.

'Positive ID,' Hughes said to Sam Gold, with a wide grin.

'Great.' Gold looked excited.

Hughes turned to Carol. 'Be warned, Miss Davis, they're all now wearing balaclavas. First of all, I'd like you to go along the line and take a really good look at their build, their eyes, their mouth, their feet, anything that might help you identify the man who attacked you. I'll invite you to go along the line again and say "Speak" to each one. But firstly tell me a phrase you'd like them to say so I can arrange that. Choose something you remember your attacker said. Listen very carefully to see if you can identify his tone, even though he'll obviously try to make it sound a bit different. I'll be listening out to see if I think any of them are trying to disguise their voices. All right?'

Carol felt nervous at the thought of seeing the man again, but she was worried it would be very hard to identify him. She wondered if Stevie would be in the line-up and felt that seeing him in a balaclava might be conclusive. She'd thought long and hard, trying to decide whether he was her attacker, but she still felt unsure. 'Yes. I understand.'

'So what should I ask them to say, Miss Davis?'

Carol thought about it, forcing herself to cast her mind back to the event that she had been trying so hard to forget. 'Michelle. Nice name,' she said, eventually. She remembered the way her attacker had practically savoured the name of 'Michelle' on his tongue.

Hughes looked at her inquisitively. 'He said that? Michelle?'

Carol nodded. 'Yes. When he asked me my name, I said it was Michelle. I didn't want to give him my real name, you see.'

'That was very astute of you, miss, if I may say so.' Hughes gave her an admiring look. 'Give me a minute to organise them to say that, then I'll call you in.' He went back through the door.

When Hughes returned a few minutes later he led her through to the adjoining room. She found it quite unnerving to see the row of men lined up in dark clothes, all wearing black balaclavas. It sent a shiver down her spine and brought the dreadful memory flooding back. The police had certainly taken great trouble to arrange this. Behind each man a number was stuck to the wall on a card. She steeled herself for the ordeal of walking down the line.

It was strange to see Paul wearing a balaclava; she'd recognise him anywhere. But she could not identify Stevie Clarke in the line-up and it seemed bad if he'd not been included. Although she found it hard to be certain, the third man did have a similar build to her attacker and his eyes looked every bit as menacing. But on her second pass down the line, when she prompted him to say: "Michelle. Nice name," she knew. True, he said it in a completely different dead-pan manner, but the tone of his voice, combined with the way he said "*Me*-shell' —with particular emphasis on the first syllable—clinched it. Feeling herself trembling for the rest of the long walk down the line, she abruptly declined the offer to pass down the line once more and was greatly relieved to be able to hurry out of the room.

Back in the adjoining room, she couldn't wait to tell Hughes. 'It was number three. I'm certain of his voice, Inspector.'

Hughes looked elated. 'I'm pleased to tell you, Miss Davis, that you picked the same man as the other young lady. We're waiting for DNA evidence to come back, but hopefully that should clinch it.' He turned to DS Gold. 'Sam. Perhaps you would enjoy arresting Mr. Gartland on my behalf.'

Gold smiled broadly. 'It would be a real pleasure, guv.'

— — ∞ — —

227

When Carol met Paul a little later at his car, which was parked a discreet distance from the police station so they wouldn't be seen together, they began to talk excitedly over each other. Paul laughed at her and signalled over the roof of the car to get in. Once inside, Carol told Paul to go first.

'I don't understand why Clarke wasn't in the line-up. Anyway. Guess what. There was someone else in it I did recognise. He's given Leah and me windsurfing lessons on the sandbank. Sasha as well, actually. While we were waiting I asked him how he came to be there and he said the police called to ask him. Said he was happy to oblige.' He paused. 'Now you. Did you manage to identify anyone, Carol?'

'Not from sight, of course, but I did when he spoke. I was certain of it then. Even better, the other girl who was attacked picked out the same guy by sight.' She beamed. 'Isn't that marvelous? Hughes reckons the DNA evidence should clinch it, when it comes back. So it's nearly over, Paul. The man we identified was apparently called Gartland.'

'Gartland? Really?' Paul stared at her in amazement. 'Are you sure about that, Carol?'

She nodded. 'Yes. Hughes asked Sam Gold to go and arrest Gartland.'

Paul was rubbing his forehead. 'But, Carol, that's the guy I was telling you about. Russell Gartland. The one who gave us windsurfing lessons.' He paused. Suddenly it all started to make sense. 'He definitely fancied, Sasha, you know. Couldn't keep his hands off her.'

They exchanged awed glances. 'So we really were wrong to accuse Stevie Clarke, then.'

Paul looked sheepish and grimaced. 'So it seems.' He paused. 'Damn! I never thought I'd feel guilty over Clarke.' He heaved a sign of resignation. 'Then this is terrible, Carol. I falsely accused someone of murder without any evidence other than his presence. And I never gave Russell Gartland a thought.'

— — ∞ — —

After sleeping a few nights under the derelict beach hut, Stevie was short of food and ready to go home. By the Wednesday afternoon he fancied some home comforts and television. The trouble was the police would be around asking him loads of questions once they knew he was back. He wished he'd stayed quiet and never told them he saw Paul Vincent fighting with his wife. He'd only done it to give Vincent more aggro. Finally he made a decision. He gathered up his things and took them to his boat.

He was not sure what he would do, so when his boat drew near to the shore and he saw Auntie Hilda waving, a new idea came to him. He'd ask her advice. She was always so understanding. Yes, the time really had come to tell someone his big secret. He waved back, excited at the thought of unburdening himself. As soon as the boat went aground, he jumped out, pulled it up the sand, stuck in the grapnel to anchor it, and headed in her direction. As he drew closer, he saw Hilda's head had its normal wobble and that seemed, in some way, very comforting and familiar. He always knew where he stood with Hilda, that was the thing.

'Where have you been, Stevie?' she asked with her shaky little smile. Even her false teeth wobbled a little. She pulled off some gardening gloves and tossed them down onto the grass. 'Tell me. What's going on?'

Stevie let himself in through her gate. He noticed her lawn needed cutting and felt guilty about it. 'Been sleepin' under the stars for a while, Auntie Hilda,' he said. 'I like to do that, sometimes. Can I talk to you?'

Hilda gave a little frown as she peered at him. 'Your mum and dad have been really worried about you, Stevie.' She sounded a bit scolding, which was not like her. But then she softened. 'You must tell them if you're going off for a few days. They worry about you. So do I.'

Stevie shrugged. 'I'm twenty-one. I can do what I like.' He wondered why she was going on. What did it matter to his parents or her? It only affected a few breakfasts; a few eggs and rashers of bacon. 'Can I talk to you?' he repeated. 'Now? It's important, Auntie Hilda.'

229

She smiled and gestured towards the house. 'Come on in then. I'll make us a nice cup of tea, then we can talk.'

Stevie sat at Hilda's kitchen table munching custard cream biscuits. He was by then feeling very hungry. What he wanted to say couldn't wait until the kettle boiled, and somehow everything began to pour out while she sat opposite, listening. He told her how he'd seen the surfing guy running after Sasha Vincent the night of the beach party. How he'd followed him in case he was up to no good with Sasha; he liked Sasha. How he'd been afraid to do anything other than hide when he saw him attack Sasha and have sex with her. 'I wanted to help her, Auntie Hilda, honestly I did, but I was scared.'

Hilda put her bony hand comfortingly over his and patted it. 'I can imagine, Stevie. You poor thing. What happened?'

Stevie went on to explain how Sasha's husband had turned up with the dog, how Sasha had fallen back and hit her head on the road when the surfing guy let go of her, how the man had attacked her husband and knocked him down, how Sasha was all silent after falling, not even moving a muscle, and how scared he'd been throughout. 'I guessed she was dead right away, Auntie Hilda. She wasn't movin' at all.' As a tear ran down his face, Hilda patted his hand comfortingly again. 'And then, dear?'

It was so easy to talk to her. Stevie rubbed his eyes with the back of his hand and continued. 'He ran off back towards the huts, Auntie Hilda. When he'd gone, I went to see how they both were. I shone my torch on the woman. I could see she was dead.' He started to sob, softly, unable to control himself any more. 'Her husband came to and shone his torch on me. It made me panic, Auntie Hilda. I didn't want anyone to know I was there, see. Otherwise they'd blame me. I always get blamed, Auntie Hilda. No one ever believes me.'

'I believe you, Stevie, dear.'

'I gave him a little knock. The husband. To keep him quiet. Then I came home.'

Stevie sobbed for a while in silence. Finally Hilda spoke. 'You should tell the police all of this, Stevie. They can find the man who killed that poor girl.'

'But they'll think it was me. Specially because I've told the police it was Vincent who did it.'

'You did what, Stevie?' Hilda sounded shocked.

Stevie felt ever worse over this. 'I told them he killed his wife. So they won't believe me now if I tell them it wasn't him. And his daughter, Leah. I told her I'd tell the police who really killed her mother and I've let her down. And she's kind.' He looked pleadingly at Hilda, tears streaming down his face. 'Oh, Auntie Hilda. What am I going to do?'

'Let me call the police for you, Stevie. You could stay here with me and you could explain it to them here. I'll stay with you, if you like. Just be honest with them. You've not committed any crime.'

'I took the girl,' he said hesitantly.

'But that's nothing against murder, Stevie. And she's all right now.'

Stevie looked up at her hopefully, but the thought of the police disbelieving him struck him forcefully again and he pushed his chair back and stood. 'I can't. That's why I've been away. I can't tell them. They'll say I'm a murderer and put me in jail for ever, Auntie Hilda.'

Hilda now also stood. 'No, no, Stevie, they'll listen if you tell them the truth. Tell them why you were scared. They'll understand.'

'Leah said that, but I can't.' He knew they were both wrong. Pushing his chair roughly aside, Stevie hurried to the back door, tore it open and went out, running down the garden. What was the point? Why had he told her all that? How could she possibly help? He was plain stupid.

— — ∞ — —

Hilda followed Stevie out into the garden and watched him vault over her wall onto the path and hurry along to his own garden. After a moment, she went back into her own house feeling desperately troubled. It tortured her to think of what she must do now. She made herself sit for a few minutes to get calm, finally summoning up the resolve to pick up the handset and dial the number the policeman had given her.

She was quickly put through to the person she'd been told to ring, a police lady called Sam Gold. Hilda explained why she was calling.

'So let me get this right, madam,' said the voice at the other end. You're saying that Steven Clarke is actually in the shed at the bottom of his garden right now?'

'Well, it's his little house, really, not a shed, dear.'

'Right. We'll send someone round right now to see him.'

'The thing is, if he sees the police coming, he'll be off in his boat again like a shot. He's been away for days now. You've got to handle him very carefully, dear. He seems very scared, so he'll run again. He's not done anything bad, you know. Please be kind to him.'

'He did abduct a fourteen year-old girl, don't forget, Mrs. Redland. Anyway. We'll be careful. Thank you for telling us about the boat. It may take some time, but I'll get a police launch to the area before anyone approaches the house. So please will you keep a discreet eye and let us know if he goes off in his boat. Could you do that for me?'

'I suppose so,' said Hilda, reluctant to be drawn further in against Stevie.

'And would it be all right if some of my colleagues came to wait in your house until the police launch is in place, madam? That way we could be more discrete, so we don't frighten him.'

'Oh dear.' Hilda really didn't want this. It would be a clear signal to Stevie she'd betrayed him if police came pouring out of her house. 'I don't think I could do that, dear.' She paused, now shaking more violently. 'Stevie trusts me, you see. I'm only telling you this for his own good. So he can explain. He's not hurt anyone, you see. He told me all about it.'

'All right, Mrs. Redland. No problem. Just let us know if you see him leave, please. You will do that, won't you?'

'Yes, I can do that. Goodbye.'

Hilda replaced the handset and went wearily across to her favourite armchair facing the window. She sank into it and began to cry. Poor Stevie. What had she done to the poor soul? Had she betrayed his kindness to her? Yet deep down she knew this was for Stevie's own good. He needed to unburden himself. He needed looking after.

— — ∞ — —

Stevie was sitting on the garden seat overlooking the harbour when he saw the fast motorboat approaching. Raising his binoculars, he confirmed it was a police launch. He'd half expected this. He'd even prepared for it, with supplies onboard and his boat moored much further along the shoreline than usual. His reaction was immediate. He hurried along the path to his boat which was moored next to Fat Joe's. Jumping in, he cast off and pulled on the starter cord. The engine roared into life, but he headed off slowly, hugging the shoreline, trying not to draw attention to himself. He planned to pull into shore again a little further along the harbour and wait for his best opportunity to get out into deeper water. At present he had the advantage because they didn't know it was him in the boat.

He had decided he couldn't face any more questioning by the police. They would get him all confused and then they'd suspect him of everything. They already had him for the kidnapping, but one mistake and they'd have him for the murder or rape as well. Why would they believe him when he'd already told them two lies? First he'd said he was at home on the night of the murder, and his mum had confirmed the lie. Next he'd called the police to say he'd seen Paul Vincent fighting with his wife that night. A second big lie. Now he needed to tell them it was the surfing guy fighting with Sasha. Three different versions to his story. So why would they ever believe him now? No, he needed to get away.

Stevie's foot rested against his can of petrol, glad he had a full tank. He was well prepared for anything.

— — ∞ — —

Paul took two cans of coke onto the balcony and cracked one open. He held it out to Leah who was lying on a sun lounger. 'Fancy a coke, Leah?'

Leah smiled up at him and reached to take the can. 'Thanks, Dad.'

Paul cracked open the second can, took a swig, and looked contentedly at the harbour twinkling in the low evening sunlight. 'Beautiful, isn't it, sweetheart?'

'Lovely.' Leah took a sip from her can. Paul was pleased she sounded lazy and relaxed.

'I got some good news just now.' Paul turned to face her. 'I had a call from Inspector Hughes this afternoon. So did Carol. They managed to hurry up the DNA testing. It proved it was Russell Gartland who killed Mum and attacked Carol and the other girl. So that's him going down for the lot.'

Leah sat upright. 'The slimy toad.' She paused to think about it. 'You know, he used to give me a funny kind of look, Dad.' She shivered involuntarily. 'Imagine if I'd taken up his offer of more windsurfing lessons. Creepy.'

Paul dare not imagine it. 'He won't be giving any more lesson in anything, that's a fact. Thank God they've got him. And thank God I'm off the hook at last. I'm sure Hughes thought it was me for most of the time.'

Leah looked uneasy. 'But truth would out, Dad. No one could really believe you did it.'

'Anyway.' Paul pulled a chair next to his daughter and sat down. He spoke in subdued tones. 'I wanted a quiet word with you, Leah; while Carol's busy. You get on well with Carol, don't you?'

Leah nodded. 'Of course. She's cool.'

Paul lowered his voice even further. 'But is she cool enough to stay here permanently? How would you feel about that?'

Leah laughed. 'Still cool. You're so old fashioned, Dad. Do you think I'm still a kid? I've seen you guys kissing and cuddling. Give me a break. Get a room.'

Paul laughed at her, somewhat embarrassed by her directness. 'Is it that obvious?'

'Hello? Is cheese yellow? It's obvious you're both so right for each other, Dad, and you know what? I'm really pleased. Especially after all the stress. And after what Mum did...' Leah swung her legs off the lounger and stretched up to give him a

234

kiss. 'Just go for it, Dad. Just go for it.' She sank back onto the lounger again, smiling.

'Some people will think it's terrible, so soon after your mother's death.'

Leah shrugged. 'So do we care? After what Mum did to us? What do they know?' She paused. 'And Mum might have done even worse things than we know.' Her face crumpled in concern.

'I don't believe we should think like that, Leah. I'm sure it was a one-off. She was a bit tipsy.'

Leah shrugged. 'No, but we both know it could be so, Dad. Look, we've all got to move on and get happy again. And you know what?'

'What?' Paul could not help loving her. She had really matured lately.

'I'll be happy if you're happy. And if you choose to be happy with Carol, I'll be even happier. She's a lovely, considerate person, Dad.' Leah's eyes really sparkled when she was happy.

'Thank you, sweetheart.' Paul got up, bent to kiss her on the forehead and headed back inside. 'I want a word with Carol now.'

Leah laughed. 'So tell her you've got my blessing.'

— — ∞ — —

Stevie cursed when he saw his plan was failing. The police launch was heading straight for him. There was no point in trying to look innocent any more, so Stevie opened up the throttle and sped off towards the harbour mouth. He wanted the option of either going out to sea or of turning back and going upriver. If he could land somewhere he could escape on foot.

He was surprised how fast the other craft was. It obviously had a very powerful engine and was on a course that soon cut him off from the sea channel and left him stranded; Mudeford shore was on one side and an immersed sandbank on the other. If he got too close to the sandbank he would run aground, although that still gave him the chance of wading ashore onto

Stanpit Marsh. Other than that he could head back down the channel towards home and make a getaway on his motorbike. But he guessed there would already be police waiting for him at home. So that was no good.

'Cut your engine, Steven. Cut your engine.' One of the uniformed policemen on the launch was using a megaphone and giving a down-gesture with his free hand. He counted three policemen on board. He stood no chance if they got aboard his boat. And he hated them calling him 'Steven'.

Stevie looked around desperately, but when the police launch did a clever manoeuvre that nudged against the bow of his boat for a moment, he did cut his throttle. One policeman held a rope, obviously getting ready to jump across to his boat, and Stevie knew he must keep clear to prevent this. Now the policeman with the megaphone was able to call across directly. 'Steven Clarke, I'm here to arrest you for kidnapping. You must not do anything to avoid arrest or you'll make things worse for yourself. Let me come aboard peaceably.'

Stevie grabbed the can of petrol and held it up. 'Look! I've got petrol. You're not arrestin' me. You're not coming aboard. I'll set fire to the boat if anyone comes aboard.'

'Don't be silly, lad.' The policeman with the rope was talking now, but he was hesitating before climbing across.

Stevie slammed his outboard into reverse, causing his boat to shoot backward, but he cut the throttle again so he could be heard. 'Look.' Unscrewing the cap from the petrol can he tossed some of the pungent liquid across the central seat.

'Don't be stupid, Steven.'

'You'll be stupid if you try to come aboard. Look.' Stevie poured petrol over his clothes. The smell was revolting, but he knew it would scare them. The engine of the police launch revved slightly as it drew a little closer. Stevie took a lighter out of his pocket. 'I've warned you. See.' He held it out for them to see. 'I've got a lighter. Lights every time. Guaranteed.' He struck a flame to show them. 'Now stay away or I'll set fire to it.'

— — ∞ — —

236

Leah exchanged a smile with Carol when she came out onto the balcony, shortly followed by her father. Carol sat in the chair he had recently vacated while he leaned against the rail, looking at them smilingly.

'Paul says you think I'm cool,' Carol grinned.

Leah was glad Carol had come into her dad's life. She grinned back. 'Telling you wasn't, though. But yeah, you're kind of cool, I guess. But so is Dad, so it's not unique.'

Her father laughed in the background. 'Go tell her, girl.'

Now Carol was laughing. 'And you really don't mind if I stick around, Leah? Sort of permanently? Is that really true?'

Leah shrugged. 'I've told Dad, already.'

'I really can't believe my turn of luck.'

'Me too,' said Leah. 'And we all need a turn of good luck now. Although…'

What?' Carol looked at her uncertainly.

'I'm not sure we entirely want you to get an acting job too quickly, Carol.'

Carol relaxed back into her chair. 'I'm not sure I'm quite so keen any more.' She shrugged. 'But who knows what might happen? But I'll not go away for very long, even if I do get a few acting breaks. I'll be picky.' She smiled across at Paul. 'I promise, Paul. I'd get too lonely without you guys.'

Suddenly there was the sound of a dull thud and they all looked instinctively across to the harbour in the direction from which it had come. A tall plume of flame flashed high above the water for a moment and then died down to a smaller flickering light. Shep shot out onto the balcony from the lounge, barking.

'Quiet, Shep,' said Paul.

'What ever's that, Dad?'

Paul shrugged. 'Who knows? Some explosion on the water, I guess. Someone in trouble.' He dashed into the lounge, reappearing a moment later with binoculars. He focussed them on the distant light. 'I can see a flame, but I can't make out very much. There's a boat nearby.'

Carol was leaning against the edge of the balcony, straining to see. 'How horrible. Fire on the water. I guess other people have worse troubles than us, now. Right, guys?' She smiled round at them.

Paul lowered his binoculars and put his arm around Carol. 'Right.' He gestured to Leah to join him at the rail, on the other side. 'Right Leah?' When she joined them, he put his other arm around her and, smiling down at her, cuddled them both tightly to him. 'Have I got a great team with you girls?'

Leah put her arm around her father and hugged him back. 'Yep. A great team. And no more troubles, right?'

Her father grinned. 'Right.'

Perhaps she would never tell him about the letter. She would have to live with this one terrible secret all her life. She looked into his sparkling eyes, delighted in his happiness, and peeped around him at Carol, equally happy as she smiled back at her. It was so funny. They were all grinning like Cheshire cats. And she felt something stirring deep within herself she barely recalled: a feeling that had been missing for far too long. Could it be the welcome return of happiness?

THE END

A Final Note from the Author

I do hope you enjoyed *Sandman*. Please visit my website at **iankingsley.com** to find background information, pictures of the true setting for this novel, and to gain advance information about future books. It also offers you the opportunity to tell me what you thought of this book. I love hearing from readers.

If you would like to look beyond the covers of *Sandman*, please go to the 'Overview, Reviews and BUY *Sandman*' page on my website and use the panel headed 'SANDMAN READERS' to enter a password that will allow you to reach the 'Beyond the covers of SANDMAN' page. You will need a good knowledge of *Sandman* in order to know the password. Because this web page contains plot spoilers, it is only intended for those who have fully read the book.

Also, if you have a moment to go to the *Amazon* book page for *Sandman*, I would really appreciate you scrolling down to the 'Tags' section and clicking tags such as 'mystery', 'thriller', 'psychological thriller' and other appropriate tags to help boost its positioning in search lists using these terms. (If visible, click the 'Search all tags' link.) And if you *really* enjoyed *Sandman*, please would you consider writing a reader review while you're there? I'd be really grateful for your support.

A Final Note from the Publisher

Books from new authors struggle to get noticed in a world where supermarket discounts limit profits and publicity budgets must be low for books not by established authors. To support new authors, please recommend the books you enjoy to all your friends. In the case of *Sandman*, that's as easy as suggesting they visit **iankingsley.com** in order to gain further information and to find out where to buy this book. Spreading the word is the only way to ensure new authors are able to write new works and publishers are able to publish new writers. If you like this author's work, please mention it during your social media networking—that way we call all help new writers to develop.

Lightning Source UK Ltd.
Milton Keynes UK
UKOW051839140113

204866UK00001B/4/P